"You're asking me why I want to make you dinner?"

Bree nodded. "Yes. Why do you want to have anything to do with me? All I've done is turn your world upside down. You should be enjoying this time before you have all the responsibilities of fatherhood."

Nick hadn't thought about it that way, and he didn't want to think about it that way. "I'm just as responsible for this situation as you are." He turned off the engine and opened the car door. "Now, come on. Let's go see what's in my fridge to eat."

He came around to her side of the car and opened her door. He reached in to give her a hand as she got out and then, as if completely natural, she leaned into him and their lips met in a kiss.

A kiss filled with promise for things to come.

Dear Reader,

Everyone has had those days. The ones where things don't go as planned. A flat tire on the way to work. You need to pick up your sick child from school, so lunch with friends is out. A flight delay. But what if that unplanned event didn't just shake up your day but your entire life?

That's what happens to Bree in *The Baby Arrangement*. She sees her life one way, with no possibility of straying from her plan to put all her energy into her expanding company. And then she meets Nick...

I hope you enjoy this first book in my new series. Stay tuned for more stories about Bree's friends. Visit lisadyson.com to find out when they'll be released.

I love hearing from readers. Please email me at lisa@lisadyson.com.

Wishing you the very best of days,

Lisa Dyson

LISA DYSON

The Baby Arrangement

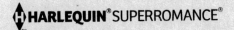

HARLEQUIN® SUPERROMANCE®

Recycling programs
for this product may
not exist in your area.

ISBN-13: 978-0-373-64023-2

The Baby Arrangement

Printed in U.S.A.

Lisa Dyson has been creating stories ever since getting an A on a fifth-grade writing assignment. She lives near Washington, DC, with her husband and their rescue dog with a blue tongue, aptly named Blue. She has three grown sons, a daughter-in-law and four adorable grandchildren. When not writing, reading or spending time with family, Lisa enjoys traveling, volunteering and rooting for her favorite sports teams.

Books by Lisa Dyson

HARLEQUIN SUPERROMANCE

Tales from Whittler's Creek

Prince Charming Wears a Badge

Resorting to the Truth
Catching Her Rival
A Perfect Homecoming

Visit the Author Profile page at Harlequin.com.

For Lila,
one of the many strong women in my life

CHAPTER ONE

How was Bree Tucker supposed to relax and kick back when she'd been so obviously abandoned?

She couldn't figure out where the heck her friend Roxie had gone. She scanned the other people around the tiki bar once more with no luck. She and Roxie had come over to order drinks, and now she was nowhere in sight.

Thinking she'd walk around the bar to the other side, Bree took a step back from the bar without looking. She immediately tripped over something and gasped as she fell backward. Somehow she ended up in someone's strong arms instead of butt-first in the sand.

Her gasp had heads turning in her direction. Great. She'd managed to attract unwanted attention from the mostly men around the bar. She turned her head to see who'd caught her, and her gaze collided with a pair of deep brown eyes with long, dark lashes. She blinked and slowly disengaged herself from him.

"Are you okay?" He was probably the nicest-looking man she'd seen since arriving on Isla de la Blanca earlier in the week for a working vacation with her girlfriends slash coworkers.

"Yes, I'm fine. And thank you for catching me. I'm sorry about that." She straightened her bright blue romper and tossed back her long hair. "I'm not usually that clumsy."

Her rescuer smiled, his eyes twinkling. A neatly trimmed dark beard set off perfectly straight white teeth. "It was my fault. I wasn't paying attention, and my legs got in your way. I'm the one who should apologize."

"But I shouldn't have stepped back without looking."

"Let's call it a draw," he suggested.

"Deal," she said, then looked around again for her friend. "Have you seen a redhead? I've misplaced my friend Roxie."

He shook his head. "I haven't seen her."

She whirled around as she checked out the nearby area again. She shielded her eyes from the glare of the setting sun off the clear azure water of the Caribbean Sea. "Did anyone see where my friend went?" she asked the men around the bar. "She's got red hair and is wearing a dark green top with white shorts."

She'd been well aware that the guys hanging out at the tiki bar had been paying a lot of attention to her, whether they were actually speaking to her or merely ogling. So she decided to use that to her advantage in locating Roxie.

"*I'll* be happy to help you find her," a sloppy drunk propped on a bamboo bar stool told her with a crooked grin before he belched and reached out to her, nearly falling off his perch.

Bree took a step back. "That's okay, I'm sure I—"

"She has all the help she needs," said an older man who appeared from nowhere, his Jimmy Buffett Parrot Head affiliation obvious from his Hawaiian shirt and straw hat with a *Margaritaville* button attached. "At your service, ma'am." He stepped forward abruptly, his drink sloshing over the rim of his glass.

"She's fine," her rescuer growled from behind her. He took Bree's elbow. "She doesn't need anyone's help." Before Bree could say a word, the man guided her away from the bar and maneuvered them through the growing number of people looking for fun.

"Hey, come back here!" called several of the men left behind.

"Wait! Where are you taking me?" Bree stumbled in the sand and nearly lost a sandal. She jerked her arm away when they were barely fifteen feet from the bar, hopping on one foot while she tried to adjust her shoe. "Stop already!"

"I was getting you out of an uncomfortable situation," he explained.

"What do you mean?" She could hold her own with a bunch of drunks. "What uncomfortable situation?"

"Those men back there," he muttered, jerking his head in their direction. "Didn't you see how they were looking at you?"

"So what?"

He continued. "You're a woman alone with a bunch of drunk and gawking men."

"And?"

"*And* some might get the wrong idea."

She ran her tongue over her bottom lip and squinted at him. "The wrong idea?"

He shook his head. "You really have no idea what kind of signals you're giving off, do you?"

She was doing no such thing. "So I'm supposed to be comforted by your macho manhandling of me for my own good?" She scowled. "Dragging me away to this secluded area where you can do whatever you want to me just because I might have tugged at my ear or scratched my leg in a way that turned you on?"

In truth, they were anything but secluded, with people barely a few feet away, but she wasn't about to admit that she'd possibly overreacted.

"How do I know you're not the one I should

be worried about?" she said. "I don't even know your name."

"Believe me, my intentions were honorable." He cocked his head and shrugged. "I'm sorry if I misread the situation." He turned to leave without a backward glance.

Good riddance, she thought as she watched him walk away. Too bad Sir Condescension thought he had to play hero, even if his overt sexiness made him extremely appealing.

Oh, well. She didn't need him sticking around, even if she had promised her girlfriends she'd try to be more open to meeting new people while on this working vacation. She just didn't need a know-it-all jerk.

Who was she kidding? At thirty-three years old, she avoided new relationships altogether. Period. She had enough people in her life, even if none of them happened to be a love interest.

Her girlfriends might think she needed a vacation fling, but this latest encounter proved Bree had been right all along. Her time would be better spent on her company's future, the only thing she truly cared about besides her girlfriends.

Bree searched again for Roxie and the others, the crowd growing more raucous as the sun all but disappeared and the tiki torches were lit. A pig had been roasting on a spit since early last evening and when she inhaled the scent in the air now, her stomach growled. She had to find the girls and then get some food.

Isla de la Blanca, off the Puerto Rican coast and named for its pure white sandy beaches, had been her coworkers' choice of a working vacation spot, not Bree's. Although, she had to admit, she hadn't gotten tired of the constant seventy-eight-degree weather and sunshine. So different from January in their hometown of Arlington, Virginia, where highs of forty-five degrees were sarcastically called *balmy.*

Her best girlfriends had all spent their free time this week getting massages and facials, frequenting the small shops and kiosks in the tiny village, as well as discovering the island's vibrant nightlife. After much coercion, and since they'd accomplished their work goals, Bree had finally agreed to put her job aside and join them tonight. At least for a little while. She still had some phone calls to return and a report to read.

"There you are!" Bree shouted, waving her hand as she made her way through already intoxicated patrons to where her girlfriends were gathered around a wicker table under the palm trees, coconut-shell cocktails with straws and paper umbrellas in their hands. Bree tilted her head at Roxie. "Why did you disappear? Didn't you see me nearly fall on my butt?"

They all chortled and spoke at once.

"It's not funny," Bree said, but she couldn't keep a straight face. "Listen, I didn't bring you all down here just so I could give a bunch of drunks an eyeful!"

Again they laughed. Bree knew when she was outnumbered, so she plopped into the single empty chair, crossed her bare legs and pretended to sulk.

"I'm sorry, Bree," Roxie said, appearing anything but remorseful. "I found a server to come over here so we could order our drinks, and then I got distracted. When I came back to find you, you were gone." She handed Bree a cocktail and pointed to the plate of food they were sharing. Their hotel offered free appetizers during happy hour and the girls had taken advantage.

"What happened anyway, Bree?" Showing her usual empathy, Hannah's voice was filled with concern. "Are you okay?"

Bree shook her head and reached for a cheese cube. "Yes, I'm fine. I just tripped and fell into some guy's waiting arms. Typical macho guy who thinks every woman is a damsel in distress."

Hannah's mouth formed an O and her dark brown doe eyes nearly popped out of her head. "Wow! Was he cute?"

"Invite him over!" Amber said, and then lowered her voice. "Unless he was a troll. Was he a troll?" Amber was nothing if not a straight shooter.

"Not even close." Bree pursed her lips as she remembered the heat that had suffused her before she'd brushed him off. Or had he been the one to brush her off? Either way, he was in the rearview mirror.

Hannah interrupted Bree's musings. "Where is he? Do you see him anywhere?" Hannah craned her neck, searching for the guy she'd never even seen.

"Was he hot?" Amber wanted to know. "I bet he was hot. You never follow up when a good-looking guy shows interest."

"Give her a break," Roxie said. "Just because the two of you are looking to hook up doesn't mean everyone is." Roxie's longtime boyfriend had recently moved to California for his job, and they were still working out the long-distance romance thing.

Bree looked around, telling herself it didn't really matter if the guy who'd caught her had disappeared. "I don't see him. He must have found someone else to annoy." She shrugged, trying to sound nonchalant, but she'd bet the women who'd known her since freshman year of college weren't fooled.

Truthfully, the man had made her heart accelerate wildly. His dark hair was full and thick, and just long enough to be sexy. He had a strong jaw under that closely trimmed beard. He was a little above average in height, with lean muscu-lature, and way above average in sex appeal in his khaki shorts, faded Dave Matthews T-shirt and boat shoes. Then again, she'd always been a sucker for guys with intense brown eyes. Too bad those eyes came with such a macho attitude.

"We could walk around and maybe acciden-tally *run into* him," Roxie suggested, using fin-ger quotes.

The others started to get up, but Bree raised a hand to stop them and changed the subject. "Not so fast. First of all, I'm not interested. Second, I want to get your opinion on something—work related."

There was a collective moan as the women dropped back down into their chairs.

"I want to offer a bartending class," she told them. "Watching the bartender over there gave me the idea."

"Bree! We worked all week on our five-year goals," Roxie whined. "You promised we'd have the evenings to actually vacation, and now you're back on the subject of work."

"Yeah!" Amber and Hannah chorused.

"And you also promised to hang out with us tonight!" Amber added.

"I know, I know. And I will." Bree held up one finger. "But I really want your opinion. We could offer mixology training for women, especially for moms who would benefit from working nights while their husbands can be home with their kids."

The other three women bobbed their heads. "I like that," Amber said. "And it would be a faster turnaround than some other training we've considered."

"Also a relatively well-paid position if you consider tips and location of the bar, like at a high-end-hotel lounge compared to a local bar or a chain restaurant," Hannah added.

Bree's private company, BeeTee, Incorporated—based on her initials—had been born during her junior year of college when she'd discovered her talent for composing résumés and guiding women into the right jobs. Her business degree, as well as her absorption by osmosis of her excessively rich and powerful father's phenomenal business savvy, had given Bree the knowledge to grow her female-based employment-and-retraining business. Two years ago, they'd branched into investing in women-owned businesses. Several years before that she'd brought her three best friends from college along for the incredible ride, knowing full well that they came with their own unique talents.

Last year the company had grossed over four million dollars, and they were well on their way to doing better this year. Bree had used her private financial resources to start up the company, but Roxie, Hannah and Amber received yearly stock options on top of their salaries as compensation for their dedication and hard work. Bree still owned the majority of BeeTee, but she ran it pretty much as if the women were full partners.

They discussed Bree's idea for a few more minutes, until Amber held up her hand and said, "Enough! We agree it's a great idea, but now it's time to play." She straightened her back and peered out at the people around them. "Let's find us some new friends." She waggled her eyebrows and fluffed her dark hair with her airbrushed fake nails. "Ooh!" Amber crowed, pointing to something behind Bree. "And here comes a splendid specimen, indeed!"

Bree took a sip of her drink, enjoying how smoothly the liquid went down her throat, and didn't bother looking up until she heard a familiar deep voice.

"Good evening, ladies," her sexy rescuer said smoothly, then tapped Bree on the shoulder from behind. "I believe this is yours."

She gasped and her drink went down the wrong way, sending her into a coughing fit.

THE WOMAN FINALLY stopped coughing and angled her head around until their eyes met. Nick Harmon dangled the earring where she could see it.

He'd discovered it when he'd gone back to the bar to get a fresh drink and felt obligated to find her.

The woman narrowed her dark blue eyes and uncrossed her incredibly long legs. He'd noticed her back at the bar before she'd fallen into his arms. How could he miss her?

"Not mine." She unstuck a strand of hair from her lip gloss and pulled back her long, golden-brown hair to show him her earrings. Not even close to what she wore.

"Oh, sorry," he said, feeling like a fool. "I found it back at the bar where you were standing and just assumed…never mind."

He went to leave, but one of the other women called out to him, "Hey, wait!"

He slowly turned around.

"Why don't you join us?" the redhead suggested as the women shifted chairs to make space for him. "I'm Roxie," she said, and pointed to the others. "This is Hannah, Amber, and you've apparently already met Bree."

"Let's just say she dropped into my life." He winked at Bree. "I'm Nick, and you must be the friend Bree lost," he said to Roxie. Then he made eye contact with each woman in turn.

They made quite an intriguing group, each an individual in appearance and sense of style. Besides redheaded Roxie with her fair complexion and dancing green eyes, there was petite Hannah with long blond hair and bangs that framed her deep brown doe eyes. Next came Amber, who had East-Asian features, straight black hair blunt cut at her collarbones with wispy bangs over a high forehead, and the impression that she was a very direct person.

Finally, there was Bree. Nick had trouble keeping a straight face. *Horrified* didn't come close to describing her expression at that moment. She didn't want him there, and she wasn't subtle about it. Her eyes nearly popped out of their sockets as she desperately telegraphed her feelings to her companions.

They were having none of it. In fact, they were completely ignoring her distress. The group seemed fun loving, so why not join them? Three out of four wanted him there. Not a bad percentage.

Besides, his cousin, Pete, hadn't shown up yet, so why not make new friends?

"What brings you ladies to the island?" he asked, determined to show Pete that he was still on his game. Pete had pressured him into coming on this trip with him, complaining that Nick hadn't taken time for himself since his life had been torn apart last spring. "Girls' vacation?" Nick guessed.

"A working vacation," Hannah said with a scowl.

"More work than vacation," Roxie grumbled,

and reached for a carrot. She gestured that Nick should help himself before dipping her carrot into the white dip on the large plate of appetizers they were sharing.

He laughed, chose a cheese cube and a raw mushroom, and then washed them down with a swig of the beer he'd brought with him. "How long are you staying?" He looked directly at Bree, who still seemed to be adjusting to his presence.

"Two more days." Bree looked down at her drink. "We leave Sunday afternoon."

"Yeah, only two more nights to have any fun on this island *paradise*," Amber said petulantly as she narrowed her gaze at Bree.

"Then you better stop wasting time." Nick tossed out his most sincere grin and rose from his chair. "Come on." He held out a hand to Bree, but she didn't take it. He kept smiling as he dropped his hand. For some reason, he felt the need to make her like him and prove that she'd been wrong about him. "There's a limbo contest and karaoke going on nearby, as well as a steel-drum band. There's also plenty more of whatever you're drinking out of those coconuts."

"Let's limbo!" The women were enthusiastic as they jumped up to join him, with Bree bringing up the rear.

"I love steel-drum bands!" one of them shouted. Nick downed the last of his beer and set his

plastic cup on the table along with the nearly devoured appetizer plate and several empty coconut shells.

The group stopped at the tiki bar to get fresh
drinks and to drop off the earring he'd found
before continuing on to search out the entertain-
ment Nick had suggested. From the way Bree
kept ignoring him and putting one of her friends
between them, she seemed determined to pretend
that he hadn't invaded her territory.

He refused to be deterred—he would win her
over. Besides, he *was* a nice guy, damn it. Everyone said so.

After several drinks and a quick dinner from a
kiosk on the street, a limbo contest on the beach
and a half-decent try at karaoke later, Nick finally
found himself alone with Bree at a corner table
in the main hotel lounge. He wasn't sure when
it had happened, but she seemed more comfortable around him. "Would you like to take a walk
on the beach?" he asked, raising his voice to be
heard. The steel-drum band had just begun another set after a short break, so conversation was
difficult.

"I should probably call it a night," she said on
a hiccup. Then she giggled, more evidence that
she'd finally relaxed.

"Maybe the fresh air will get rid of your hiccups," he suggested, enjoying Bree even more in her calmer state.

She giggled again. "That's silly." She picked up her empty coconut shell and considered it. "Did someone drink all of this?"

"You could say that." He grinned automatically and caught her hand in his. She smiled and didn't pull away, a dreamy look on her face with her eyes shuttered to mere slits.

"You know, you're not half-bad," she said. "I'm starting to get used to you."

"Gee, thanks." He laughed at her backhanded compliment. "You're not so bad, either." He meant the words. Once she'd given in and let herself enjoy her surroundings—live in the moment— she was fun to hang out with.

He wondered what it was about her that had made him think she was so vulnerable. Now he only saw her as damned attractive and overtly sexy. Not that he was looking to hook up, no matter what his cousin thought he should do.

So what if she had a slender body with just enough curves to make his own body react. And so what if her long, medium-brown hair had shades of gold that sparkled when light hit them. Just because the long layers rested against those delicately toned, bare upper arms didn't mean he wanted to kiss every inch of them.

The sudden urge to run his fingers through her

silky locks that she liked to toss made his fingers curl into tight fists, and he reined himself in.

"No, really," she said. "When we first met I thought you were pretty bossy and a know-it-all. But you actually seem like a pretty nice guy."

He grinned, blaming it on the sweet mixed drinks she'd been downing. He'd consumed more alcohol than he normally did and he was beginning to feel it. He suspected she didn't imbibe this much very often, either. She presented herself as always in control—of both herself and situations.

A short while ago, her friends had mysteriously disappeared after excusing themselves, one by one, to go to the bathroom. Nick checked his watch. The last woman had left nearly ten minutes ago. Either there was an emergency in the ladies' room or Bree's friends had deliberately abandoned her.

He chose the second option as having a higher probability. As protective of her as they seemed to be, he supposed this meant he had their approval as a chaperone. Of course, it wasn't like they'd been left alone in the woods. There were plenty of people still enjoying the tropical night.

"You have the nicest smile," Bree told him. "Thank you for catching me earlier. Have I thanked you already?"

"Yes, you have." He'd been absently rubbing his thumb over the back of her hand.

His cell phone vibrated in his pocket. He checked the caller ID, not surprised when he read it. "Excuse me a minute." He rose, touching Bree's bare shoulder and speaking close to her ear. "Promise you'll be here when I get back?" The citrus smell of her hair was nearly his undoing.

She nodded, held up three fingers in a mock salute and said, "I promise."

Damn. She was nearly irresistible.

"Hey, Pete," Nick greeted his cousin on the other end when he found a quieter spot to talk. "I've been trying to reach you. What happened to you earlier? I thought you were meeting me at the bar. After all, this weekend getaway was your idea."

"There was a problem on the boat and it's taking longer than expected." Nick and Pete had flown to San Juan, Puerto Rico, using Pete's airline miles. Then Pete had borrowed a friend's boat for them to come to Isla de la Blanca. Nick probably wouldn't have let himself be talked into coming if most of the trip hadn't been free.

"You need me to come back to the marina?" Pete had told Nick to go to the lodge without him so he could take a quick shower first.

"No, I've got it," Pete said. "There's a guy here who's helping me out. Shouldn't be too long now."

"Get here as soon as you can. You'll be happy to know that I met a group of really fun women."

"Excellent. Be there soon."

By the time he made it back to the table, he was second-guessing what he'd told Pete. The other three women were still nowhere in sight. Bree was alone—her head was on her folded arms and her eyes shut.

CHAPTER TWO

BREE LIFTED HER HEAD when she heard Nick move his chair as he returned from taking his phone call. She was tired and would have preferred to go to bed, but she'd promised the girls that she'd let her hair down while they were on vacation. She didn't think she'd had that much to drink. After all, how much alcohol could there be in those sweet drinks? Still, she felt a little wobbly when she stood up.

"Maybe some fresh air is a good idea," she told Nick. Afterward, she could go to bed with a clearer head.

"Let's go." He offered her his arm and she didn't refuse.

They stepped through the automatic doors and Bree drew in a deep breath, trying to counter the effects of the alcohol.

The air was humid, but the continuous breeze off the ocean was refreshing.

They followed a masonry walkway that led to a narrow boardwalk, and from there they walked down the few steps onto the sandy beach.

"Hold on a sec," Bree said, stopping abruptly. "I need to take my shoes off if we're going to walk on the sand."

They both slipped off their shoes and left them next to the stairs before heading to the water's edge.

The sky was clear and Bree saw more stars than she could count, wondering what constellations she was admiring.

"That's Orion, the Hunter," Nick said as if reading her mind. "Those three stars together make up his belt." He pointed to another cluster of stars and took a step to the side as if trying to keep his balance. So she wasn't the only one who was feeling the alcohol. "And that's Cassiopeia," he added.

He'd taken her hand somewhere between the lounge and the beach, but she didn't mind. In fact, she kind of liked it. She decided to blame her nonchalant attitude on too many sweet drinks.

"You're probably making that up to impress me," she teased.

"Is it working?" Nick chuckled, a pleasant sound that made Bree smile. "I promise, those are definitely Orion and Cassiopeia." He spoke as he looked toward the sky, wavering slightly. "Legend has it that Orion had women trouble. When he wooed Merope, the daughter of King Oenopion, she rebuffed him. One day he drank too much wine and tried to take Merope by force, so the king had Orion blinded and banished."

"Imagine if today's sex offenders met the same fate." Bree was fascinated by the tale. "So this guy, Orion, was blind forever?"

"No, eventually he regained his sight with the help of Hephaestus, the god of the forge. Not sure how a blacksmith can restore sight, but that's what I learned."

"What are you, an astronomer or something?" She knew very little about him aside from his skill at rescuing falling women.

"Nope. Just an Eagle Scout."

"Eagle Scout, very impressive. I'm sure your parents are very proud."

"They were," he told her in a more subdued tone.

"You make it sound like past tense." Bree cocked her head, waiting for his explanation.

"Sorry. My mother still brags about me." He paused. "My father died almost two years ago."

"I'm sorry." Her own father had been absent so much of her life that it sometimes felt like he was deceased. And he lived only a half hour away from her.

He shrugged off her condolence. "It was very sudden and there are times I still can't believe he's gone. He actually taught me how to navigate with the stars, and he did all the venture camping trips with me."

She tried to lighten his mood. "So I don't have to worry about getting lost, and you'll protect me from bears?"

That made him laugh, an enjoyable male sound. "I doubt we'll come across any bears on the beach, and as long as we stick next to the shore I'm pretty sure I can get us back to the main lodge."

Her head had cleared a bit and she didn't feel quite as out of control in the fresh air. At some point during the evening, she had stopped resenting Nick's intrusion on her girls' working vacation and begun having fun. He hadn't made a good first impression, but she had been willing to rethink her initial opinion of him.

Maybe the girls had been right about her needing to have a vacation fling. She wasn't about to seduce him, but he was definitely entertaining to have around.

"Someone mentioned earlier that you were all here on a working vacation," he said. "So what kind of work do you do?"

This was a subject she loved to talk about. "I own a company that helps women get ahead in their jobs. We offer training and guidance for women already in the workforce, as well as for those coming back into the workforce."

"Isn't that a little sexist, just focusing on women's issues?"

"Isn't it sexist for men to be paid more than women for the same job? Or for women to be passed over for promotions because they're of childbearing age and might require maternity leave?"

"Whoa! I've obviously struck a nerve. Sorry," he said. "I just wondered why you don't offer the same services to men. But you've explained it perfectly."

She relaxed. "I'm passionate about my company and what we do for women. Two years ago we even started loaning money to women to start up new businesses. So far, it's been very successful."

"That's great! When did you start the company?"

"Technically, about thirteen years ago."

His eyes widened in surprise.

"But I was still in college then," she added. "I didn't actually incorporate until two years later."

They were silent for a while, the pounding of the waves crashing on the shore making for a pleasant soundtrack.

"What brought you here?" she asked as they continued walking. "I didn't even know this place existed." The island was small, no more than a few square miles, but with all the luxuries imaginable. So far, four days into the trip, Bree had no complaints.

"Someone recommended it to me," he said as he looked at the sky.

"And you just had to check it out?"

"Something like that," he said cryptically, and then looked down at her. "Would you believe I just needed to get away?"

She shrugged. "But why here?"

"Why not? From where I'm standing right now, it seems like I chose wisely."

She stopped walking at those words.

He stopped, too, and turned to face her.

Their eyes met and she forgot to breathe. He took both of her hands and pulled her to him, wrapping her arms around his waist. His body was solid, and the heat coming off him suffused her in a cocoon of warmth and comfort.

She rested her cheek on his chest. The pounding of his heart and the hard muscles beneath his T-shirt were difficult to ignore.

He tipped up her chin with his finger. Her eyelids closed as his mouth descended on hers. Their first contact was chaste, but her lips hummed with expectation. She ran her hands up his back, enjoying the play of his muscles as he tightened his embrace.

He slanted his mouth over hers, deepening the

kiss and stealing her breath away. His hand on her lower back held her securely.

But then Nick ended the kiss abruptly, leaving Bree to question her kissing ability. "What—" she gasped, realizing how truly out of practice she was at this man-woman thing.

"I'm sorry," he said. "We should get back. Your friends will wonder what happened to you." He grabbed her hand and tugged her in the direction from which they'd come.

"Slow down," she cried, trying to keep up. Her foot landed on something sharp. "Ouch!" She liberated herself from his grasp and hopped on her good foot.

"What happened?" he asked, when she sat down hard on the damp sand.

"I think I cut my foot on something," she sputtered. Then she mumbled under her breath, "As if you cared." Not only was her pride hurt, but now she'd done a number on her foot if the pain she felt was any indication.

"Bree, I'm sorry. It's not you," he began. "I—"

"Save it." She'd never been as good as her friends were with the opposite sex. Up until this moment, she hadn't really cared.

She brushed the sand from her cut foot to discover she was bleeding. The moon and stars were bright, but not bright enough to see how deep the cut was. "It's bleeding."

Without another word, he picked her up and carried her back to where the light was brighter and set her down.

"You might need stitches," Nick said, after examining her foot.

No way. That would mean needles and she didn't do needles. "I'm sure some antibiotic ointment and a bandage will do."

"Let's get a second opinion," he said as he lifted her again and proceeded to carry her to the hotel. He inquired at the front desk about a nearby infirmary, and was directed to the resort's clinic, just a short walk away. He was also given a towel to wrap around her foot.

"Really, Nick, I'll be fine." Being carried around by a strong, sexy guy might be some girl's fantasy but not hers. She was just plain embarrassed.

He ignored her pleas, as well as her demands to walk on her own. And about five minutes later she was seated in front of a nurse, who was irrigating the sand and debris from Bree's wound.

"All this fuss is ridiculous," she said to Nick.

"Humor me," he said from the fake leather chair in the corner of the exam room. His arms were crossed, the ankle of one leg resting on the knee of the other. Thankfully, he'd picked up their shoes on the way to the clinic, donning his but not even allowing her to carry her own shoes, which were now on the floor next to his chair.

"The wound is pretty deep," the nurse stated. "The doctor will be in to stitch you up in a few minutes. When was your last tetanus shot?"

Bree's heart stopped. Stitches *and* a shot? "In high school," she mumbled. There hadn't been a need for one since then. She wasn't exactly an outdoorsy kind of gal.

The nurse raised an eyebrow. "And you're thirty-three now?"

Bree nodded her head and frowned.

The nurse made a note in Bree's chart. "I'll be back with the booster when the doctor has finished stitching you up."

"It's not that bad," Nick said when the nurse left them alone. He must have seen her panicked expression. "They'll numb you and——"

The doctor knocked before opening the door, a syringe visible in his hand.

"Numb me? With a needle?" She was suddenly light-headed. "I don't feel so well."

Then everything went black.

NICK FOUGHT OFF CONSCIOUSNESS without success the next morning when bright light stabbed through his eyelids to penetrate the center of his brain with white-hot fire.

He moaned in agony, brought his hand to his head and squinted at the source of his torture.

A sliver of daylight shone through the room-darkening drapes where they hadn't closed completely.

He rolled from his left side to his back and realized he wasn't alone. He wasn't even on the tiny bunk on the boat, which meant this wasn't his bed. His head jerked to his right, the pain slicing through his skull again.

"Bree!" he gasped. They were in her cottage.

"Hmm?" She lay on her right side, her back facing him.

Nick knew the minute Bree regained consciousness, because she rolled to her back before abruptly sitting up straight. Her hands flew to her head and she moaned. She pulled up the sheet to protect her modesty, but there was no need.

She was fully dressed in the shorts and tank top she'd changed into after they'd gone to the hot tub.

How had he—they—ended up in such a compromising position?

"What happened?" Bree demanded in too loud a voice for his ears to tolerate. Her hand flew to her temple and she lowered her voice. "What are you doing here?" She got out of bed and looked around the room as if there was an answer. "Did we—?"

Nick lifted the sheet to look at his lower body. Definitely fully clothed, too. "I wish I could remember, but I don't think so."

"You don't remember?" Bree's bug-eyed expression would have been laughable if there had been anything funny about the situation. "Believe me, if we had—you know—there'd be no way you wouldn't remember."

"Right back atcha," he countered.

Bree turned away in a huff, nearly losing her balance on her one good foot before she grabbed on to the bedside table. "Why are you in my bed?"

He sat up too quickly, his head throbbing from the effort. "I have no idea. I'm going to take a guess and say we both passed out last night. Or very early this morning."

He had this nagging memory of Bree being anything but prudish as she—

Damn. Why couldn't he remember?

It was more than eight excruciating months since he'd had sex, and here he was with no memory of what could well have been a truly memorable experience. Never mind. He'd obviously passed out before anything happened or they wouldn't still be fully dressed.

Unless…

"Do you remember anything about last night?" he asked tentatively. "Did we—?"

"You really don't remember?" She glared at

him and then turned away before answering. "Of course we didn't do anything." Her words said one thing, her attitude another. She didn't have a clue, either.

He looked on the floor around the bed and then walked over to check the wastebasket. No sign that they'd used protection. He could only hope they hadn't been completely stupid. "So do you remember everything?" he asked.

She stomped toward the bathroom in a huff, her hurt foot preventing a full demonstration of the desired impact. She stopped short, put her fingertips to her temple and then faced him. "I'm going to take a shower. I expect you to be gone when I come out." Her words were succinct, and, judging by her wincing, her head obviously hurt to utter them.

Bree didn't wait for his reply and slammed the bathroom door behind her. He felt the noise pound like something was trying to escape from his head, and at the same time he heard her moan.

Instead of leaving, he came around the bed to talk through the closed door.

They had to talk. If not now, then later if she needed time to pull herself together. He had to fill in the missing pieces. He couldn't leave things between them like this. He'd really enjoyed their time together—at least what he remembered—and he didn't want her to think of him as a bad guy.

He checked the bedside clock. It was just after nine, so they had at least eight blank hours. The last thing he recalled was planning to bring Bree back to her room after the doctor stitched up her foot. But when they heard her girlfriends frolicking in the hot tub, they'd made a detour to see them. After that, a blur.

Nick had opened his mouth to speak when the sunlight streaming through the crack in the drapes shone on a napkin with an embossed *W* and an anchor on the dresser across the room. He walked closer and his breath caught in his throat.

He was beginning to remember.

Damn, damn, damn.

They'd all gone back to the boat, where they'd done shots. It came back to him now.

Pete had come to the hot tub when Nick had texted him where they were. Pete then invited everyone to the boat. It was obvious that he'd made a liquor run, because the booze had been free-flowing.

Nick also remembered that Bree had refused to take any pain medication since she'd already been drinking, so Nick had figured the shot or two she'd had afterward would at least dull her pain. But from the look of her this morning, she must have had more than he'd known about.

From the other side of the bathroom door, Bree let out a yelp.

"Is everything okay, Bree?" Nick yelled over his shoulder, and opened the door to check on her while mumbling softly to himself. "'Cause it sure as hell isn't okay out here."

BREE HUDDLED IN the corner of the large bathroom, trying to ignore her queasy stomach and aching head. She kept her eyes focused on the creature in the glass-enclosed shower stall.

Nick came straight through the bathroom door she'd neglected to lock after slamming it, his gaze taking in the room until it stopped on Bree. "What's wrong? Is it your foot?"

Bree's hand shook as she pointed to the shower stall. "In there." She hated that she needed his help, but there was no way she was touching that slimy creature.

Nick stepped closer to the stall and laughed. "It's just a harmless frog. I've seen them all over the island, either live or painted on something. It's called a coqui, I think, named after the sound it makes."

"Don't tell me," she grumbled, the slightest sound piercing her brain, "you earned a merit badge on frogs, too."

"If you don't want my help—" He turned to walk out.

"No, no, please." She'd get down on her hands and knees to beg if that was what it took.

He reached for the shower-door handle.

"Don't open the—" she yelled without thinking, sucking in a breath when her head reminded her to lower her voice. "It might escape."

"It won't hurt you, Bree. In fact, it's probably more afraid of you than you are of it."

"Isn't that what people always say about small creatures who are venomous or carry disease?"

He ignored her and opened the shower door a little at a time. Bree squeezed her eyes to mere slits as he stepped carefully inside the stall, shutting the door behind him. He cornered the frog and carefully picked it up. Cupped in Nick's large hands, the frog looked smaller than she'd originally thought. Maybe two to three inches at most.

"What are you going to do with it?" she asked when he stepped out of the shower.

He held the frog gently in one hand. "I'll take it outside and release it." He winked at her. "Don't worry, I won't do it too close to your cabin." He gestured to her bandaged foot with his head. "Don't forget, you can't get that wet."

"I know. I thought it might be easier to take a bath." She gestured to the separate tub. Truthfully, she'd forgotten that she had to keep her foot dry. That seemed to be the least of her problems.

The total loss of memory about what had happened last night was her major concern.

"There's probably a plastic laundry bag somewhere if you'd like me to seal up your foot."

That sounded like a better idea. A long soak in the tub would feel wonderful, but if she wanted to wash her hair, the shower would be best. "Good idea, but I can handle it myself."

Bree heard Nick go outside and she searched the room for the laundry bag while trying to put two and two together. The hard part was that she had no two and two to put together. Her memory was completely blank.

She had drunk a lot more than she usually allowed herself, that much was clear. After she'd passed out in the doctor's office, embarrassing herself beyond measure, she remembered coming to and finding the doctor almost finished stitching her foot. Nick had actually been very sweet by distracting her while the nurse gave her a tetanus booster shot. Bree moved her arm tentatively, happy that it didn't hurt too much, at least not yet. Although nothing was as bad as her headache at the moment.

She remembered Nick walking her back to her cabin. But wait a minute… They'd stopped walking when they'd heard laughing in the distance and Bree had recognized her girlfriends' voices.

So they'd followed the sound to the hot tub. Right, the hot tub.

Amber had been curled up in a towel on a lounge chair, an empty champagne bottle on the ground next to her. Hannah had sat on the edge of the pool, dangling her feet in the water. Roxie. What had Roxie been doing? Oh, right. She'd been in the hot tub with a couple of other people.

She remembered something else, but had no clue how much time had passed between the two memories. There was something about a boat. Had they been on a boat?

The rest was a blank until she woke up this morning next to Nick. At least they'd been fully clothed.

Had they slept together? Evidence pointed to them doing just what Nick had suggested. Sleeping or—more precisely—passing out.

Nick walked back into the cabin then, ending her musings. He headed directly to the small kitchen sink in the corner of the cabin and washed his hands.

"Have you been tested?" she asked.

He spun around. "Tested?"

"Yes. Have you been tested for…for STDs?" The thought that she might have been so stupid made her stomach roil.

"Did you remember something from last night?" he asked, instead. He turned away to finish washing his hands as if she'd merely inquired about the time.

"I don't like to take chances in case something happened between us. Just answer the question. Have you, or have you not, been tested recently?" She could barely breathe, anticipating his reply.

He dried his hands on the towel hanging on the side of the upper cupboard and finally faced her, a dead serious look on his face.

"Yes, I've been tested. You don't have to worry." He was hiding an emotion that Bree couldn't quite decipher.

"You don't have to worry about me, either," she said quickly, in case that was what his reaction was about. Her gynecologist tested her yearly, but you had to be having unprotected sex to contract an STD.

That counted her out since she hadn't had sex since—

"Did you find a plastic bag?" he asked.

She was happy to change the subject. "No, I got distracted." Trying to remember if she'd screwed up last night.

He walked to the closet next to the bathroom door and opened it. He reached in for the dry-cleaning bag hanging there. "This will work perfectly. Do you have a rubber band or something to go around your leg to seal it?"

She nodded and hobbled to the bathroom where she had a hair scrunchie she thought would fit over her foot and ankle. He'd followed her and she handed it to him.

"Sit down over there." He pointed to the closed toilet.

"I told you I can do it myself."

"I heard you the first time," he said. "But if your head feels anything like mine, then it's going to explode if you lean over."

As much as she wanted to argue, she knew he was probably right.

She took a seat and watched the top of his head as he dealt with the plastic bag, wrapping it tightly enough around her ankle to keep out water. He looked up at her and asked, "Is that too tight?"

She shook her head, and that same vague memory came to her as his gaze met hers. She couldn't wrap her head around it because it didn't make sense. "Were we on a boat last night?"

"A boat?" he asked. "You remember being on the boat, too?"

So there *was* a boat.

She nodded slightly. "We were all there. You, me, my friends." She paused. "Wait. There was another guy there, too."

"Pete. Pete Buchanan."

She nodded. "Yes. That sounds familiar."

"He's my cousin, although he's legally my brother. My parents raised him after his mom and dad were killed in a car accident when he was eight."

"Oh, that's terrible," she said. "So it was his boat we were on?"

"No, we borrowed it from a friend of his who lives in San Juan. This vacation was all Pete's idea. He thought I needed to get away, stop focusing on work so much."

"Sounds familiar," she said. "That's exactly what the girls said to me. 'Go have a vacation fling,' they said. 'You work too hard.'"

"I guess we have that in common," he said quietly.

He was being very nice to her, and she hadn't been as thankful as she should be. In fact, she'd been openly hostile. Opening her mouth to speak, she was suddenly very aware that he still had his hand on her calf. Their eyes met and she couldn't look away. Without thinking she put her hand to his bearded cheek, remembering the softness of it when he'd kissed her on the beach.

She wanted him to kiss her again. In fact, she wanted more than a kiss. She wanted him. All of him. She wanted to take her girlfriends' advice and have that vacation fling.

With Nick.

She leaned in and he did, too. When their

mouths met, she knew for sure that nothing had happened between them last night except for that kiss on the beach. She definitely would have recalled the electricity between them.

Nick rose, pulling her up with him until they were both standing. He deepened the kiss and her body kept screaming that she wanted more.

He suddenly lifted her, and her legs wrapped around his waist. He carried her to the bed without removing his mouth from hers. She touched him everywhere she could reach—his back, his hair, his face, his arms, his butt. She couldn't get enough.

He caressed her, as well, his large hands learning her body. When he stopped kissing her suddenly and pulled back to look her in the eyes, she groaned. She didn't want him to stop. She didn't want this to be a repeat of how he'd ended their kiss on the beach.

"Are you completely sober?" A strange question to ask her at this moment.

"Yes, I'm sober. Why?" She ran her hand down his chest to his abs, lingering on the button at his waistband.

He grabbed her hand and held it in his. "I'm serious. I don't take advantage of inebriated women. I'm pretty sure neither of us was in good enough shape to do anything last night, but if you're sure you're sober enough to consent—" he grinned and waggled his eyebrows "—then I plan on taking full advantage."

She grinned back. "Would you like it in writing or is my word good enough?"

His answer came in his extremely adept actions. Words were definitely unnecessary.

CHAPTER THREE

QUITE A WHILE LATER, after a most satisfying time in bed, Bree and Nick moved their activities to the shower. Still breathing hard, Nick reached around Bree's wet and sexy body to turn off the water. She was facing away from him, and when she leaned back into him, she ran her hands up and down the outside of his wet thighs. He kissed the side of her neck and pressed his hand to her abdomen. He slowly inched upward until he cupped her breast, teasing her nipple between his thumb and forefinger.

He kissed her shoulder and groaned. "You feel so good," he whispered close to her ear before reaching for a towel for her and then one for him.

"Need help?" he asked when she turned toward him as he toweled off his hair.

She grinned back. "I think you've been quite enough help, thank you."

He opened the glass shower door and exited, wrapping his towel around his waist and securing it.

"I'm starving," he said as his stomach growled. "Want to grab breakfast?"

When she didn't say anything, he turned to look at her. She'd wrapped her towel around her body and now held on to it tightly between her breasts. She seemed to be surprised by his question.

"It's just a meal," he said. "I could use some coffee and about a gallon of water. Plus food."

"I know. But…the girls will be expecting me." She removed the wet laundry bag from her foot and tossed it into the trash can.

"Sure. I understand. I hope they're feeling better than we were when we woke up." He grinned. "My head still feels like it could explode any minute."

"Could have fooled me," she quipped as she ran a comb through her hair. "Your head didn't seem to bother you a little while ago."

He chuckled. "Yeah, I think I may have found the perfect hangover cure."

She smiled at him in the mirror and he felt an unfamiliar twist in his gut. He really enjoyed being with her. "Maybe we can get together later today. You're here until tomorrow, right?"

"Right. We leave tomorrow. I don't remember what time. I'll have to check and see what the girls have planned." She sounded hesitant.

"Is something wrong?" He suddenly felt slightly unsure of himself.

She hobbled past him to the bathroom door and turned to face him. "No, nothing's wrong." She smiled, a pleasant smile. Almost a sympathetic smile. One to let him down easy? "I've had a great time with you, Nick—"

"But that's it," he finished for her. He raised his hands. "Hey, I get it. A vacation fling and all that. What happens here, stays here." He could feel his blood pressure rising as he spoke. "We both have lives to get back to."

"You're not upset, are you? I thought you'd be relieved that I'm not going to become clingy just because we had sex."

He should be feeling relief. He'd come here for the same reason. To relax for a few days before returning home to the problems that were mounting for him there.

He didn't need to add another to the list.

"You're right. Anything more right now isn't an option for me anyway."

"Same here," Bree said. "My friends say I'm married to my job."

"And what do you say?"

"I say I'm dedicated to my company and have no time or interest in a relationship."

AFTER NICK LEFT, Bree limped around her cabin as she slowly got dressed. She could tell that Nick hadn't liked that she'd been the one to say that nothing would come of the good time they'd had together. She really liked Nick, but she also knew that being in a relationship would take up too much of her time and she wanted to focus on her company right now.

She braided her wet hair and made her way toward the breakfast buffet in the main lodge of the resort, although she had no appetite. Which was surprising after all the physical activity she and Nick had engaged in. In fact, the mere thought of food had her stomach reacting negatively. What she really wanted was coffee. Maybe that would help this awful hangover, because the large amounts of water she'd consumed in her cabin hadn't done a thing for her.

As soon as she entered the large dining room, she nearly left again but was stopped by her friends waving to her. The smell of the food was upsetting her stomach even more. She was definitely avoiding alcohol for the near—and far—future.

Maybe she just needed dry toast and some precious coffee. She was well-known for not being able to function without several cups of the stuff during the day. So she headed to her friends' table, and they pulled up another chair for her to join them. They all started speaking to her at once.

"How are you feeling?" Hannah wanted to know.

"You don't look so good," Amber said, not hiding the truth. "Is your foot bothering you?"

"Why don't I get you a coffee," Roxie suggested, and left the table before Bree could reply.

"My foot's the least of my problems. Can someone tell me what happened last night, please?" She looked directly at Amber and then Hannah. Although after what had taken place between her and Nick this morning, it didn't matter so much whether they had done the nasty during the night. She'd just like to fill in the missing hours in her memory bank.

"You don't remember?" Amber asked, while Hannah seemed to go slightly pale.

"I wouldn't be asking if I remembered."

Roxie set a cup of black coffee in front of Bree. One whiff of it nearly did her in, and she pushed the cup away.

"You *really* must not be feeling well," Hannah said unnecessarily. "You never turn down coffee. Can I get you something else?"

When Bree could answer without gagging, she said, "Maybe dry toast."

"I'll be right back."

"Thanks," Bree whispered as Hannah left the table.

"Maybe you should go lie down for a while," Roxie suggested.

Bree shook her head. Her hands flew to her temples as she reminded herself not to shake her head unless she wanted the feeling of a jackhammer through her skull. How had she managed to have incredible sex with such a terrible hangover? Obviously, her body had compensated for her discomfort. Not that sex with Nick had been anything but spectacular.

"I'm not going anywhere until I find out what happened last night." She paused, squinting her eyes. "Were we on a boat?"

The women grinned. "Yep," Amber said. "Nick and his cousin, Pete, took a boat here from San Juan. Too bad you don't remember anything because you were having a great time."

"Yeah, but you weren't very good at the drinking game we were playing," Hannah said as she set a plate with dry toast in front of Bree. "That's probably why you don't feel so good now."

Bree gave her a forced smile, knowing better than to nod her head. "Nick told me about Pete. They were raised as brothers after Pete's parents died."

A collective "oh" came from her friends.

"See, Rox, all the more reason for you to give Pete a chance," Amber told her.

Bree looked to Roxie. "You and Pete?"

Roxie shook her head vehemently. "No way." She looked at Amber and addressed them all. "You know Jim and I are still together. Things may be a bit rocky, but there's no way I'd cheat on him."

The women had been a little relieved when Jim moved away, hoping that he and Roxie would eventually call it quits. It wasn't that they didn't like Jim—they just didn't think his and Roxie's relationship was one that would last. Jim was a nice guy, but he could be picky. There were restaurants he wouldn't try because he was sure he wouldn't like the cuisine. He hated horror movies and Roxie loved them. And, worst of all, he had a problem with her spending any free time with Bree, Hannah and Amber. He wanted her all to himself.

"We all know you'd never cheat on Jim. Maybe Pete just wants to be friends." Bree picked up a piece of toast, even though she didn't really want it, hoping it might soak up whatever was upsetting her stomach. She took a few bites and kept them down with difficulty. Thinking she might be able to drink the coffee now, Bree pulled it closer. But as soon as the aroma reached her, she pushed it away again.

If she tried to drink it, she'd never keep it down. So now, on top of a hangover, she'd probably have a caffeine headache, too.

"I don't think friendship has anything to do with whatever Pete wants." Roxie shook her head vehemently. "Even if Jim weren't in the picture, Pete's not my type."

Bree came to her friend's rescue and changed the subject. "I think I'll take Roxie's advice and go back to my cabin to rest," Bree said. "Maybe I'll feel better when I wake up." She rose slowly, the room tipping slightly as she did. "Please promise me that you'll never let me drink that much again." She gave a little wave and slowly made her way out of the room.

WHILE NICK HEADED to the marina from Bree's cabin, he wondered why he cared whether Bree wanted to spend more time with him or not. It wasn't like he would ever see her after this. He didn't even know where she lived.

There was a lot they didn't know about each other. He realized that they hadn't even shared last names.

"Hey, buddy," his cousin said from the galley when Nick came aboard the boat. "You must have had a good night." From the way Pete looked this morning, he had probably been just as drunk as Nick and Bree.

"I wish I could remember it," Nick said as he helped himself to a cup of coffee. "I know we were doing shots here, but I don't remember how I got to Bree's cabin."

"Ha! The girls walked both of you back to the

lodge. Seemed like they were trying to get you two together."

Well, they'd succeeded, hadn't they? "And you weren't part of that conspiracy?"

Pete put up a hand. "Hey, I've been telling you for months that you need a social life, but I can't take credit for whatever happened between the two of you." Pete cocked his head to the side. "So what *did* happen?"

"We woke up in bed together—"

Pete perked up.

"—fully clothed."

Pete's shoulders slumped. "Damn, I thought you were gonna say—"

"I know what you thought. But I'm telling you what happened." At least part of it. For some reason, he wanted to keep his time with Bree to himself. For now. Possibly for always.

Besides, what difference did it make, since he'd probably never see her again?

"Sorry to disappoint you," Nick said, remembering that Bree had been anything *but* disappointing. He sat down with his mug of coffee.

"You're the one who should be disappointed," Pete said.

"Why's that?"

"She was supposed to be your first step to taking back your life."

Nick leaned forward, his eyes open wide as he asked, "What are you talking about?"

"Getting Tracy out of your system."

"Oh." Pete had been saying the same thing for months. He'd never been a fan of Nick's ex, and having her call off their wedding the week before the date hadn't ingratiated her to Pete. "Doesn't matter anyway. She's really dedicated to her career and says she has no time for relationships."

Pete nodded. "That's right. I remember Roxie—who, by the way, is damn hot—telling me about what their company does. Helps women, lends them money and stuff."

"Yeah, that sounds about right."

Pete's eyes widened. "Hey, I think I've got the answer to all your problems."

"I doubt that."

"Listen. Bree's company lends money, so why shouldn't she loan some to you to save your restaurant?"

Nick shook his head. "Did you miss the part about how she only loans money to *women*? That kinda leaves me out of the running."

"Maybe, maybe not."

"Please tell me you're not thinking I should sleep with her to make a good impression?" He was pretty sure he'd already lived up to her expectations.

"I wasn't, but that's not a terrible idea. Seriously, though, she'd probably lend you money if she got to know you better."

Well, that wasn't going to happen.

"*And*, there's also the fact that while the restaurant isn't completely female-owned, it is partially female-owned."

"What do you mean? You and I own the restaurant." What was Pete talking about?

"Okay, now don't get mad, Nick. But you know how we needed help when things went south?"

"How can I forget?" After his ex, Tracy, dumped him, he'd gone into a funk, not paying enough attention to what was going on at The Fresh Pantry, the restaurant he'd opened three years ago. To make matters worse, at the same time, he'd found out an employee was stealing from him and his food supplier had been overcharging him. His world had imploded all at once, and now he was struggling to keep his restaurant afloat.

"So I went to Auntie Em," Pete said, referring to Nick's mom. "She was happy to help."

"What money did she use?" Please don't say she borrowed from her 401(k).

"She took a loan from her retirement account," Pete said.

Nick slumped over. "I can't believe you went behind my back—both you and my mom. Why didn't you tell me this before?"

"Because Auntie Em didn't want you to know. But now you need to know so that you can hit up Bree for a loan. See how it's all working out perfectly?" Pete looked hopeful.

How could he ever ask Bree for money now without her thinking he'd slept with her for just that reason? What a mess.

CHAPTER FOUR

NICK HAD BEEN home from the island almost two weeks, and every single day his cousin had asked him the same question.

As soon as he saw Pete enter the restaurant's professional kitchen, Nick stopped chopping herbs for a new pork marinade he was trying out and waited for it.

"Have you called Bree about loaning the restaurant money yet?" Before they even left the island, Pete had looked up Bree's company online and discovered that it was located in Northern Virginia, not too far from where Nick's restaurant was located.

Pete had obviously come straight from his engineering consulting office because the top button of his pale green dress shirt was open and his navy-and-green tie was loosened and hung at an odd angle. Thanks to Pete's hard work over the past several months, the company he worked for had been awarded a big government contract. But now that he didn't have to put in so much overtime, Pete had more time to bug Nick about talking to Bree.

Nick sighed and began chopping garlic while he spoke. "For the last time, I'm not going to ask Bree for financial help." He hadn't told anyone, including his cousin, about sleeping with her, and he planned to keep it that way. The only problem with that plan was that Pete wasn't buying Nick's reason for not calling Bree.

If he called her at all, it would be to ask to see her again on a personal basis, certainly not for money. But he hadn't called her yet because she'd made it clear on the island that she didn't want him to. She'd brushed him off again when she and her girlfriends and Pete and Nick had met before leaving the island. Not that he could blame her. She seemed to want to keep their very brief fling a secret *and* in the past.

His body reacted to the memory of their one morning together, and he nearly sliced his finger.

He hadn't been able to get her off his mind since he'd returned home, and it wasn't only the sex he recalled. Their sniping banter had been very entertaining. He'd never had that kind of connection with Tracy. Bree had lit a fire in him with just a spark from her sharp tongue. Maybe that was what Tracy had realized when she'd called off their wedding—they had lost their spark...or maybe it had never been there.

"Are you even listening to me?" Pete asked in a tone that revealed his frustration.

Nick blinked and looked up from the cutting board. "Sorry. What did you say?"

"I said I don't buy that you won't ask Bree for money because you don't want to take advantage of your friendship. I know that you haven't had *any* contact with her since we left the island. Not much of a friendship."

Nick agreed that was a weak excuse, but it was the only one he'd been able to come up with. That and the fact that Bree's company lent money only to female-owned businesses. Even though Nick's mom had a partial stake in the restaurant, she wasn't the majority owner. He didn't know why Pete wouldn't just drop it.

"Nick, don't you realize you'll lose this place without financial help?" He spread his arms wide to encompass the restaurant Nick had opened by using every penny he had.

"We're still pulling in a solid number of customers every night, even on weeknights," Nick said.

Pete shook his head slowly. "That's not enough, buddy, and you know it. The restaurant needs a shot of cash now or you'll lose the lease on the building."

Nick gritted his teeth. He blamed himself for the mess they were in. He'd been so focused on his breakup with Tracy and paying off wedding expenses that he hadn't seen what was going on around him. He'd let things get out of his control, and you couldn't run a successful business like that. But learning a few weeks ago that he might lose his restaurant had been a wake-up call.

"I'm working on some other things, Pete." That was true, but they were pie-in-the-sky ideas that would take time before they produced a profit— nothing that would bring in fast cash. "And don't forget that restaurant week starts in a few weeks. That always brings in customers."

"It's just not enough, man. We need cash now."

"Hello, boys." Nick's mother appeared just in time to stop the conversation. She was in her mid-sixties but was often told she could pass for late forties. He'd witnessed younger men flirt with her while she worked at the restaurant's hostess station, a job she'd taken on part-time when they'd opened. She'd been his most dedicated employee, only taking off the week his dad passed away.

"Hi, Mom, what are you doing here?" Nick asked as she presented her cheek for his kiss. The restaurant was closed Mondays, which was why he'd thought he'd have the kitchen to himself to work on new recipes.

"Can't a mother come by to see her son?" Her tone was slightly haughty but mostly teasing. She looked at Pete. "I even lucked out and get to see both of my sons at once."

Nick rolled his eyes. "You work here, Mom. We see each other every day." He set down his knife. "So what's up?"

His mom smiled and winked at Pete. "He always sees through me," she said.

Pete grinned. "I have to say I'm also wondering what you're up to, Auntie Em." Nick's mother's given name was Emily, but most people shortened it to Em. When Nick's parents had adopted Pete after his own parents died in a car accident when he was eight, Nick's mom suggested Pete call them Mom and Dad if he was comfortable doing so. Pete had acquiesced when it came to Dad, but, after seeing *The Wizard of Oz*, he'd always called Nick's mom Auntie Em and wasn't about to call her anything else.

His mother pursed her lips and narrowed her eyes at Pete, probably surprised that he hadn't automatically taken her side against Nick for once.

"As a matter of fact," Nick's mother said to Pete, "I'm glad you're here, too." She began digging through her purse until she came up with a few slips of paper. "A friend of mine is opening a pop-up restaurant tonight, and I'd like you both to come with me." She looked expectantly at them. "It's more like an open house or cocktail party. My friend is showcasing her tapas menu and wants to generate some financial interest in the restaurant she's hoping to open."

Nick looked at Pete, who shrugged, and then back at his mother. "Who is this friend?" With his restaurant in the heart of Old Town Alexandria, Virginia, he was usually pretty savvy about what was going on with other restaurants in the area.

She didn't meet his eyes, instead concentrating on moving things around in her purse. "No one special. Just someone I met at my yoga class. She's a lovely woman. We went for coffee the other day, and she invited me to come tonight and to bring a few people."

"No reservations required?" Nick was suspicious of the whole setup. His mother had been a matchmaker her entire life. And since Pete had a new woman on his arm every week or two, her attention was fixated more on Nick's lack of female companionship. She claimed she wasn't getting any younger and wanted grandchildren.

She held out the slips of paper she'd taken from her purse. "I was waiting for you to agree to come. Here's a ticket for each of you. The address and time are right there." She paused, then looked from one man to the other. "Would you like to bring someone with you?"

"No, thanks," Nick said.

"I might," Pete said, catching Nick off guard.

"You would?" Nick narrowed his eyes at Pete.

"Sure. Why not?" Pete took a second ticket from Nick's mother. "I've got someone in mind."

"Well, darn," she said to Pete. "I was thinking you and Pinar, tonight's pop-up restaurateur, might hit it off."

"You did?" Nick stopped short before asking why she thought the woman was right for Pete and not Nick. Never mind. He wasn't interested anyway.

"Yes, dear," she said, tilting her head at his question. "Oh, well, I guess I'll see you both later, then." She waved over her shoulder as she hurried out the back door that led to the alley behind the restaurant.

"What do you suppose that was all about?" Nick asked Pete when they were alone again.

Pete shrugged. "Beats me. You know how she is."

He certainly did, and that's exactly why he was concerned.

LATE MONDAY AFTERNOON, Bree entered the main conference room at the BeeTee office. Roxie, Amber and Hannah were already seated, silent as they were busy on laptops or cell phones.

She pulled out her chair at the head of the table, setting her glass of water down in front of her as she lowered herself into her seat. "Would you mind moving your coffee cup?" she asked Amber, who sat to her right.

Amber's head jerked up, and she narrowed her dark eyes as she moved the cup. "You're still not able to drink coffee?"

"Are you sick?" Roxie asked, looking up from her phone to join the conversation from her place next to Amber. "You haven't been right since the island. That was two weeks ago."

Hannah added in her two cents. "Yeah. You've never been able to survive without coffee."

Bree shrugged. "I don't know. Just the smell of it makes me nauseous. Ever since we got back from vacation."

"But a hangover doesn't last two weeks," Roxie pointed out. "Maybe you should see a doctor. Could be an ulcer or something."

Bree waved away her suggestion. "I'm fine. I've probably just upset my stomach lining with so much alcohol and now I'm paying the price." She paused. "Maybe it's a good thing, healthwise. I've not only given up alcohol but coffee, too. I'm sure this is just temporary." She consulted the list of discussion items she'd brought with her. "Let's get started. I'd like to get home and freshen up before we head to dinner."

The women nodded in agreement and got down to business. They spent the next hour on each of their departments. Roxie, the most outgoing of the group, was head of marketing. Amber was head of technology, a role in which her confidence and skill served her well. And Hannah was the artistic one of the group who consulted with clients about their websites and corporate logos.

Bree had been blessed with a group of friends who got along so wonderfully while having entirely different talents to offer BeeTee. And they worked well together when it came to making big decisions.

"Everything sounds good," Bree announced after they'd each finished briefing her. "Is there anything else I should know about Pinar Garcia and her restaurant?" They'd already decided to back her restaurant, but hadn't told Pinar yet. Going to her pop-up tonight was just a formality to see how she handled a hungry crowd.

"Nothing new," Roxie said. "Her background check came back and all seems fine. Nothing more than the student loan she's nearly repaid and no criminal record."

"Glad to hear it." Bree gathered her things and paused before standing. "What time is dinner?"

"Six to nine," Hannah said. "Why don't we meet at The Tides around six thirty?"

"Sounds good to me," Roxie said. "Pinar said they have our names at the door."

Bree nodded and the others began talking about what they were going to wear this evening. She left the conference room and headed back to her office. She had one last phone call to return before going home.

The advantage of locating her company in Arlington, Virginia, was the ability to walk home from work to her high-rise condo. The two-block distance was usually not a problem weatherwise except for early February days like today with freezing rain. If given the choice, she would rather take a long soak in her tub and then put on her comfy PJs than go out tonight. But this was her job, and this was important. She blamed her recent lack of energy on working too hard without her usual high doses of caffeine, as well as it being the most dreary month of the year.

By the time she reached the restaurant later, there was a line of people to go in.

"Come to the front." Roxie had appeared behind her. "You don't need to wait out here."

Bree wasn't the type to use her influence when it meant others couldn't benefit, as well, but she did as Roxie suggested. After giving her name to the woman at the hostess desk, Bree said to her, "Several people are standing outside getting wet. Is there any way you can get them inside quicker?"

The young hostess appeared startled. "I'm so sorry, Ms. Tucker." She came around the podium. "I'll make sure they get inside. There's probably enough room for them to wait in the entrance-way. And I'll try to get them checked in faster."

Bree nodded her approval. "Great. We want the patrons to enjoy the food and not be turned off before they get to try it."

"Nice going," Roxie said when the girl was out of earshot. "The hostess, I think her name is Calista, is Pinar's younger sister. I'm not sure she has much experience, so I'll keep an eye on her."

"Good idea," Bree said. "Let's check out the food. I'm starving."

"Me, too."

The restaurant was set up with the eatery's usual tables and chairs, but a long table with food on it buffet-style had been added at the far end of the room. The idea for Pinar's pop-up restaurant was to offer a tapas-only dinner, but not in a formal dinner style. Instead, diners could mix and mingle, stand or sit, whatever they preferred. More like a casual cocktail party than a sit-down dinner, which was a nice nod to the origin of tapas. Pinar had explained that the small plates had been initially designed to cover glasses of alcohol, specifically sherry, to keep the fruit flies away.

The decor in The Tides restaurant was nautical, but definitely on the tasteful side—no large fish hanging from the ceiling or nets filled with crustaceans. Instead, the pale blues and greens on the walls were a nice backdrop to ocean vistas in framed photographs, as well as oil and water-color depictions of calm seas.

Bree had been to The Tides many times. Her favorite dish was their mahimahi in a bourbon sauce, quite different from the Spanish tapas laid out on the table in front of her for this pop-up restaurant event.

She recognized some of the food, like empanadas and olives stuffed with anchovies. But others were new to her. Pinar had been smart to put little signs in front of each platter to tell diners what they were eating.

There was a potato dish with a sauce she couldn't identify, and chorizo cooked in wine that she could probably make a meal of by itself.

"How do you think it's going?" Pinar had made her way through the throng of people to the corner where Bree stood with her plate of food. "We have a good turnout, even with the bad weather."

Bree nodded. "Lots of hungry people." She gestured with her plate. "Great food, too." Although she hadn't done more than nibble because her stomach still wasn't feeling quite right. There was a smell she was detecting that seemed to be causing the upset to increase. No need to tell Pinar that, though. She had enough to think about.

Pinar colored slightly at Bree's compliment. "Thank you. I'm so glad you approve of the menu."

"I do. I think this is a great start for your restaurant. Why don't you make an appointment with me some time this week, and we'll discuss the terms of your contract."

Pinar's eyes widened. "Thank you so much! You don't know what your financial help means to me."

Actually, she *did* know, but she didn't correct Pinar. "I'm glad we'll be able to provide it. You have a good product and deserve to have a chance to make a go of it."

Pinar was still speaking when Bree's attention was drawn across the restaurant to the entrance. Her eyes must be deceiving her because the two men talking to the hostess looked exactly like—

Nick turned in her direction and their eyes locked. It *was* him. What was he doing here? What were the odds that they'd be in the same place at the same time?

She couldn't tear her eyes away, even as he left his cousin behind and walked straight toward her.

ROXIE COULDN'T BELIEVE IT. She must be seeing things. Was that really Pete with a girl on his arm? The same man who had been all over Roxie just two weeks ago on Isla de la Blanca and claimed he couldn't wait to see her when they got back to Virginia?

She ought to give him a piece of her mind since she hadn't heard a word from him since. Straightening her back, she took a step forward and stopped abruptly. He hadn't seen her yet. Maybe she should just play it cool and act like she didn't care.

Because that was the truth. She didn't care what he did or with whom he did it. She was in a relationship. A long-distance one, but still a relationship. Even though she hadn't heard from Jim in over a week, she was still unavailable to Pete. Besides, he was obviously a playboy who collected women like some people collected coins.

Except it looked as if the "coins" he gathered in the form of women were casually tossed into a fountain when he got bored with them.

She was just glad she'd kept things between them casual, a harmless flirtation. She didn't need to be another one of his easy conquests.

"Isn't that Pete?" Amber approached Roxie from behind, peering over her shoulder.

Roxie shrugged, acting as if she didn't care. "So what if it is?"

"Sorry. I'm just stating the obvious." Amber moved to stand next to Roxie. "Did you see who arrived with him?" She motioned with her head.

Roxie turned her head slightly, not terribly surprised to see that Nick had come in behind Pete. The woman was clinging to Pete as if she might lose him forever if she let go. Just two weeks ago, Roxie had been the one who'd had his complete attention.

Well, good for him.

Amber spoke again. "Uh-oh. Bree just saw Nick and she doesn't look pleased."

Roxie narrowed her eyes at Amber. "Do you think something happened between those two?"

Amber shrugged. "Not that I know of, but she doesn't look happy with him. And not a *casual-* friends kind of unhappy, either."

"You're right about that. She practically has steam coming out of her ears."

Amber grabbed Roxie's elbow and pulled her toward Bree, who was headed in Nick and Pete's direction. "Let's get closer so we can find out what's going on."

Roxie went willingly, wondering why Bree and Nick hadn't connected before now if something had gone down between them. They'd been home from their vacations for two weeks. And it had also been plenty of time for Bree to mention to her best friends if something had happened between Nick and her.

Amber stopped several feet away from the pair, causing Roxie to almost run into her. "Stay right here," Amber instructed. "We don't want to be too obvious."

There were too many other people around for them to hear the conversation. "We need to move closer," Roxie said. "I can't tell what they're saying."

"Watch their mouths," Amber said. "They're so focused on their conversation that they don't even know anyone else is around. Intense." Amber squinted and spoke out of the side of her mouth. "Nick is saying 'I wasn't lying to you.' Now Bree says, 'You lied by omission.'" Amber turned to Roxie. "What do you suppose that means?"

Roxie shrugged. "Beats me. Maybe he's married and he *forgot* to tell her?" She used finger quotes to make her point.

Out of the corner of her eye, Roxie saw Pete with his chick du jour. She was determined to act nonchalant, no matter how much she wanted to walk over to him and demand an explanation for why he hadn't contacted her. But when it came right down to it, he had nothing to explain. He was free to do whatever he pleased.

And so was she.

Amber was reading lips again. "Something about living in DC and she's shaking her head." Amber looked at Roxie. "Did they talk at all back on the island?"

Roxie had had enough. She grabbed Amber's

elbow and pulled her away. "This is crazy. All we have to do is ask Bree what's going on. I'm sure she'll tell us."

Amber gave her a look that said she was definitely unconvinced. "Just like how she told us what happened between them on the island? Because you don't argue with a guy like that unless there's something more than just a casual friendship going on."

NICK WATCHED AS Bree spun around and walked away from him, her anger evident from not only her words and attitude but her abrupt end to the conversation, not letting him explain.

"Wait a minute." He took a few steps forward to follow her. "Wait a minute!" he repeated, and his command had her turning to face him.

"What?" Her question dripped with insolence.

"That's it? You find out we live within twenty minutes of each other and you get mad and walk away?"

"What am I supposed to say? You lied to me." She lowered her voice. "And now I understand why."

What did she understand that he didn't? They'd never talked about where they lived. He only knew she lived here because Pete had checked out her company online. "Go ahead, tell me why you think I lied, even if I didn't."

She kept her voice quiet. "You figured if I didn't know where you lived, then after we slept together I wouldn't expect anything from you. DC is a big place. What were the odds that we'd run into each other?"

"You couldn't be further from the truth," he told her. "You never asked me where I lived and I only knew you lived outside of DC because one of your friends mentioned your company's name to Pete. Besides, back on the island, you acted like you never wanted to see me again. So what difference does it make where I live? We had never run into each other before the island, so I assumed we'd never run into each other in the future."

Her eyes widened. "Assumed?" Her loud exclamation had heads turning their way. "Assumed?" she repeated softly. "You've got to be kidding." With that, she spun around again and walked away.

Damn, if she didn't look good enough to eat, wearing that emerald-green formfitting dress. Even angry, she was hot.

He shook his head to clear it of thoughts he shouldn't be having.

How exactly had they ended up at the same place tonight? What were the odds? He glanced around, considering those people in the restaurant who might have arranged their *accidental* meeting.

His mother was speaking with the chef—Pinar, he believed was her name. His mother had given him the ticket, supposedly a friendly gesture from Pinar. And as far as he knew, his mother had never met Bree. Besides, she had insinuated that she was inviting Pete to introduce him to Pinar. As if Nick had been more of an afterthought in the invitation.

At least, that was what he'd thought until right this moment. Pete hadn't seemed especially excited about coming tonight, but maybe he was just acting his part. Had Pete planned this reunion with Bree all along so Nick could ask her for financial help? His mother could have just been a pawn in Pete's plan.

The more he thought about it, the more he was convinced that he'd been tricked into coming. He ought to leave right now, if not for the fact that he was starving. He also liked to keep up with local food trends. Not to mention that he didn't want to leave things so badly with Bree.

"Hi, Nick."

A hand touched his arm and he turned to see a familiar petite blonde looking up at him. "Hey, Hannah. How are you?" He hoped he'd gotten her name right. For some reason he had trouble keeping Bree's friends' names straight.

She smiled at him. "I'm fine. Just surprised to see you."

He forced a smile. "Not as surprised as I am to see all of you." He nodded in Bree's direction. "So how did you end up here?"

"The chef, Pinar Garcia, is our client. We're here to decide whether we should help finance her new restaurant."

That made perfect sense. Maybe this meeting between Bree and him had been accidental all along.

"So how did you hear about the pop-up?" she asked. "Do you know Pinar?"

He shook his head. "No, we've never met. But, apparently, she takes the same yoga class as my mother. Pinar gave her some tickets for tonight."

"Ah, I see. And your mom coerced you into coming," she surmised with a grin.

"That about sums it up. When she came into my restaurant today she admitted to having an ulterior motive."

"An ulterior motive?" Hannah cocked her head to one side.

He nodded. "She's become a matchmaker, hoping for grandchildren. Right now, she's got Pete and Pinar in her sights."

Hannah laughed. "Good for her." She glanced around the room and then back at Nick. "You said *your* restaurant? Are you a chef or the owner?"

"Both."

Hannah nodded. "Where is it?"

He swallowed the last sip of his watered-down soda now that the ice had nearly melted. "It's called The Fresh Pantry and it's in Old Town. We serve American classics with a twist, using fresh, local ingredients. Meat loaf, steaks, fried chicken, pastas. Then we have things like spaghetti and tacos that have become Americanized." He shrugged. "You get the picture."

"Sounds great. We'll have to come by."

He took a business card from his wallet and held it out to her. "When you call for a reservation, make sure you mention that you're a friend of the owner." He smiled, wondering if she'd bring her friends, including Bree, with her. He wasn't sure how he felt about that after tonight's run-in. "How's the food here?" he asked, instead. "I haven't had any yet."

"Delicious." She took his arm. "Come on, let's get you some."

He allowed himself to be led, but abruptly stopped when the crowd separated and he came within a few feet of Bree. Roxie and Amber stood with her. From the concerned expressions on their faces, he inferred that something was wrong with Bree.

"Do you need some air?" Roxie was asking her. That's when Nick noticed how pale Bree was. She didn't answer as her eyelids fluttered closed. She began to crumple to the floor and would have injured herself on the hardwood if Nick hadn't stepped forward quickly to catch her.

CHAPTER FIVE

BREE BLINKED A few times. Nick's face was right in front of her. "What happened?" She turned away from him to glance at the people surrounding her. Roxie, Hannah, Amber. Behind them was a different backdrop—not the restaurant she'd been expecting. An office, judging by the desk and computer over Nick's shoulder. She was pretty sure he'd carried her to wherever she was now because he still held her in his arms. "Where am I?" She avoided turning toward Nick again because that would put their faces only inches apart.

Hannah took a step closer and put a hand on Bree's forearm. "You passed out, Bree." She glanced at Nick and then back at Bree. "If not for Nick catching you—"

Bree turned her head in Nick's direction without thinking. "You caught me?" She blinked, wishing he would stop gazing at her with those intense brown eyes. This close to him she could see tiny flecks of gold. They triggered memories she preferred to keep filed away. "How?" She paused. "How could you have caught…? Weren't you on the other side of the room?" She realized too late that her comment might be construed to mean that she'd been keeping an eye on him.

Which, unfortunately, had been true. She'd had an innate urge to keep track of his movements.

Nick's mouth was moving now, but she had trouble understanding his words because she was so enamored with the way his lips moved. He was saying something about seeing her legs begin to fold.

Hannah spoke up again. "Thank you so much, Nick. Bree could have really been hurt if she'd hit the floor."

"Yes, thank you, Nick," Bree echoed, without putting much feeling into it. "This is the second time you've been there to catch me before I fell."

"The second time?" Hannah asked.

Bree made the mistake of glancing at Nick again and this time they locked gazes. She cleared her throat, unable to look away. "Yes, the first time was on the island. Remember—I told you guys—that's how we met."

Nick nodded slightly and his lips twitched.

Jerk. She knew where his mind had just gone. And now she was thinking about them in bed again, too.

"Would you please put me down now?" As much as she enjoyed being held by him, she needed to remember that he'd been deceitful by not telling her he lived near her, and just a few minutes before she'd been telling him exactly what she thought of him.

He carefully set her down in an office chair that someone had rolled in front of him. "She could probably use some water and a cool compress," he said to the room at large.

"I'm fine," she insisted, but was glad she was seated.

Amber handed her a glass of water, and she sipped it.

"Thank you all for your help." She kept her tone businesslike and turned away from Nick to address Hannah. "How do I get back to the dining room?" She was beginning to feel the small office's walls close in. She stood up slowly, not wanting to further embarrass herself. It took a few seconds to right herself, especially since she was wearing four-inch heels.

Hannah gripped her elbow. "I'll show you the way. Why don't I get an Uber to take you home?"

Bree shook her head. "No, I'm fine. I don't want to go home." That wasn't completely true, since she still felt a little light-headed, but she blamed that on having too little to eat. "I'll get some food and then I'll be okay."

When they reached the dining room doorway, a mature, petite woman with blond hair came rushing toward them. "I wondered where you were."

The woman was speaking to someone behind Bree, and that was when she realized Nick was trailing behind her.

"Hi, Mom," Nick greeted the woman.

Mom? His mother was here?

Nick put an arm around the woman's shoulders and guided her away from Bree, who could still hear the woman's questions as they kept walking. "She passed out? And you caught her? Who is she? Do you know her?"

Bree couldn't hear his answers, because he was speaking much quieter than his mom.

"Bree?" Roxie sounded as if it wasn't the first time she'd addressed her. Bree hadn't even seen her approach.

"What?" Bree answered.

"I think you should go home."

This overblown concern needed to end now. "And I think you're all worried about nothing. I got a little dizzy because I haven't had enough to eat today and it's warm in here. That's it. Period. The end." She paused for effect. "Now I'm going to get a plate of food. Anyone else?"

Only Hannah came with her, leaving Amber and Roxie alone, probably to discuss how to convince Bree to leave. Well, she'd show them. She grabbed a plate and added one of everything to it. Like before, the smell of the food didn't sit well with her, but she was determined to get something into her stomach.

"There are a few chairs over there if you'd like to sit," Hannah offered.

"Lead the way," Bree said.

As soon as they sat down, Bree contemplated her plate. Maybe it was the mixture of smells that caused her stomach to flip-flop. She obstinately picked up an empanada and took a large bite. The taste was delicious as long as she didn't inhale. She put the rest of the savory turnover back onto her plate, thinking she'd try something else next. She chose a stuffed olive and that was a huge mistake. Before she could even take a bite she had to swallow, carefully controlling her gag reflex. She dropped the olive back onto her plate and stood up. "I need to go to the ladies' room."

Hannah pointed to the hallway where they'd just been. "On the right. Want me to come with you?"

Bree didn't have time to speak—she just shook her head and took off before she embarrassed herself again. This time it would have been by throwing up in the middle of the restaurant.

NICK HAD BEEN keeping an eye on Bree from across the room. And not just because something was obviously wrong with her, though he would never admit that if asked. She'd made it clear on the island that she wasn't interested in pursuing anything with him. Which made her anger over them living in the same city even more perplexing.

But people didn't faint for no reason. Now, as she hurried back down the hallway to the restroom, he had a hunch—from her greenish complexion and her hand over her mouth—that she was about to puke her guts out.

He leaned down to whisper in his mom's ear. "Mom, would you do me a favor and go into the ladies' room to check on Bree? I don't think she's feeling well." His mom had stayed by his side while they'd sampled the food.

She handed him her nearly empty plate. "Of course." She gave him a questioning look. "You never answered me before. This woman is someone you know?"

He could hear her matchmaking gears turning. "She's someone I met recently. I'm just concerned, that's all."

His mother nodded and left to check on Bree. She'd continue the interrogation later, he was sure.

"Hey, hero." His cousin nudged him as he came to stand next to Nick.

He rolled his eyes at Pete's teasing. "Knock it off." He noticed Pete was alone. "Where's your date?"

"She's around." Pete shrugged. "She's just someone I met in line for coffee yesterday."

Nick slowly shook his head. "You're such a player."

Pete chuckled. "Speak for yourself. Hey, I gotta say, that was a great way to get close to Bree. Sweep her off her feet."

"She passed out, knucklehead."

"Sure, sure. But now you've got an in. She owes you. Play on that when you ask for financial help."

"Shh!" Nick looked around to see if anyone might have overheard Pete. "Keep your voice down."

"But you're gonna do it, right? You need help right away, so running into her tonight must be fate." Pete urged, "Don't wait too long. The restaurant's in real trouble, you know."

Nick knew it, but he didn't want to ask Bree for help, period. Nick spoke quietly. "I told you, I have other ideas that I'm working on to bring in more money."

"Maybe *I* should ask Bree," Pete suggested. "You're obviously too chicken to bring up the subject. Or maybe you're too tongue-tied when she's around." He switched to a singsong tone. "You *like* her!"

"No!" The word came out louder than Nick had anticipated. He lowered his voice. "No, don't ask her. I'll handle it." Which wouldn't mean asking Bree for a loan, even if Pete took it that way.

Man, he had enough to worry about with the restaurant, and now his cousin wouldn't give him a break on this loan idea.

Pete finally left Nick when Pete's date came to drag him off to show him something. Nick stood by himself for a few minutes until his mom and Bree returned to the dining room. His mom gave him a look that said he'd been right about having her check on Bree, who had lost the green tinge to her complexion but now was beyond pale.

His mom turned Bree over to her friends, who had stepped forward en masse to help. They must not have seen how sickly she'd looked as she'd hurried out of the dining room.

"She's probably got some kind of stomach bug," his mother said to him when she returned to his side and retrieved her plate. "We'll be lucky if we don't all come down with it, too."

"Are you blaming her for coming tonight?" That wasn't like her.

"No, no," she said as she swallowed her bite of food. "It's not her fault. She said she was fine before she came, just tired. Smelling the food was what did it to her." She took another bite of food. "You know, it reminds me of when I was pregnant with you."

Nick stared at her, his heart suddenly beating at an alarming rate. "What do you mean?"

Mom shrugged. "I don't know her situation, but with the fainting, nausea and actually losing her lunch, she could be pregnant. She has all the symptoms. I guess I should have asked her, but it's a pretty personal question to ask a stranger."

Nick couldn't speak. His ears were ringing, and his own stomach had started doing somersaults.

Lucky for him, his mom was oblivious to his discomfort. She continued talking. "If she really doesn't have a stomach bug, I hope it's not food poisoning because we all might be the next victims. Then again, if she's pregnant and doesn't know it, then I hope it's a nice surprise for her."

"THERE'S SOMETHING WRONG with Bree," Roxie told Amber and Hannah after they practically forced Bree into an Uber to get her home. Trying to get her to agree to one of them accompanying her had been impossible.

They stood on the sidewalk outside the restaurant watching the car drive away. The cold rain had stopped, but everything was wet, and there was a chill in the air.

Hannah nodded, her expression serious as she rubbed her hands on her upper arms. "I know. She hasn't been right since we got back from vacation."

She cocked her head. "Do you think she might have picked up a tropical virus or something?"

Amber scowled. "I don't know. I guess that's possible."

"We should probably get her to see a doctor," Hannah added.

Roxie frowned. "Like she'd ever take our advice."

"True," Amber agreed.

"But we should still try." Hannah's empathetic side was showing. "This has been going on for too long. I'm worried about her."

"Me, too," Amber and Roxie said at the same time.

"What if it's a parasite?" Hannah shivered.

"Ew!" Amber scrunched her face while Roxie shuddered at the idea.

"Let's go back inside," Roxie said, feeling the chill through the thin sleeves of her dress. "Bree will want a full rundown of the event later."

"You're right," Amber said as she took a few steps and reached for the door handle.

As Amber was opening it, she saw Nick heading to the exit. Roxie had to admit that he was one fine male specimen. Not that Roxie was interested, but he was perfect for Bree. If only she would stop working so hard and give herself a chance for fun.

"Where's Bree?" Nick exited the restaurant,

and Amber closed the door when none of the women moved to go back inside.

"She went home," Hannah told him. "She wasn't feeling well."

He nodded. "I know. I was there." His demeanor was no longer calm and confident. "You let her drive herself?"

"No," Roxie said, annoyed that he'd think they'd allow Bree to do that after she'd fainted. "She went by Uber. I'll drive her car home."

"I need to speak with her," Nick said. He pulled out his phone. "What's her address?"

"Whoa!" Amber stepped forward when she heard his request. "We don't give out personal information."

Nick nodded slowly. "I understand. But this is important. I need to ask her something."

"Whatever you need to ask her will have to wait until she's back in the office." Roxie narrowed her eyes. "Unless you have her cell phone number?"

"No."

Roxie shrugged, not surprised that Bree hadn't given him her number. She was adamant about never allowing herself to be distracted by romantic relationships. "I guess you're out of luck, then. Try her at work." She pulled a business card from her purse. "Call the main number and ask for Bree."

Nick didn't seem happy with his limited choices, but Roxie couldn't help him any more than she already had. She had a sudden idea, of which the benefits might be twofold. BeeTee was looking for a venue and it might help push Nick and Bree together. "You have a restaurant, correct?"

"Yes," Nick said slowly with a definite hint of suspicion. "Why?"

"It has a full bar?"

He nodded.

"Great. We're looking for a place to hold bartending classes. Would you be interested in us 'borrowing' your bar?" She paused. "We'd pay you, of course."

Nick seemed to consider the idea. "It would have to be on Mondays when the restaurant is closed."

"That's perfect!" She was excited about moving forward with Bree's idea from vacation. "Can I come by to check it out, maybe during the midafternoon lull on Saturday or Sunday? Then we can figure out the details and I'll have a contract drawn up."

"Sounds great."

"Hey, what's going on out here?" Pete exited the restaurant and joined the group, his flavor of the week clinging to his arm. "I wondered where you got to," he said to Nick. Pete looked directly at Roxie and said, "Hey, Rox. How's it goin'?" He had the nerve to punctuate his question with a wink.

"Peachy," she said.

"Okay, then." He looked at the woman on his arm who, on closer inspection, appeared to be even younger than Roxie had first thought. "Ready to go?"

The girl bobbed her head, and Pete tipped an imaginary hat to Roxie before he and his date headed in the direction of the nearest parking garage, where he'd probably left his car.

The three women looked at Nick when he said, "Please, are you sure you can't get in touch with Bree for me tonight?"

"She needs to rest," Hannah told him.

"But tomorrow's Saturday. She won't be in the office, will she?"

Roxie chuckled. "She will be unless she's tied down or she's too sick. She tends to work seven days a week if no one stops her. That's why we insisted on a working vacation on the island."

Nick rubbed his bearded cheek as if considering his options. "Okay. I guess I'll try her at the office in the morning." Nick said goodbye and went on his way.

He sounded resigned, but Roxie didn't honestly think that would be the end of it.

NICK WALKED TO his car in the parking garage several blocks away. He'd wanted to speak with Bree's friends about her possible pregnancy, but how did you bring that up?

Did you just come out with it? *Hey, so is Bree pregnant or what?* Yeah, that would have gone over well. And what if she wasn't? He'd have sounded downright stupid. He didn't even know how much they knew about what had happened between Bree and him.

He got into his car, wishing he had some way to contact Bree.

At least now, with Roxie's proposal to use his bar for teaching, he not only had an extra source of income but he might even run into Bree once in a while.

NO SOONER HAD Bree exited the Uber car, entered her building and pushed the elevator button for the seventh floor, than she began receiving text messages from her girlfriends.

Make it home okay? came from Roxie.

Do you need anything? was Amber's text.

And then Hannah, Feel better. Call if you need me.

Bree would have been annoyed at their concern if she didn't love them so much and know they were merely worried about her.

Privately, she was becoming a little concerned herself. She'd never fainted before. Ever. She didn't count what had happened when she got her foot stitched. She hated needles with a passion. She shivered involuntarily.

But this hadn't just been a little dizziness. It had been full-out, *almost*-drop-to-the-floor—if not for Nick—passing out. Followed by throwing up the few morsels she'd been able to eat.

She must have some kind of bug. There was no other explanation. Maybe something she'd picked up while on their island vacation. Although none of the others had come down with any type of illness.

Bree sent a group message to her friends saying she was fine and that she was going to bed early. By the time she'd stripped off her dress and heels, slipped on a nightshirt, brushed her teeth and washed her face, she realized it wasn't even eight o'clock. But her body felt like it was midnight.

She crawled into bed, glad her stomach had finally settled down. She was positive she'd be awake before the sun came up, so she didn't set her alarm. Even though tomorrow was Saturday, she wanted to get into the office bright and early to get some work done with few interruptions.

The next morning, Bree awoke to the sun shining into her bedroom. She sat up, trying to remember what day it was and why she'd been sleeping during the day. Then she remembered going to bed very early last night. She must have been really tired if the sun was up before her.

She turned her alarm clock toward her. "Eleven o'clock!" She felt her eyes nearly bug out. "This must be a joke." She grabbed her cell phone from her nightstand and checked the time. Exactly the same. She'd slept for fifteen hours.

"How could that be?" she said aloud as she got out of bed and headed to the bathroom. She was normally lucky to get six hours a night. That was all she needed to function. She couldn't even remember sleeping longer than seven hours while in college.

She showered and dressed in jeans and a sweater since there would be no meetings with clients. She needed to catch up with her never-ending email and review the financial statement she'd been avoiding.

No matter the weather, she preferred to walk to her office, stopping at the coffee shop on her way. Today was no different although, since she'd returned from vacation, the smell of coffee had gone from soothing to distressing. She ordered her usual yogurt parfait with chai tea instead of the espresso she used to order.

She was about to walk out of the coffee shop with her combination breakfast and lunch to go when a woman about Bree's age suddenly doubled over in what appeared to be pain.

"Are you okay?" Bree asked her, setting her things down on a nearby table so her hands were free. Except for a man at a back table with his nose in his computer, she and the woman and the two employees were the only ones in the coffee shop.

The woman moaned and looked like she was about to tip over.

"Here, sit down." Bree pulled a chair closer. She guided the woman into it. "Can I call someone for you? Do you need an ambulance?"

The woman slowly raised her head and deliberately breathed in and out. "I'm pregnant," she said. "I think there's something wrong."

Bree froze. She knew nothing about pregnancy or pregnant women. When she could finally speak, she said, "Do you need me to call someone? A doctor maybe or an ambulance?"

The woman nodded, tears beginning to fall down her cheeks. "Thank you. I hate to make a fuss." She sucked in a breath. "I had a miscarriage before my first child and—" The woman doubled over.

Bree pulled her cell phone out and called 911, explaining the situation. "What's the address here?" she shouted. One employee called out the exact address and Bree repeated it to the 911 operator.

The pregnant woman doubled over again and all Bree could do was rub her back, hoping to soothe her through her pain.

"The ambulance will be here soon," Bree told the woman quietly. "Just hang in there. You'll be fine."

The woman sobbed openly now. Bree didn't know what to say or do. Thankfully, she heard a siren coming, though it seemed to be from a long distance away. Making it through the Arlington traffic wouldn't be easy, but at least it wasn't a workday.

By this time, the other employee had come over to see if there was anything she could do. "Why don't you stand at the door and flag down the paramedics," Bree suggested. She didn't want to leave the woman in the young woman's hands, not that Bree had any experience when it came to pregnant women in pain.

Another two long minutes went by before Bree finally stepped back as the professionals took over. After the ambulance left with the woman, Bree could have kicked herself. She hadn't even gotten the woman's name, and now she'd never know what happened to her and her baby.

CHAPTER SIX

THE NEXT MORNING, after a terrible night's sleep, tossing and turning while dreaming of multiple screaming babies, Nick called Bree's office.

No answer.

He pounded his fist on the kitchen counter, hard enough to make his coffee slosh in the cup. What was he going to do? Still considering his options, which seemed few, he decided to take a shower before going to his restaurant.

While in the shower, he came to the conclusion that he was worrying about nothing. Or, at least, worrying prematurely. If she really was pregnant, he might not even be the father.

But what if she *was* pregnant and the baby was his?

Finally Monday morning arrived, after he'd driven himself crazy all weekend trying to get in touch with Bree. Nick stood at the elevator bank in the modern, ten-story building where Bree's company maintained its offices. The elevator door opened and he entered, pushing the button for the fourth floor. According to the directory in the first-floor lobby, BeeTee leased the entire floor.

His plan was to go directly to Bree's office.

"I'm here to see Bree Tucker," Nick told the male receptionist when he reached the correct floor.

"Do you have an appointment?" the young man in a dress shirt, vest and bow tie asked. He appeared barely old enough to vote, and, frankly, Nick was surprised to find a male working at a female-dominated company. He could only assume it must be equal-opportunity employment coming into play.

"No, I don't, but I'm sure she'll see me."

The receptionist narrowed his eyes at Nick, obviously disagreeing with Nick's statement. Then he made a phone call, all the while keeping his eyes on Nick. "This is Todd at the front desk. Gentleman here to see Ms. Tucker. Says he doesn't have an appointment." He looked at Nick. "Your name?"

"Nick Harmon."

Todd repeated the name into the phone. He looked up at Nick, covered the mouthpiece and whispered, "Her assistant is checking with her." He returned to listening to whatever the person on the other end was saying. "Okay, thanks." He hung up the phone and looked up at Nick. "I'm sorry, but she won't see you without an appointment."

"If I can just have a minute with her—"

The receptionist held up a hand to stop him. "I'm sorry, sir. There's nothing more I can do."

"Can I call her?" Nick hadn't expected to have this much trouble getting through to Bree.

"I'm sorry, but that's not possible. I can put you through to her assistant to make an appointment, if you'd like?" He looked to Nick for an answer.

Nick considered his options. Then he remembered that Roxie had asked about using the bar in his restaurant for training. She was supposed to come in to check it out over the weekend, but he hadn't seen her. He pulled her card from his wallet. "If I can't get in to see Bree, then what about Roxie Sinclair?"

"Sure. I'll see if she's available," the young man said as he dialed.

"Tell her it's in regard to the training we spoke about Friday evening."

The receptionist repeated Nick's words into the phone. "Okay, I'll send him back." He hung up and then gave Nick directions to Roxie's office.

"Hi, Nick," Roxie greeted him when he reached her office. She held out a hand to shake his. "I wasn't expecting to see you today."

"I know," he admitted. "And to be honest, I have an ulterior motive. I actually used seeing you as a way to get to Bree. She won't see me without an appointment."

Roxie laughed. "Sounds like her." She gestured to a straight-backed chair near her industrial-looking desk. "Well, while I have you here, let's discuss actual business, and then I'll see if I can get you in to see Bree."

That sounded like a good idea, so he agreed. Thirty minutes later, they'd come up with a plan that would benefit both of them. Nick's restaurant might get the financial boost it needed, though he'd been careful to keep that piece of information to himself.

"So why do you need to see Bree?" Roxie was definitely a straight shooter.

So he was mostly honest with his answer. "I wanted to check on her after she was so ill Friday night. Have you seen her? Is she okay?"

"I haven't seen her this morning, but I know she came in over the weekend." She gestured to a mountain of files on her desk and scowled. "She left me a present."

Nick smiled. "I hope that means she's okay."

"Me, too," Roxie agreed. "We've been concerned about her health since we came back from vacation. I'm worried that she picked up a virus there. Or even a parasite." She grimaced.

His eyes widened. "A virus or parasite, of course." Internally, Nick sighed with relief. Why hadn't he thought of that? It was so logical. "Has she seen a doctor?"

Roxie shook her head. "Not that I know of. She keeps telling us she's okay."

"And then she goes and passes out and throws up," Nick concluded.

"Right." Roxie grinned.

"What are *you* doing here?" Bree asked from the doorway.

Nick spun around to face her and his entire body went *boing*. Damn, she was beautiful. She wore a sheer, sleeveless white blouse over a matching camisole tucked into black pants that not only hugged her curves but kissed them tenderly. Her strappy black high heels made her legs appear six feet long. His mouth went dry as he began to speak. "Roxie and I were discussing using my restaurant's bar for training." His hands itched to touch the soft hair that curled past her shoulders and onto her breasts. "Also, I've been trying to contact you to see how you were doing after Friday night, but you're a difficult person to reach." All in all, Bree appeared to be fine physically, unlike the last time he'd seen her. "How are you feeling?"

Bree held her arms out. "As you can see, I'm fine. Thank you for asking." Her tone wasn't the least bit friendly. "You own a restaurant?"

"I do."

"He's a chef in Old Town," Roxie clarified.

"What's the name of your restaurant?" Bree asked.

"The Fresh Pantry."

Her eyes widened with interest. "The Fresh Pantry? I've heard good things about it."

He smiled. If only good reviews could fix his financial problem. "That's nice to hear. You should come by sometime."

Bree cocked her head slightly to the side. "I might just do that." She paused, appearing oddly flustered for a few seconds. "So you and Roxie came to an agreement about using your restaurant?"

Roxie answered. "We did." She looked at Nick. "I told him I'd have a contract drawn up and messenger it over to the restaurant tomorrow." Nick nodded his approval.

"I'm glad you could work it out," Bree said almost robotically.

"Me, too." The two words were all he could manage. Feeling tongue-tied was not normal for him.

"I'm just going to go check on something," Roxie said as she left the office, obviously giving Bree and him some privacy.

They stood staring at each other until Bree blinked and looked around. "Did Roxie leave her own office?"

Bree's question stopped him from taking a step closer to her. "Yes, she did."

He cleared his throat, needing to utter something coherent. "So let me know when you want to come to the restaurant," he said as he regained his composure. "I'll make sure you get the best table."

"I guess that's almost as important as the food," she quipped.

He tried not to take offense. "I like to think that eating out is a complete experience. Not simply the food or the atmosphere or the service. The whole package." Nick wasn't purposely trying to sell her on his work ethic—he merely spoke the truth.

"Then I'll look forward to deciding if you and I *see* eye to eye when it comes to a great eating-out experience." She gave him a smile that said, *Bring it on.*

He never passed up a challenge, especially when it came from a beautiful woman.

SHORTLY AFTER NICK LEFT, Bree returned to her own office. She was no sooner sitting behind her desk than Roxie appeared in the doorway. "So did he ask you out?"

"Who?" She pinched her lips shut when they began to twitch, and she didn't look Roxie in the eye. As if Bree didn't know exactly who Roxie was talking about.

Roxie stepped into Bree's office and closed the door for privacy. "Don't be coy. What happened after I left?"

Bree's face heated from the memory of the few minutes Nick had been there. "Nothing happened." Which wasn't a lie. But if she hadn't broken the mood, something could have happened. If she'd wanted it to.

"I don't believe that." Roxie's green eyes staring at Bree finally penetrated her invisible shield.

"Okay—"

"I knew something happened!"

Bree smiled. "I was telling the truth. Nothing happened, except for him giving me 'the look.'" Her insides felt funny as she remembered.

"The look?" Roxie's eyes grew round. "That's a big deal."

Didn't Bree know it. She and the girls had come up with a definition of what they called "the look" back in college. It was when a guy got that "I want to kiss you" look and you, in turn, could barely breathe.

"It was probably just my imagination." Although Bree didn't really believe that.

"I doubt it," Roxie said. "I mean, we may have discussed business, but it was obvious that he was really here to make sure you were okay."

"Okay?"

"He was worried about you after seeing you so sick Friday night."

Bree covered her face with her hands. "How embarrassing." Although it was nice to know he'd been concerned.

Roxie laughed. "Hey, at least he was there to catch you before you hit the floor. Now *that* would have been really embarrassing."

Bree nodded. "True." She needed to change subjects. She didn't want to get caught up in some fairy tale about her in a relationship with Nick. "So tell me about this agreement you and Nick came up with for bartending classes."

"Sure. It's perfect, actually! He's more than happy to have us use his bar on Mondays when the restaurant is closed. Even if he has prep going on in the kitchen, we won't be in the way."

"What about an instructor? Did you find one?"

Roxie nodded vigorously. "I did. She's been running her own bartending school for several years and she's agreed to do three two-hour classes for us. One a week beginning next week, as long as the students have already taken her online responsible-bartender class. And she'd prefer no more than five or six in a class. Otherwise, the students don't get enough practice time."

"What does the online course teach?" Bartending was an area Bree wasn't familiar with. She'd never thought about it beyond ordering a drink at a bar.

"Things like understanding state liquor laws, checking IDs, overserving. It's a four-hour course, but you can take more time if you need it. Establishments like their bartenders to have the certification because it can lower their insurance rates."

"Sounds good," Bree said. "Do we have a list of women who might benefit from the training?"

"We do," Roxie said. "In fact, Nick mentioned that he'd like to get his bartenders certified, too, and we can get a discount on the online course if we do it through his restaurant. He might also have someone who works for him interested in bartending. She's a line cook now but has mentioned wanting to make more money because she's a single mother with a GED."

"Let's include her, then. She sounds like the kind of woman we're trying to help. Why don't you contact all those interested so they have the week to take that online class before next Monday?"

"I'll do that." Roxie narrowed her eyes at Bree. "Are you all right?"

Bree straightened. "Of course I'm all right. What would make you think otherwise?" Could Roxie really see that Bree was feeling nauseous again? She'd thought she'd hidden her distress well.

"You're just a little pale," Roxie said. "And with how you've been feeling lately—"

"Don't start in on that again," Bree begged. "I've had just about enough of people worrying about my health. I'm fine."

"If you say so."

"I do."

Roxie left then, and Bree sat alone in her office. Unfortunately, her first thoughts were of Nick. Here he was again, insinuating himself into her life. And coming by simply because she hadn't felt well on Friday night? Bree wasn't sure if that was good or bad. Maybe she'd just need to wait and see.

TUESDAY MORNING NICK was nearing his restaurant when his cell phone rang. "Hi, Mom," he said when he pushed the button on his car's dashboard to use Bluetooth.

"Hello, Nick," she replied, sounding slightly miffed. "Are you at the restaurant?"

"Almost. What's up?"

"I was wondering about tonight's reservations. Can you look and see if we can fit in a table of twelve to fifteen? I forgot that it's your uncle Frank's birthday and Aunt Lois asked me weeks ago about reserving a table. And, of course, I completely forgot."

"I'm sure we can figure something out," Nick

reassured her, wondering why she hadn't used their online reservation service but not asking. Actually, he'd been considering canceling the service to cut down on expenses, but he found that most people preferred it over calling the restaurant for a reservation. The last thing he needed was to stop customers from choosing his establishment. "What time did they want?" Probably prime time, but at least it was a Tuesday and not a weekend night.

"Lois was thinking seven since it's a workday."

Of course she was. "Let me check and I'll call you back, Mom." He pulled into his reserved parking place in the alley behind the restaurant.

"Thank you," his mother said on a sigh before hanging up.

He shut off the engine, locked his car and entered the restaurant through the back door, turning on lights as he went. He walked straight through the kitchen and booted up the computer at the hostess desk. While he waited, he took a good look at the space. His assistant manager had taken charge of a thorough cleaning of the restaurant yesterday while they were closed and everything appeared as it should.

As soon as the computer was up and running, he checked the evening reservations and added the large party for his mother. And then another name on the reservation list caught his attention. Sinclair. Wasn't that Roxie's last name? He pulled out his wallet where he'd placed her business card. Yep, Roxie Sinclair. The reservation was for four people at seven o'clock. He'd make sure she got top-of-the-line treatment. Not that he didn't want all of his guests treated well. But since she was obviously someone he might do more business with in the future, he would oversee her table personally. He also had to admit he wondered if Bree would be one of the four.

Pushing that thought to the side, Nick got on with his day, which went surprisingly fast. Lunch service was good and before he knew it, his staff was prepping for dinner. The lunch and dinner menus weren't that different from each other, mainly smaller portions for lunch, and he'd added a few more expensive entrées, like marinated rib eye and creamy seafood casserole, with lobster, crab and shrimp, to the dinner menu.

Since he had family coming, he decided to add a special dessert to the menu for the evening. Uncle Frank, the birthday boy, was Nick's dad's older brother and the two of them had loved their mother's tiramisu. Her recipe had been passed down after his half-Italian grandmother's death several years ago, along with other family recipes she'd made like lasagna and fettuccine Alfredo.

Nick was so busy that he lost track of time until his mom came into the kitchen and hugged him.

"Thank you," she whispered in his ear. "I really appreciate that you made room for our group."

Nick kissed her cheek. "Not a problem. Just make sure the check is paid by eight because we have another party coming in then."

"What!"

He bit the inside of his cheek to keep from grinning. The panic on his mom's face was well worth it. He patted her shoulder. "I'm kidding, Mom. You can stay as long as you want."

She let out a visible sigh. "Don't do that to me. You want me to have a heart attack?"

"Go." He turned her toward the door to the dining room. "Have a good time. I'll come out to greet everyone soon."

She nodded, started to leave and then stopped. She faced him. "Oh, I forgot to tell you. That woman who fainted last week at the pop-up? She's at table four." She shrugged. "I guess she got over whatever made her sick."

Nick watched his mother disappear through the doorway and realized his mouth was open. He shut it and slowly turned back to finish what he'd been doing, but his sous-chef had taken over.

"I'm going to say hello to my family," Nick told Fernando. "I won't be long."

"Don't worry about it, boss. I'll cover for you."

Nick knew that was true. He brushed off his white chef jacket with his name embroidered under the restaurant's name and looked down to make sure he was presentable. He refused to admit that he was more concerned about how Bree would see him than anyone in his family.

He straightened his shoulders and headed to the dining room. There she was at table four, not too far from Uncle Frank's birthday celebration. Roxie was on Bree's right and across from them were Hannah and Amber. Visions of what had transpired between him and Bree floated through his brain. He shoved them away, pasted a smile on his face and went to wish Uncle Frank a happy birthday.

Everyone was talking at once, and Uncle Frank rose as soon as he saw Nick, pulling him into a bear hug. "Good to see you, Nicholas." The table grew quiet as the group focused on Nick.

"Happy birthday, Uncle Frank." He clapped his uncle on the back and turned to Aunt Lois to give her a hug. "Thanks for coming," he said.

"Thank you for accommodating us." Aunt Lois pointed at Nick's mom. "Em's the one who suggested it."

Nick's eyes widened as he and his mother locked gazes. "She's pretty good at plugging the restaurant," he said to Aunt Lois.

He went around the table, greeting his cousins and his other aunt and uncle in attendance. When he got to his mother, he leaned down to whisper in her ear, "We'll talk later."

"I figured as much."

As he stood to his full height, he caught Bree looking at him from her table. He nodded his acknowledgment.

"You're going over to say hello, aren't you?" his mother asked, obviously noticing the interaction between Bree and him.

"Of course," he said through gritted teeth, knowing his mother was trying to take his attention off the part she'd played in hosting the family dinner at his restaurant. Not that he minded having the extra customers. It was the last-minute notice that bothered him.

He returned to Uncle Frank's end of the table. "I made a special dessert for tonight to celebrate your birthday. I hope you enjoy it."

Next he turned to Bree's group. Seeing that they were focused on their menus and not deep in conversation, he stepped to the end of their table. "Good evening." He smiled at each woman in turn, ending with Bree. "I'm glad to see you all here." He didn't notice any of the others in particular, but he couldn't help looking more intently at Bree. He couldn't see below her waist, but she was dressed in what she'd probably worn to work that day. Her dark brown, long-sleeved blouse made her dark blue eyes appear almost black.

She had two buttons open at the neck, exposing a hint of cleavage. Her brown leather jacket was hanging on the back of her chair.

The women all smiled back and spoke at once, except for Bree. She didn't seem as happy to see him. Not a surprise. She'd thought she was having a vacation fling with him and now here he was in front of her for the third time in ten days.

"I see you all have drinks." Amber and Hannah had red wine. He couldn't help noticing that Bree was drinking water. Designated driver? He pointed to Roxie's drink. "Our signature martini?"

Roxie nodded, picked up her glass and smiled. "It's delish."

He gestured to his family's table. "Today is my uncle's birthday and I've made a special dessert for the occasion. I'd love to bring you all some after dinner, as well, if you'd like. On the house."

Again, they spoke at once, except for Bree, chattering about how nice it was for him to offer.

"What did you make?" Hannah asked. "Unless it's a secret."

"I haven't told my uncle specifics yet, but I made my grandmother's tiramisu. It was a favorite of my uncle, as well as his brother...my dad."

"I love tiramisu," Amber said in a stage whisper. "Is that other man at the table your dad?"

Nick sobered. "No, my dad passed away almost

two years ago. The other gentleman is also my uncle. He's married to my dad's sister."

The women gave him sympathetic looks.

"Hey," he said. "I didn't mean to bring down your party."

"I don't see Pete at the table," Roxie said. "Isn't he your cousin or your brother or something?"

Nick nodded. "He's actually related by blood to my mother's side of the family, but then my parents adopted him when he was eight and now everyone considers him family. You know how he is—he's usually the life of the party. Unfortunately, he had a work thing tonight."

"That's too bad." Amber looked directly at Roxie when she spoke.

Nick pointed to the menus they'd been perusing. "What are you planning to order? Do you have any questions about the menu?"

The women asked questions and wanted suggestions, so he spent the next few minutes going over the menu with them. "I'll get your server over here to put in your orders. Enjoy!" He took a last glance at Bree, left the table and went into the kitchen.

When it was time to serve Uncle Frank's dessert, Nick helped his staff bring the individual plates to everyone at the table.

"This looks just as I remember it," Uncle Frank told him, his eyes glowing with unshed tears at

Nick's surprise dessert. He took a bite and closed his eyes, a stream of liquid escaping down each cheek. He bowed his head and covered his face with his hands.

Nick was overcome with emotion, too, and patted his uncle on the shoulder. "I'm hoping it tastes like you remember it?"

Uncle Frank looked up at him and gave him a sad smile. "Exactly. Thank you so much. You're a good boy for doing this for me."

Thankfully, everyone else at the table began talking as they ate their own portions of tiramisu. Some recognized the recipe and others were too young to have tasted Nonna's food.

Nick finally made his way back to the kitchen, grateful that he had such a competent sous-chef to cover for him tonight.

One of the restaurant's longtime servers entered the kitchen. "Table four is ready for their dessert," he said to Nick, who nodded before getting the plates he'd put into the fridge to make sure they had enough for Bree's table.

He handed the server two plates and Nick followed behind with the other two as they went back into the dining room.

"This looks wonderful," Hannah said as the dessert was placed in front of her.

"I love tiramisu," Roxie said, rubbing her hands together in preparation for tasting it.

"I noticed your uncle was a little emotional when you brought out the dessert." Bree's words surprised him. Not only had she noticed the exchange between his uncle and him, but she was actually speaking to Nick for the first time that evening.

"He was." Nick spoke directly to Bree, wishing they were in a more private place than they were right now. "Food can bring back memories just like familiar smells do. It's one of the things that drew me to cooking."

Bree nodded and took a bite of the dessert. He was about to leave, but his ego got the best of him. Surely she'd love it.

Instead, she covered her mouth as she sprang up from her chair and headed quickly to the ladies' room.

CHAPTER SEVEN

"I TOLD YOU I'm fine," Bree said to Roxie for about the hundredth time the next day. They were seated in the waiting room of Bree's doctor. Roxie—and Amber and Hannah—had insisted Bree see a doctor first thing this morning. Bree wasn't sure what Roxie had done to get this last-minute morning appointment, but here they were.

"And I—we—told you that people who are fine don't pass out or throw up for no reason."

Bree rolled her eyes. "I know. But I don't feel sick at all right now." At least it was only Roxie accompanying her to the doctor. They wouldn't let her go alone, probably not trusting her to go, so she'd compromised by allowing only Roxie to go with her rather than the three of them.

"Then let Dr. Strickland agree with you and we'll all stop bugging you."

"Promise?"

Roxie gave her a resigned smile. "Promise."

"Bree Tucker?" A young woman in light blue scrubs stood at the door leading to the back of the office.

"Right here." Bree rose. She turned to Roxie, who was about to stand up, too. "I can handle this on my own. I'll get a notarized statement saying I'm healthy if that's what you need."

"Go ahead." Roxie sat back down in the plaid-upholstered chair, crossed her legs dramatically and picked up the magazine she'd been browsing. "But I'll know if you're lying."

Bree was already through the door to the back when Roxie made her threat. "Thanks for the confidence," she murmured.

The nurse who showed her to an examination room took her vitals while asking why Bree was there.

"Because my friends forced me to." At the young woman's surprised expression, Bree explained. "I've had some unusual things going on. But I feel fine," she added quickly. "My friends are just concerned because I've had an occasional upset stomach and I passed out last week."

"Sometimes friends worry too much."

"Don't they?" Bree was glad to see she had at least one person who understood.

The nurse made notes on a computer screen and then walked to the door. "Dr. Strickland will be in shortly."

"Thank you."

While she waited for the doctor, Bree checked

email on her phone. She was replying to one when the doctor knocked and then entered the room.

"Good morning, Bree," the midforties, female doctor greeted her. "What brings you in today?"

Bree explained for the second time what had been going on over the past few weeks while Dr. Strickland typed something into the computer.

"And when did this begin?"

Bree tried to remember. "I was fine on vacation, so it started right after that. In fact, the first time I felt queasy was the last day of vacation."

Dr. Strickland narrowed her eyes. "And where was this vacation?"

"We were on a small island off the coast of Puerto Rico. Isla de la Blanca. My friends and I were there for a working vacation."

"Have any of them had similar symptoms?"

"No, they've all been fine. In fact, I feel fine right now. It all just comes on at the oddest times." She remembered something. "I did cut my foot and needed stitches while I was there, but it healed quickly."

The doctor asked a few more questions about the cut and then listened to Bree's heart and lungs with her stethoscope. "Let's have you lie back on the table."

Bree did so and the doctor checked the lymph nodes in her neck and felt around her abdomen.

"Have you gotten your period recently?"

Bree had to think. "I'm not sure when it was. My ob-gyn put me on a low-dose birth control pill for my irregular periods. I just take the pills and don't think about when my last period occurred."

The doctor nodded her head. "Yes, I see that birth control medication noted in your chart. And you're taking the pills every day at the same time? You haven't missed a dose?"

"Like clockwork."

"Good. You can sit up now. I'm going to have some blood drawn to make sure you didn't pick up something on that island. It's also possible that you're having a reaction to the birth control pills. We should have the results later today with our on-site lab."

Great. Needles again. "If it's something I contracted on the island, do you think I'm contagious?" Bree asked.

"I doubt it, since your friends have shown no symptoms."

"Should I be worried?" Bree hadn't actually considered herself sick until the doctor started asking her so many questions.

"Let's not jump the gun. We'll see what the tests show." The doctor put her hand on the doorknob. "The lab tech will be right in. Make sure the front desk has a current number to call you and we'll go from there."

"Thank you."

Bree dreaded needles, but then, who didn't. Not long after the doctor left, the lab tech came in. Bree couldn't help remembering how supportive Nick had been on the island when she'd cut her foot. She almost wished he was with her now. Fortunately, taking her blood was quick and nearly painless, and Bree was back in the waiting room in no time.

Roxie stood up when Bree returned. "What did the doctor say?"

"She took blood and I should know later today if I picked up something while we were on the island."

Roxie nodded. "Good. I'm glad you'll get some answers."

Bree scowled at her. "You mean you're glad *you'll* get some answers."

Roxie shrugged. "Yeah, that, too."

"Let's get back to work."

As much as Bree was trying to stay calm for Roxie's sake, inside she was panicked. She'd brushed off her symptoms until now, but what if she had something with no cure? Would it get worse and worse? Would she not be able to work? She wasn't sure how she'd manage if she didn't have her job to occupy her days.

Those were the thoughts that plagued her when she returned to her office, having departed from

Roxie at the elevator. As long as someone was around to distract her, she was fine. It was these times alone that made her thoughts spin out of control.

On their way back to the office, she and Roxie had stopped at a local deli to pick up lunch. Bree sat down at her desk, opened her foam container, and the smell of the pickle next to her sandwich nearly did her in.

She shut the lid quickly and shoved the container away from her. She closed her eyes and took a few calming breaths, hoping the nausea would go away. Finally, after a few minutes went by and she'd drawn on every bit of self-control she could muster, she felt normal again.

Around midafternoon, feeling hungry since she'd skipped lunch, she decided to go down to the deli on the first floor to get some yogurt or an energy bar. She couldn't bear to repeat opening the container with that pickle inside.

She was almost out the door when her phone rang. "Bree Tucker."

"Bree, this is Dr. Strickland. I have the results of your blood test."

Bree's heart beat double-time. She lowered herself into her office chair and waited for the news. "You know what's wrong with me?"

"The good news is that you're not contagious

and you *will* get over your symptoms in the next few months."

"Months?" She couldn't keep this up for that long.

Dr. Strickland laughed. "I decided to do a pregnancy test along with checking for other things. And, guess what? You're pregnant."

Bree was dumbfounded, unable to form a sentence.

The doctor finally broke the silence. "Are you okay? I take it this is a surprise. I hope it's a good one."

"Um—"

When Bree didn't say anything, the doctor continued. "I would suggest seeing your ob-gyn, who can help you keep your symptoms to a minimum. Is there anything else *I* can help you with?"

"Are you sure? Could there be a mistake?" This was either a mistake or a joke. A bad joke. She couldn't be pregnant. Pregnant! She was married to her job. Her company was her baby. She had no need or desire to have a physical human being in her life. Especially one who would rely on her for its every need.

"I had the lab run it a second time. There's no mistake. And blood tests for pregnancy are the most accurate—more reliable than the drugstore urine tests."

"Okay." She paused. "Thank you." Bree hung

up and turned her chair to stare out the window. She placed a hand on her abdomen and for the first time in her life, she had no plan for what to do next.

LATER THAT DAY, Roxie, Amber and Hannah went for drinks at a hipster wine bar down the street from their offices. Roxie had made the decision to not include Bree so they could talk about their friend's health situation. With its dark wood and rosy lighting, the bar seemed a good place to have that discussion.

"So we still don't know what's wrong with Bree?" Amber took a sip of her cabernet.

Roxie shook her head. "Before I left the office, I asked if she'd heard from the doctor, but she hadn't. She was supposed to know the results of her tests today."

"That doesn't mean there's something horribly wrong with her," said Hannah, ever the optimist.

"What if she's gotten her results and doesn't want to tell us?" Amber suggested in her glass-half-empty way. "Maybe it's such bad news that she's not ready to share it with anyone."

"I really doubt it," Roxie said honestly. "She's usually pretty open with us. I think she just hasn't heard anything yet."

"Good evening, ladies."

Pete Buchanan. He had come up to their table

and stood behind Roxie. She hated to admit it, but she'd recognize the man's deep voice anywhere.

"This is quite a coincidence." He'd taken a few steps to the right and now he looked directly at Roxie. "We seem to run into each other often these days."

"We do." Roxie took too large a swallow of her Pinot Grigio, hating that he had an obvious effect on her. He was dressed as if coming directly from work. Dark pants and a white dress shirt with the top button open and the sleeves rolled up to reveal strong forearms. His dark, thin tie hung slightly loose. On some men, she'd say the look was slovenly. On him…

"Are you here alone?" Amber's surprising question jolted Roxie from her reverie. "You're welcome to join us."

Roxie stared at Amber with wide eyes, trying to mentally clue her in on how Roxie didn't want to be anywhere near Pete. Besides, he probably had some girl with him. His flavor of the week. And Roxie didn't need to see that right now.

"Thanks, that would be great!" Pete said, oblivious of Roxie's discomfort as he pulled up a chair from another table and sat so close to Roxie that the heat from his leg warmed her entire body.

Pete took a long drink of the red wine he'd brought with him and then said, "So where's your fourth? Don't you travel in a pack?" He laughed at his own joke.

"She's still at work," Roxie said quickly, before Amber or Hannah could say anything.

"How's she feeling these days? Better I hope. The last time I saw her was when she was at the pop-up, but I heard she was feeling a little under the weather at The Fresh Pantry last night, too." He looked at each of the women. "She's okay today?"

"She's fine," Roxie told him, wishing she could think of some other subject to talk about.

"She went to the doctor this morning," Hannah shared. "We'll find out soon if she picked up something while we were on the island."

Pete raised his eyebrows. "I hope it's nothing serious. That was a few weeks ago."

The women looked at each other, their silent expressions communicating their own concern.

Pete hung around for a little while and chatted on general topics, but left when some of his buddies showed up.

"You're really into him, aren't you?" Amber asked Roxie as soon as Pete was out of earshot.

Roxie felt her face heat. "No way. He's not my type."

"Since when?" Hannah said. "He's a living, breathing male who seems to show up when you're least expecting it, and you can't stop looking at him."

"Not true."

"It's absolutely true," Amber verified.

"I told you, I'm not interested in him."

At least she hadn't admitted to her girlfriends what she couldn't admit even to herself.

TWO DAYS LATER, Bree was finally seen by her ob-gyn. If she hadn't pushed for the appointment, she would have had to wait several weeks. The person making the appointment was adamant that there was no need for urgency unless she was having symptoms of bleeding or cramping. Bree pushed the truth a little and said she was unable to keep any food down. That wasn't the complete truth, but close. She'd already lost the two pounds she'd put on while on vacation and, according to everything she'd read, going below her ideal weight wasn't good for her or the baby.

Once she'd gathered her wits after receiving the news, she'd read what seemed like a million internet articles on pregnancy. She also bought several digital books on the subject that she'd read before coming this morning to see her ob-gyn. She liked to be well-informed.

Sitting in a paper gown on an exam table was the last thing she wanted to be doing that morning. But she needed to make sure she was physically okay and then talk to the doctor about her options. She believed wholeheartedly that women should be able to choose what was best for them, and she'd realized over the past two days that ending the pregnancy wasn't the right choice for her.

There was a knock on the door and her grandmotherly doctor entered the exam room. "Hi, Bree, how have you been? I see from your chart that you were just in a few months ago for your yearly exam. What's up?"

"I'm pregnant." That was the first time she'd said the words out loud. She'd told no one, not even her closest friends when they'd kept bugging her about getting her test results. "My internist did a blood test trying to figure out what was wrong with me and she also did a pregnancy test that came back positive. Twice."

After Dr. Bell did an exam and pronounced everything as it should be, she and Bree spent the next few minutes discussing the symptoms Bree had been having. From her reading, Bree knew that she wasn't as bad as some. *Hyperemesis gravidarum* was the medical term that had made the news when Kate Middleton suffered from it. Bree felt really bad for her now that she was experiencing a much weaker case than the mother of the presumptive future King of England had suffered through.

"We've gone over what you can do to alleviate the nausea and vomiting, so do you have any other questions?"

Bree inhaled deeply. After much consideration, she'd come to what she thought was the right conclusion when it came to the pregnancy. "Yes, I do. This situation has been a complete surprise, and I've made a decision that I think would be best for both the child and myself."

Dr. Bell didn't say anything, simply waited for Bree to continue.

"I think adoption is the route I'd like to take." There. She'd said it. "I'm just not mommy material. I run a growing company that takes up most of my time. I don't think it would be fair to a child to have me as its mother." What did she know about being a mother anyway? Her father had seen to that, forcing her own mother to be absent from Bree's life.

The doctor nodded. "I understand your concern. Where does the father stand in this matter? Does he agree?"

"I haven't told him and I don't plan to." Nick was supposed to have been a vacation fling, not the father of her child.

The doctor's pale blue eyes widened. "He has a right to know. Wouldn't you want to know if you were in his place?"

She hadn't thought about it that way. "I guess so."

The doctor nodded. "Good. Then go tell him

and if you both agree, then I can point you in the right direction for adoption. Besides, he'll have to eventually sign off if you go through with the adoption."

Bree felt the panic boil her insides. How was she going to tell Nick? What would he say? Would he blame her? She'd been on low-dose birth control pills, fully expecting them to prevent pregnancy. Ha! That was a joke.

If only one of them had remembered to use a condom that time in the shower...

"Bree?" The doctor sounded like she'd been trying to get Bree's attention.

"Yes?"

"I want you to start on daily vitamins. They might make your stomach troubles worse, so take them with food. I'll also send you home with specific instructions on what you need to avoid eating during your pregnancy. The list has gotten quite long."

Bree already knew about that from her voracious reading up on pregnancy.

After Bree dressed and left the doctor's office, she got into her car and turned on the engine. Before pulling out of her parking space, she decided to make a call before she chickened out.

As soon as Roxie answered, Bree asked, "Can you get Hannah and Amber and meet me in my office in about fifteen minutes?"

"Sure, what's up?"

"I'll fill you in when I get there."

"Is this about your health? Did you finally get the results of your tests?" Roxie sounded panicked, which was probably to be expected. Bree had held out on them for the past two days, avoiding them whenever possible, and they probably weren't going to be very happy with her.

"Everything's fine. I'll explain soon." Bree ended the call before she blurted out her news, which was not the way she wanted her best friends to find out.

The women were waiting for her in her office when she arrived a short time later. Bree closed her office door, not wanting anyone to overhear before she was ready to go public. Since she wasn't keeping the child, she wanted her pregnancy a secret for as long as possible.

"Thanks for coming," she said as she sat down in her desk chair. "I've just come from the doctor and, before you get all riled up, I'm fine."

They let out a collective sigh.

"Then what's been wrong with you?" Roxie wanted to know.

Bree swallowed, knowing she had to tell them, but once they knew, it wouldn't be her secret alone. "I'm pregnant."

No one said a word.

Bree looked at each woman in turn. Roxie's

green eyes were ready to pop, Amber's jaw had dropped open and Hannah had covered her gasp with both hands.

Finally Roxie spoke. "I guess that answers the question about what happened between you and Nick on the island. Have you told him yet?"

"You're assuming he's the father," Bree said.

Roxie scowled. "Come on, who else could it be? You don't date, have a limited social life, and unless you've got some secret life you haven't shared, then Nick is the father of your baby."

Amber and Hannah were also giving her knowing looks.

"Okay, so it's Nick's," she admitted. "And, no, I haven't told him yet. I have a long way to go, and telling him isn't a priority right now."

"We're going to be aunts!" Amber's excitement came seemingly out of nowhere.

"And we can shop for those cute little outfits," Hannah added.

"And noisy toys," Roxie said with a grin. "The kind that drive parents crazy."

Bree watched the excitement on her friends' faces and was loath to set them straight. "I have more to tell you."

They grew serious. "Is everything okay?" Hannah asked. "Is the baby okay?"

"Everything's fine," Bree assured them. "It's

about me and the pregnancy. I've decided to put it up for adoption."

Again, three sets of eyes stared at her in what appeared to be disbelief. She continued speaking. "I've thought about this a lot and feel this is the best thing for everyone concerned."

"Then I feel even more strongly that you must tell Nick as soon as possible," Amber said. "He should have a say in what happens to his child."

"He will have a say, just not yet," Bree said. At the raised eyebrows she was confronted with, she added, "I promise I will tell him." Unless she could figure out a way around it.

AFTER THE FRIDAY-NIGHT dinner rush, Nick went into the restaurant's office to make a private call to Bree to find out how she was doing after his dessert had obviously upset her stomach. Her friends had told him they thought it was because it was a coffee dessert and coffee had been upsetting her stomach since they'd been on the island.

He'd tried once again to get through to her office today, but had no luck. Then he'd tried Roxie and, much to his surprise, she'd offered him Bree's cell number. He wasn't sure what had changed, but he hadn't been about to question it.

"Hello," Bree said.

"Hi, Bree. This is Nick. Nick Harmon." He wasn't sure why he was adding his last name or why he felt a little nervous talking to her. They'd slept together, seen each other naked. "I hope I didn't call at a bad time."

"How did you get this number?"

He didn't want to get Roxie in trouble. "I have my ways," he said in what he hoped was a jovial tone and not menacing.

"Was it Roxie?"

She must be psychic to figure it out so quickly. He changed the subject. "I wondered how you were feeling after the tiramisu upset your stomach the other night."

"Oh, right. Sorry about that," she said. "I'm feeling much better, thank you for asking."

"So now that you're healthy, would you like to come back to the restaurant again?" Where had that come from? It sounded like he was asking her out. Maybe he was. "I promise not to serve you a coffee dessert again."

"Well—"

"I'd like to make up for your bad experience. Your evening was cut short and I can't have you judge my restaurant by that one night." He knew he was babbling and didn't know how to stop. "Whatever night works for you, I'd love to have you as my guest."

"Actually, I have something to talk to you about. Maybe Sunday night?"

He wasn't sure he'd heard correctly. "Sunday

night? That works. You can bring your friends if you want."

She was quiet for a few long seconds. "No, I'd like to come alone. Can you join me if we do it later in the evening?"

"I can do that. Is nine o'clock too late for you?" He couldn't believe she was agreeing to come. Maybe she'd had time to remember their good times on the island—not counting the time they'd spent in bed—and was interested in continuing their new friendship. Or whatever it was that they had.

"Nine is perfect. I'll see you then."

She disconnected and he stared at his phone. How had that happened? He'd only wanted to check up on her, make sure she was doing okay.

And now they had a date. A real date. Well, sort of. He wasn't sure she considered it a date.

Kind of backward since they'd already slept together, but he found that made looking forward to Sunday night even sweeter.

CHAPTER EIGHT

SUNDAY AFTERNOON, BREE was startled awake from her slumber by the ringing telephone. She'd never been one to sleep during the day, but this pregnancy had made it a necessary habit.

She threw off the afghan she kept on the chair in the corner of her bedroom where she took her naps because she refused to climb into her perfectly made bed in the middle of the day. She stumbled to her cell phone, which was clear across the room on her antique oak armoire. Roxie's name was on the caller ID. "Hi, Roxie."

"Hey, you're not answering your texts," Roxie said. "Are you okay?"

"Sorry. I'm fine. Phone was on vibrate." Bree inhaled deeply to wake herself up and also to not sound like she'd just wakened. Not that she'd committed a crime, but sleeping during the day was certainly out of character for her. "What's up?"

"I was reminding you that we're getting together at my house to watch *Love for a Lifetime*. The new season starts tonight." The four women had taken turns hosting weekly viewing parties for the reality television show since it began three years ago. They drank wine, ate snacks and made snarky comments about the contestants, who were looking for love, whether it cost them their pride or not.

"I forgot the season premiere was tonight. I'm sorry, I've made other plans."

"Plans?" Roxie sounded suspicious. "What kind of plans?"

Bree didn't want to share that she was having dinner with Nick, no matter how innocent it was. She knew Roxie would blow it out of proportion. Before Bree could explain why she'd agreed to have dinner with Nick, Roxie would have the two of them married.

"I'm having a late dinner with a friend." That sounded innocent enough.

"How late? The show starts at nine. Can't you come after dinner?"

"That's when we planned to meet."

"Why so late?" Roxie asked. "I thought you've been going to bed early since you're…you know."

"It's called pregnancy, Rox. There's no getting around it. I'm pregnant. I've accepted it and so should you."

Roxie didn't say anything at first. "I'm trying to, Bree." She paused. "It's just that this situation isn't that simple."

"Not true. For the next eight months, I'm pregnant, and I have to deal with the symptoms and limitations. After that, it'll have a good home, I'll go back to my regular life and this will all be in the past." Her doctor had given her a provisional due date of mid-October even though Bree could pinpoint the exact day she'd gotten pregnant. So she figured that by Halloween, all would be back to normal.

"This isn't a business contract, Bree. You can't treat it like it doesn't affect you and the baby and Nick and everyone else around you."

Bree disagreed, but didn't want to argue. "Like I said, this is the way it is for now."

Silence. Roxie finally asked, "So you're definitely not coming to the watch party?"

"I don't see how I can. I'll record the show and catch up with what happened. Then we can talk about it over lunch one day this week."

"Can't you do dinner some other night? We'll really miss you." She paused. "And who did you say you were meeting for dinner?"

Bree grinned. "Good one, Rox. You know I didn't say." She hesitated and then decided it didn't matter if Roxie knew or not. As long as she didn't read anything into it. "I'm meeting Nick at his restaurant. He's sorry about the tiramisu incident and wants to make it up to me—"

"Nick! You're having dinner with Nick?"

Bree should have known that Roxie would get excited at the prospect of the two of them getting together.

"It's not what you think."

"He's your baby daddy. What else can I think? Are you telling him about the pregnancy tonight?"

"No."

"But it's perfect timing."

"I only agreed to dinner because I have a business proposition for him."

Roxie was silent for several seconds. "So you're eating that late because he'll be working?"

"Right. The restaurant closes at nine on Sundays, so we'll have the place to ourselves as soon as the patrons clear out."

"How romantic!" Roxie was clearly out of control. This was not the levelheaded woman Bree was used to. Amazing what news of a baby could do to a person.

"*Romantic* is the last thing I'd call it. I told you I need to discuss business with him."

"Whatever," Roxie said on a sigh. "I guess I'll talk to you at the office in the morning."

"Absolutely."

They disconnected and Bree walked across her bedroom to smooth out the quilt on her bed. Then she folded the afghan and placed it across the back of the chair where it belonged. She looked around her bedroom to see that everything was in its place before heading to the updated kitchen she used only for making coffee and reheating leftovers.

Until this morning.

After her extensive reading about pregnancy, she'd decided that eating out so much wasn't healthy for her or the baby. So she was going to teach herself how to cook some nutritious meals.

She opened the refrigerator to retrieve a yogurt, not ready to test her cooking skills twice in one day. At lunchtime, she'd burned her finger while attempting to scramble an egg, followed by burning the egg when the smell turned her stomach. All would have been fine if she'd turned off the burner before sprinting to the bathroom.

She opened the yogurt and got a spoon from the drawer, hoping it would hold her until dinner. Just in case, she'd bought crackers to keep in her purse. Several of the pregnancy websites said eating them would help with the nausea that seemed to be never ending.

Heaven knew she needed all the help she could get in that area.

Especially if she was going to keep this pregnancy news a secret from Nick until she absolutely had to tell him.

SUNDAY DINNER SERVICE went smoothly at The Fresh Pantry, but you couldn't tell that from the way Nick's insides felt.

Why was he this nervous about having Bree here for dinner? Maybe it was because he was so out of practice when it came to women. Dipping his toe into the dating puddle was one of the things on his to-do list. Right after getting his restaurant back into the black.

He hadn't been completely honest with Bree when he'd invited her to dinner. He had let her believe it was more of an apology than a date. Maybe he should think of it that way, too. After all, if he eventually needed her company's financial help because his attempts to find new revenue weren't panning out, then dating her might appear as though he were creating an inside track to her money.

No matter how unorthodox the invitation had been, he needed to take small steps in that direction and avoid large leaps. Keeping it on a friend basis was probably the best plan for everyone.

"Hey, Nick." His mom popped her head into the kitchen while he was prepping for the meal he hoped Bree would enjoy.

"Hi, Mom."

She'd been acting as hostess tonight, filling in for the part-time college student who normally worked weekends. His mom usually worked the lunch crowd Tuesdays through Saturday. Since his dad passed away almost two years ago, his mom had gone from part-time to full-time, probably feeling the need to keep busy.

"I'm going to take off now," she said, before stepping over to where he was chopping dill. "Trying out a new recipe?"

Should he tell her the truth or let her think what she wanted?

"I've got a friend coming for dinner after we close."

Her eyes grew wide. "A female friend, I hope?" Another sly comment to remind him how anxious she was for him to get married and give her grandchildren.

Heat suffused Nick's face. "Yes, a female friend."

"Anyone I know?"

"Actually, it's Bree. The woman who passed out at the pop-up."

"And the one who didn't like the tiramisu." His mom nodded approvingly. "I take it she's feeling better now?"

"I hope so."

"Well, you enjoy yourself." She came around to give him a kiss on his cheek. "You deserve it."

"Thanks, Mom."

After she left and there were only a few staff members finishing up, Nick made sure a table was set for two and that everything was perfect. He'd even paired a special wine for the main course.

After the last customer had left around eight thirty, the front door had been locked, and now Nick went to unlock it for Bree. He stepped outside onto the sidewalk to see if she was close by and saw her immediately. She wore a black peacoat that was unbuttoned, and underneath she had on a long, high-necked sweater with a coordinating scarf and dark, skinny jeans with black knee-high boots.

She looked perfect.

"How long have you been out here waiting for me?" she asked as she approached. "You're not dressed for the weather." She gestured to his long-sleeved Henley that he'd changed into from his chef jacket.

"I'm fine." She had no idea how overheated he felt once he saw her heading his way.

He held the door open for her and then locked it from the inside. He showed her to the table he had set for them. She removed her gloves and put them into her coat pockets before taking off her coat and hanging it on the back of her chair.

"Would you like a drink to start?" he asked when she was seated. "I've got wine for the entrée course, unless you'd like some now?" He thought he saw her cringe slightly, but it must have been his imagination. "Or maybe a cocktail from the bar? I'm a pretty good mixologist, if I say so myself."

She smiled and tossed her luscious hair back over her shoulder, which made him smile in return. "I'll just have some water right now, please," she said.

"I'll be right back."

When he returned, he carried a tray with water for each of them, as well as a special amuse-bouche. "To start us off, I've made an ahi tuna tartare amuse-bouche. I hope you like it. We don't serve amuse-bouches here at the restaurant, so this was a nice opportunity for me to do something different." He placed a small, shallow bowl in front of her and she laid her linen napkin on her lap.

She inspected the food carefully, making him feel self-conscious. "What exactly is in this?" She looked up at him, waiting for an answer.

He grinned. "You haven't even tasted it yet, and you're already trying to figure out the recipe?"

Her lips twitched. "No, no. It looks delicious. I'm just…um. I have some food allergies and I like to know ahead of time what I'm eating so I don't have a reaction."

"I guess I should have asked about allergies, but I didn't think of it." Although with the way she'd been feeling every time he saw her eat, he knew he should have at least wondered about food sensitivity.

He pointed to the different layers of the approx-imately one-inch cube that he was very proud of. "The bottom layer has a mixture of avocado and lemon juice. Next is the tuna tartare—"

"Raw fish," she said, her eyes widening. "And what's on top and in that sauce?"

"Crispy rice and shallots on top, but the sauce has soy if that's a problem for you." He took his seat across from her.

"No, I'm good with soy." Then she proceeded to pick apart the layers, nibbling little bits from her fork and pushing the tuna off to the side. She suddenly lifted her head and looked at him. "What?"

He shook his head and couldn't help but chuckle a little. "If you only knew how intricate that was to make."

"Sorry." She had the decency to appear regret-ful that she hadn't enjoyed the food the way he would have liked.

"So I guess you don't like sushi, since you're not eating the tuna tartare."

She raised her eyebrows. "I love sushi!" Before he could figure out why she loved sushi and not what was in front of her, she said, "Um…but only California rolls."

Her choice of the one kind of sushi that had no raw fish in it answered his unasked question.

Now he only hoped she wouldn't be as picky with the rest of the food he'd prepared.

BREE *LOVED* SUSHI! *All* sushi! In fact, it was her favorite carryout food from the Little Sushi Bar a block from her apartment. Watching what she ate during this pregnancy was going to be more difficult than she'd expected.

She needed to be more careful when it came to what she was putting in her mouth and also the words coming out of it. The last thing she wanted to do was make Nick suspicious.

"So the reason I accepted your dinner invitation—"

Nick raised his hand. "Excuse me just a minute," he said as he rose. "I need to check on the next course."

Bree nodded and took several long swallows of her water while she waited for him to return.

As soon as he left the kitchen and headed her way, she knew she was in trouble. He was holding the bottle of wine he'd mentioned, as well as a basket of bread. What was she going to say? He'd seen her drink alcohol on the island, so she couldn't say she didn't like it or her religious beliefs didn't allow her to drink it.

He set down the bread on the table and showed her the wine label. "I chose this wine to go with our entrée."

Cabernet sauvignon. Her absolute favorite red wine. She even recognized the label as one she occasionally splurged on.

"I've been letting it breathe back in the kitchen. Would you like me to pour you a glass?"

She swallowed. "I'm afraid I'll have to pass." She stumbled through her reasons. She didn't want to hurt his feelings. She'd already picked at his amuse-bouche that, under different circumstances, she would have devoured as it was meant to be devoured—all together in one bite.

He seemed to be waiting for her to continue with an explanation.

"I'm taking medication and it wouldn't be good to mix it with alcohol." There. That was a perfect reason.

"So they put you on medication for the symptoms you've been having?"

She hadn't expected a follow-up interrogation. She could be snotty and say it was an antibiotic for a UTI, but that wasn't her style. Even if they *had* already seen each other naked. "I took an antihistamine…for my allergies."

"Oh! I understand completely." He paused, his brow furrowing. "But I'm surprised you're having allergy problems this time of year. I know spring can be tough for some people, but I didn't think winter was such a problem."

"Yes, well, I—" How could she get herself out

of this one? She had zero allergies. What were some things people were allergic to all year round? She couldn't think. "Cats," she blurted. "I'm allergic to cats and I was visiting a friend with cats this afternoon. She has lots of cats. She's a cat lady." *Shut up, Bree.*

"I see. Well, I'll keep that in mind." He'd taken a seat again and offered her a roll. "Unless you have a gluten allergy? Or dairy? We use real butter."

Bree smiled and put a roll on the small plate he'd provided. He was being extremely nice. She wished she could just come out and tell him the truth about the pregnancy, but she wasn't ready to do that yet. He would just complicate things and she had enough going on with her company and now this pregnancy. "Thank you." She buttered a small piece of the warm roll and took a bite. "This is delicious." At least that was no lie.

"They're an old recipe of my grandmother's," he said. "Several of the recipes we use come from her." He scowled. "Like the tiramisu the other night."

She could feel herself blush and she put her hands to her face. "I'm so sorry about that. I'm sure it was delicious. I'm just not a coffee person." At least not since he'd gotten her pregnant. Before that, she couldn't survive without her caffeine of choice.

He smiled at her. He was so handsome with his flirty brown eyes and straight, white teeth that had probably worn braces early in his life. No wonder she'd decided to have that vacation fling with him.

"You were telling me why you accepted my dinner invitation," he reminded her. "I'm sure it was to experience my charming disposition and delicious food. Correct?" His eyes were dancing and she couldn't help but laugh.

"Well, there is that, but I had another reason, too." She took a sip of her water. "I don't remember how much I told you about my company when we were on the island—or what Roxie has shared with you—but we began by retraining women for jobs and helping them move up in their current jobs."

"So you started the company, right?"

She nodded. "Back in college. I found I was good at advising my girlfriends on how to compose a better résumé and before I knew it, their friends were coming to me, too, and so it began."

"A self-made woman. Very impressive." He sounded sincere, which was a point for him.

"Thank you. I think I learned a lot from my father by osmosis." She paused. "He's Cal Tucker of Tucker Industries." She didn't feel the need to mention that he always made the Forbes list of the wealthiest people in the United States.

"Oh! Sure. I think someone mentioned he was your dad. So is that how you were able to start your own business?"

"Absolutely not." That came out more adamantly than she'd meant for it to. "I used a small inheritance from my paternal great-aunt to get started. It wasn't much, but there's no way I'd take money or anything else from my father."

"You don't have a good relationship?"

"I haven't seen or spoken to him in almost a year. So yes, I'd say we don't have a good relationship." What would her father think of her pregnancy? She could only guess how disappointed in her he'd be.

A timer on Nick's cell phone went off. "Hold that thought." He rose and placed his napkin on his chair. "I hope you like the main course. It's a chicken dish that's one of my favorites."

"I'm sure I'll love it."

He wasn't gone very long, and it turned out that he was right about the chicken. She loved it. The chicken was moist and seasoned well, and the farro and asparagus were also delicious complements. She was so busy eating that she'd completely forgotten about the conversation she'd been having with Nick, until he reminded her.

"So you were telling me why you accepted my invitation," he said, after several minutes of silent eating.

"Oh, right." She swallowed the bite she had in her mouth and patted her lips with her napkin. "This food is so good that I forgot what we were talking about." She took a drink of water, glad he'd refilled it when he'd brought in the chicken. "So my company has a client, Gabriella, we'd like to help, which is where you come in. She has a restaurant that's failing, and I was hoping you'd come on as a consultant to figure out what she's doing wrong."

He stared at her a few long seconds. "Consultant?"

"Yes, we'd pay you a generous consultant fee." She named the standard figure for this type of job. When he didn't respond, she added, "It's negotiable if the amount's a problem for you. And you can work around your restaurant schedule." She raised her hand to encompass the room. "You've got a great restaurant here, so you obviously know what it takes to be successful in the business."

IF ONLY, NICK THOUGHT.

Bree's offer made him feel like a fraud. If only she knew how deep in the hole they were.

"You can think about the offer," she said when he didn't reply.

"I accept." He heard the words come out of his mouth and couldn't quite believe he'd said them.

What could he tell someone that would improve their restaurant to make it profitable? *Don't do what I did?*

"You do?" she asked excitedly. "That's great! I'm so glad." She took another bite of food, followed by a long drink of water.

"Would you like a soda or something else to drink?" He'd never thought about offering her anything different until now. "I'm sorry I didn't ask sooner."

"No, no, water's fine. I prefer it."

They spoke for a few more minutes about his job as a consultant and he found it an interesting idea. The extra money coming in would certainly go a long way to help cover this month's rent.

"Why choose me as your consultant?" he asked. "You're a female-oriented firm. Why not hire a woman for the position?"

"Good question." She nodded. "I believe in hiring the best people for the job, no matter whether they're male or female. I've tasted your food twice now and seen how this place operates, and I think you are the best candidate for the job."

"Thank you. I appreciate your confidence." He only wished he had as much faith in himself. He *did* know how to run a restaurant. He'd just been trying to balance too many things at once and lost control. Deceitful employee and distributor, canceled wedding plans that had left him with bills, as well as having to buy out his ex's half of their condo all came at once. If he'd suddenly suffered locusts and a drought, he doubted he would have noticed.

"Besides," she added. "You accept the job and I'll forgive you for letting me drink so much after I cut my foot."

"I think I've already paid you back by catching you in my arms twice." He winked.

Her cheeks turned pink.

He continued. "Forgiven?"

She nodded and took a long drink of water instead of speaking.

"Then I accept the job," he said.

By the time he brought out dessert, a chocolate-raspberry torte—he hoped he couldn't go wrong with chocolate—Bree seemed to have relaxed in his presence. Before this, she'd been much more standoffish than he'd expected after their time on the island. Hopefully, this signaled a new beginning for them.

"I'd offer you an after-dinner drink or coffee, but I already know the answer," he said when they'd finished their dessert.

She patted her lovely mouth delicately with her napkin. "Dinner was delicious and that dessert was the perfect ending. Thank you so much."

He smiled. "You're very welcome. I hope we can do it again sometime." That came out before he'd thought it through, but he liked the idea. A lot.

"Um, sure," she said as she got up from her chair and pushed it in. "We should probably go have dinner or lunch or something at Gabriella's Latin-fusion restaurant so I can introduce you and you can take a look at the place."

That's right. He was going to be working for her. Sure, it would only be a few hours here and there. But then she would also be using his restaurant's bar to train bartenders. Maybe they needed to keep this a business relationship, after all. At least for now.

He helped her on with her coat and walked her to the front door. He was about to unlock it when she turned to him and he leaned in to kiss her without thinking too hard about it. He'd been wanting to kiss her from the moment he'd seen her walking toward him on the sidewalk.

She pulled back slightly and stared at him in surprise, their faces inches apart.

But then she shocked him by grabbing his head with both hands and kissing him like he'd never been kissed before. His body came alert the moment their kiss deepened. She tasted sweet and hot and he wanted her. Oh, how he wanted her.

He'd explored every inch of her while they were on the island. He wanted to do that again and again.

His fingers slid through her hair to her neck and she pressed her body against his. He'd only begun to know her body intimately, and he wanted to increase that knowledge and use it to make her cry out in pleasure.

She pulled back then, pressing two fingers to her slightly swollen lips. "I'm sorry. I don't know what got into me."

He'd like to be the one to get into her, but kept his inappropriate commentary to himself.

"I should go," she said softly.

"You don't have to." And he meant it.

"Yes, I do." She gazed up at him. Even in boots with high heels, the top of her head only came to his chin.

"Have you forgotten how good we were on the island?"

She blushed. "How could I forget?"

He placed his hands on her hips and brought their pelvises together. "We could continue where we left off."

She seemed to be mulling it over. "I'm sorry. I just don't have time to get involved with anyone. What we had on the island was a vacation fling, and now we're back to reality."

He didn't say anything. What could he say? His body was screaming its disagreement, while his head had to agree with her. Business and pleasure weren't a good mix. Maybe after their business arrangement ended and his own business was on the mend, he could revisit a personal relationship with her.

"Good night, Nick." She laid her hand on his cheek and their eyes met for an instant. She was out the door before he could offer to walk her to her car.

CHAPTER NINE

MONDAY MORNING, AFTER a staff meeting that lasted longer than she'd planned, Bree was gathering her thoughts at her desk when her assistant rapped lightly on her office doorway.

She looked up. "What is it, Jen?"

"Your father's on the phone," she said. "Todd sent the call back to me. Should I put him through?"

Her father was calling? Bree had mentioned him last night for the first time in months. Maybe he was like Beetlejuice. Had she said her father's name three times to make him suddenly reappear in her life?

What could he want? She'd never even heard from him on her last birthday, even though he only lived thirty minutes away. Instead, his personal assistant had sent her an extravagant gift, much like the one Bree had received the year before. "Put him through," she said reluctantly, wondering why he hadn't simply called her cell.

"Hello, Aubrey," her father said when she answered, already annoying her by his use of the name she'd never liked. Now that she thought about it, maybe he hadn't called her cell because he knew she might ignore his call.

"You know I prefer Bree," she said evenly. "It's my legal name now."

"Oh, right, I always forget. I never understood why you disliked the name I chose for you."

Because, as in regards to so many other things, you've never really listened to me, that's why. "Like I've told you before, it sounds too much like Audrey and that was the name of the cat I had as a little girl that your driver ran over."

"That does sound familiar," he said offhandedly. "So you're probably wondering what I've been up to."

She didn't need to reply because she was sure he would tell her. Not that she'd wondered about it a bit.

"Well, I have big news," he said when she remained silent. "You have a new stepmother."

Yippee! "Another one?"

"Don't be snippy."

This made number four or was it five? She couldn't keep track because as soon as she met one of his wives or girlfriends, the next time she saw him he would be with someone different. She had stopped caring a long time ago. "Congratulations, I guess."

"We got married at the courthouse first thing

this morning and I'm anxious for the two of you to meet."

Great. At least he hadn't invited Bree to the wedding. She'd been saved from that torment. "Why do you want me to meet her?"

"I think you'll have a lot in common," he said.

Did that mean they were close to the same age? The older Bree got, the younger the women in her father's life had become. She was aware of that only because his picture was plastered on grocery-store gossip rags and she couldn't help but see them.

"Besides, she's part of your family now."

"So what were you thinking? How and when would you like us to meet?" Bree asked.

"We're flying to Aruba on Wednesday for our honeymoon, but I thought maybe you could come to dinner tonight."

"Tonight? At your house?" Bree hadn't been invited to dinner at the house in probably four or five years.

"Yes, at my house. Can you make it?"

Her dad tended to meet her at restaurants and then leave early with a business problem as an excuse. Of course, he always paid the bill before he took off while she'd finish eating her meal alone. She'd get sympathetic looks from the waitstaff because her father was immediately recognizable. When she had been younger, his behavior had made her angry. But as the years went by, she'd decided it was his loss that he really didn't know her very well.

"I guess that would work." Her calendar was clear, not that she had much of a social life beyond her girlfriends and her company. And she liked it that way just fine.

"Great. We'll see you at seven? I'll send a car for you."

"Thank you." That would save her having to drive through DC traffic at rush hour to get to his mansion along the Potomac River.

She was ready to hang up when her dad said, "Oh, and I'm supposed to tell you that you can bring a date, if you'd like." Funny how he had to be reminded that he had no idea about what went on in her personal life.

"That's okay. I'll come alone." She couldn't imagine disliking any man enough to put him through a few hours with her father.

They disconnected and Bree stared at the phone, wondering why she'd agreed to endure the torture of a dinner with her dad and her new stepmommy.

Maybe she'd come up with a viable excuse not to go by the time she left work.

"Hey, what's with you?" Roxie asked, and Bree realized she was still staring at the phone.

She looked up to where Roxie stood in the doorway. "My dad called."

"You're kidding." Roxie entered Bree's office and closed the door so they could speak freely. "What did he want?"

Bree put on a fake smile and said perkily, "He was calling with great news. I have a new step-mommy! Turns out they went to the courthouse this morning to get married."

"And you weren't invited?" Roxie's tone was sarcastic, as she knew all about the relationship between Bree and her father.

"Thankfully, no." Bree leaned back in her chair. "But he wants me to come to dinner to-night to meet her before they fly to Aruba on their honeymoon."

"Aruba?" Roxie's eyebrows rose.

"Yeah, same place he took his last wife on *their* honeymoon."

"At least he's consistent," Roxie joked.

Bree chuckled. "There is that."

Roxie changed the subject. "How was dinner last night?"

Bree rolled her eyes. "Oh. Stressful. At least at first."

"How's that?"

"Did you know there's a big long list of things you can't eat while you're pregnant? So every time I turned around, Nick was offering me one of them, and I had to make up excuses why I couldn't partake."

"All the more reason to just tell him about the pregnancy."

Bree shook her head. "No way. I'm not ready to tell him about it now or maybe ever. Only if I have to for the adoption to take place. But I can't think about that just yet." Right now their business arrangements were short-term, but she'd need to make sure they didn't enter into any contracts that would cause him to be around when she began to show. Bree knew she was playing with fire.

Roxie shook her head, not keeping her opinion to herself as usual. "Speaking of Nick, I had another reason for coming in here," she said. "I'm going over to The Fresh Pantry to observe the bartending class for a while. It's from one to four. Want to come with me?" She paused. "Unless last night was a total bust, and you're afraid to see Nick so soon."

"I'm not afraid, but I will pass," Bree said. "We had a very nice dinner, even with all the little lies I had to tell him." She would savor the memory of their kiss and keep that tidbit to herself. "I even have him thinking about coming on board as a consultant. We have that client, Gabriella Carrera with the Latin-fusion restaurant that's not doing well. I thought Nick would be perfect to go in and take a look around and see what she might be doing wrong."

"Good idea, but is it really wise to hire your baby daddy? Unless you've changed your mind in the last two minutes and you're going to tell him about his new title?"

"No, I haven't changed my mind. And I don't think it'll be a problem." As long as she made a concerted effort to avoid seeing him later in her pregnancy.

"Just don't be surprised when this all blows up in your face."

If she survived dinner with her dad and his new wife tonight, then weathering this pregnancy with Nick around would be a breeze.

WHILE ROXIE WAS DRIVING to The Fresh Pantry, she thought about Bree and Nick. It was probably just as well that Bree hadn't come with Roxie to observe the bartending class. The more time the two of them spent together, the more likely it was that Nick would figure out Bree was pregnant with his child.

Even if Roxie thought he should know, there was no rush to tell him since him knowing wouldn't change a thing. Except that he'd insinuate himself into Bree's life, and she claimed she didn't have time for that. She was probably right on that count. Bree spent most of her waking moments on work.

Once at the restaurant, Roxie set herself up at a table in the corner of the empty restaurant and opened her laptop, hoping to get some emails answered while she listened to the class going on at the bar.

So far so good. Everyone who'd signed up was in attendance, and the instructor Roxie had hired seemed to be very good. Nick had made an appearance before they'd begun, and he'd given Roxie the Wi-Fi code so she could work online. He'd disappeared into the kitchen after that.

Roxie became so engrossed in her work that she wasn't paying attention when someone came walking over to her table. "Well, look who it is," Pete said. "I didn't expect to see you here today."

Roxie hit Send on the email she'd just written and looked up at Pete, her mouth watering at the same time she hated herself for noticing how sexy he was. She was in a committed relationship, she reminded herself. "I didn't expect to see you here today, either."

He grinned and took a seat. Not the one across from her, but the one right next to her. He crossed his legs, placing one foot on the opposite knee, while his other foot came to rest touching Roxie's.

She tried to ignore her body's reactions, but wasn't completely successful.

"I like your hair like that," he said.

"It's the same as always," she retorted. "But I'm sure that's a line you use often."

His eyebrows shot up. "You think it's a line? No way." He reached out to touch a lock of her hair before she could move away. "Redheads are hot." He wove his fingers through her hair, and even though he wasn't actually touching her beyond her hair, she had goose bumps rising on her scalp.

"Come on, you know you're a player. Hair color makes no difference." She cleared her throat. "You've got a different woman on your arm every time I see you."

He grinned and shrugged. "I can't help it. I like women. They're fun to be around." He abruptly dropped the lock of her hair. "Just like you."

She laughed. "I am *nothing* like the women you parade around with. I'm not a 'buy me dinner and disappear before the sun comes up' kind of gal."

"Whoa!" He laughed then, too. "Come on, give a guy a break." He leaned in. "Just to prove you're wrong about me, have dinner with me tonight. I promise no funny stuff—unless that's what you're into—and I'll even call you tomorrow and prove I can stay focused on one woman."

"No way," she said automatically.

"Why not? Afraid you might be wrong about me?"

"I *know* I'm not wrong."

"I keep telling you we'd be great together," he said.

"And every time you say that, the next time I see you, you have another female on your arm. I don't want to be one of your flavors of the week." Then she added, "Besides, I'm already involved with someone." She mentally scolded herself because those should have been the first words out of her mouth when Pete started flirting.

"Hey, Pete, what's up?" Nick had come out of the kitchen and stood next to Roxie. "Leave work early?"

"I had a meeting down the street and just came in to say hey." He gestured to Roxie. "I never made it to the kitchen after seeing this lovely lady."

"Please." Roxie felt her stomach turn. Not in a good way. "And you wonder why I think you're a player."

Pete scowled, but Nick laughed so hard that the bartending class all turned in their direction. He lowered his voice. "Hey, how's Bree doing today anyway? I hope she's recovered from being around all those cats. Must be tough to be allergic like that."

"Cats?" Roxie tried to remember what Bree had told her about last night. "Right, her cat allergy. Yeah, she's a sucker for a stray cat. I keep telling her to ignore them, but she insists on getting near them to make sure they're okay."

"Stray cats?" He squinted. "I thought she said she visited her friend with a lot of cats. Called her a cat lady."

"Oh, right!" Roxie nodded, swearing to stay out of this mess from here on out. "She went to her friend's house. Anyway, she just loves cats, even though she's highly allergic."

Nick narrowed his eyes and seemed to be analyzing her answer. Then he said, "Come on into the kitchen, you two, so we don't disturb the class."

Pete rose, but Roxie declined. "That's okay. I have some work to do here. You boys go play." She looked pointedly at Pete.

"Fine, but just wait one second—so you've got a boyfriend? I guess that means dinner's out?" Pete asked.

"You guessed right," she said, and tried with all her might to concentrate on her laptop and not his gorgeous butt as he walked away.

WHILE BREE WAITED for a call from the driver her father was sending, she double-checked her outfit. She'd chosen a teal knit dress with tan suede booties. Dressing appropriately for dinner at her father's was one of the first lessons drilled into her as a child.

She also checked her purse for crackers—just in case. And she stuck a small bottle of mouth-wash into it in case she threw up. She had to be prepared because the last thing she needed was for her father to discover she was pregnant. He would have all sorts of advice to dole out and who knows who he'd leak it to. Next thing, she'd see her picture in print while in the grocery-store checkout line.

Not at all fair to Nick to find out that way.

She still had a few minutes before getting picked up, so she called Nick while she was thinking about him. "Hi, Nick," she said when he answered. "This is Bree."

"Hi, Bree." He sounded surprised to hear from her.

"I wanted to follow up on our conversation last night about you being a consultant. Did you get the contract I couriered over this afternoon?"

"I did."

"Well?"

"I think it looks good, and I'll get it signed and back to you in the morning."

She sighed in relief. "Great! This makes me very happy. I think you'll do a wonderful job for us and Gabriella."

"I hope you're not being too optimistic. I cer-tainly can't work miracles."

She placed a hand on her abdomen. "I think

you're wrong about that." She moved ahead before her emotions got the best of her, something else she'd had to deal with recently. She'd never been one who cried when those sappy commercials came on the TV. Now she constantly needed tissues nearby to sop up her tears. "Also, I was wondering if you're free for lunch tomorrow?"

"Tomorrow?"

"Yes, I'd like us to have lunch at Gabriella's Latin-fusion restaurant so you can see what's going on."

"Sure. Let me see what I can do. Maybe a late lunch so I'm still here for the midday rush at The Fresh Pantry?"

"That would work." They set a time and she gave him the address. "See you tomorrow."

About a minute after they disconnected, the driver called to say he was downstairs. She grabbed her purse, looked at her laptop and decided not bring it. She couldn't get online while they drove, so why bother. She had her phone and she could make the reservation at Gabriella's on the way to her father's.

The drive through traffic was slow, but Bree was in no hurry. After making the late lunch reservation and letting Gabriella know by email that they were coming, she leaned her head back on the plush leather seat and closed her eyes.

"Ms. Tucker?"

She jolted awake when the driver called her name. "Yes?"

"We're here." He'd parked the car in front of the huge house on the circular driveway and had opened her door for her.

Bree blinked several times. She must have fallen asleep. "Thank you." She struggled to grab her purse and get out of the car. She straightened her coat and fluffed her hair, knowing she needed to look perfect when she entered the house.

The butler was waiting for her at the front door. He greeted her with a big smile. "Good evening, Ms. Tucker. So good to see you."

"And you as well, James," she said, giving him a hug. If not for the staff her father employed, she would have had a childhood devoid of love and affection. "How is your wife?"

"Very well," he replied. "She sends her best wishes."

"Aubrey!" Her father interrupted the conversation before she could ask about James's children, who were a few years older than Bree. "Come in, come in! James, take her coat so she can come meet her new stepmother."

Normally, she would have allowed him to take her purse to keep with her coat and scarf, but this time she held on to it. Just in case.

Rather than hugging like most fathers, he greeted her with a healthy pat on the back as he guided her past the formal living room, one of the many rooms she'd never been allowed to enter as a child. They continued toward the back of the house to what her father referred to as the den.

"Linda, I'd like to present my daughter, Aubrey."

"Bree," she automatically corrected as she reached out to shake hands with a woman she could have described before seeing her. She was blond, curvaceous and probably late thirties. Actually older than his last wife. "Nice to meet you."

"Oh, I'm so happy to meet you, too." She was a bubbly one. "Cal has told me so much about you."

"Really?" She looked to her father, wondering what he knew about her that he could tell someone.

"Let me get you a drink," he said. "What would you like? And there are canapés on the coffee table. Help yourself."

"Water will be fine," Bree said as she and Linda took seats on the brocade chairs in front of the massive stone fireplace. "So how did you two meet?" That seemed like a safe question.

"Great story," her father said over his shoulder as he poured her a glass of water from the bar in the corner of the room.

Expecting to hear that he had met her in Vegas, and that she'd been his massage therapist or a bartender or showgirl or something worse, she was nearly blown away when he said, "She's one of my accountants."

"Really?" Bree asked. "And it was love at first sight?"

"Oh, no." Linda laughed, an infectious laugh that made Bree smile. "We butted heads several times and your dad was going to fire me."

Her dad jumped in. "Until she finally convinced me that her way was the right way." He walked over to his wife and kissed her temple. "And the rest is history."

Bree didn't know what to say. "Well, congratulations on your marriage. I haven't had time to buy you a present yet—"

"No need," her dad said. "We're just glad you're here tonight."

His simple statement was an unexpected gift to her, and she blinked away her sudden tears. Damn those hormones.

A short while later, they were called in for dinner. Her father took his normal place at the head of the long table that could easily accommodate sixteen or more. Linda sat on his left with Bree on his right.

The first course was served, and thankfully Bree had no problem eating any of the food.

By the time the entrées came out, she began wondering why her father hadn't offered her wine. He had a huge cellar with thousands of bottles that he always served at meals. Not that she could drink any, but he didn't know that.

When one of the kitchen staff appeared with a silver wine cooler with a bottle in it and a towel around it, she began to panic. It had been too good to be true! Maybe she could use the medication excuse she'd used last night with Nick. Satisfied that she could handle the invitation to enjoy the wine, she was startled when she realized the wine was actually nonalcoholic sparkling cider.

"You're probably wondering why we're not having wine or champagne to celebrate tonight," her father said, as if reading her mind. "Well, we have some other news to share." He poured the liquid into each of their fluted glasses, then looked at Linda and smiled. He seemed truly happy. He turned to Bree with his glass raised. "Tonight we're celebrating both our marriage and the upcoming birth of our child!"

All Bree could do was stare in stunned silence. Her mouth wouldn't work and she couldn't even swallow the lump in her throat. Her father clinked her glass with his and she immediately downed the entire thing in one gulp, wishing it was alcoholic after finding out that both she and her stepmother were having babies at the same time.

LUNCH SERVICE AT The Fresh Pantry the next day went smoothly, and by the time Nick met Bree at Gabriella's Latin-fusion restaurant, he was starving.

As soon as he saw Bree sitting at a table in the dark restaurant, he realized he wasn't just starving for food. He was starving for her, too. Their kiss the other night had lingered in his mind at the oddest times.

"So what do you think?" she asked when he came close enough. Today she was dressed in a black business suit with a pale pink blouse, and all he wanted to do was unbutton it to find out what she wore underneath.

"What do I think?" He realized she was asking about the restaurant and not about what he'd really been thinking. "The place looks nice," he said as he took a seat at the round booth with its red tufted vinyl bench. "A little dark for my taste, but then Latin-fusion food is spicy and flavorful, so the atmosphere works."

"I've ordered a bunch of different items for us to try so we can get a feel for what they're serving." She pointed to the things she'd chosen on the menu.

They stuck to business as they shared portions of food. Stuffed tomatillos, mole chicken on skewers, and chorizo and bean burritos were just some of the selections they tasted.

"I'm not having a problem with the food," she said. "I think it's all pretty good. What do you think?"

"I agree. But the portions are large and I'm wondering if she's charging the right amount." He explained to Bree about profit and overhead costs and how important it was to keep food costs low to stay in the black.

"I'm stuffed," she said when they'd finished tasting everything. She sat back in the booth and sighed in pleasure as she closed her eyes. Nick folded his hands on his lap to keep from reaching out and caressing her neck like he was itching to do.

Suddenly, she moaned and pitched forward, clutching her abdomen.

"Are you okay?" he asked in alarm.

She shook her head as if unable to speak.

"Do you need me to take you to the bathroom?" he asked, trying to find a way to help her.

"No," she whispered as she shook her head, still hunched over as if in pain.

He waited a few minutes, hoping she'd feel better, but she seemed to be in more agony. "Do you need a doctor?"

"I don't know." She spoke so softly that he could barely hear her.

"An ambulance? Or can I take you to the hospital?" He wondered if this was related to the other symptoms she'd been having, but he knew that now wasn't the time to burden her with questions.

She moaned again and doubled over. He couldn't let this go on. He couldn't watch her in pain like this. He had to help her.

"I'm calling 911," he said as he reached for his phone.

She said, "Okay," and he knew she must be in pretty bad shape to go along with him calling an ambulance.

When his call was answered, he relayed the information and address. While the operator stayed on the line after dispatching an ambulance, he asked Bree, "Do you want to stretch out on the bench while we wait?"

"No. Can't."

"They should be here soon."

She nodded slightly and mumbled words he didn't understand. "This must be how the...the woman...at the coffee shop felt."

CHAPTER TEN

BREE RODE IN the ambulance, the entire time suffering the worst cramping she'd ever had and wondering when it would end. She'd been hooked up to an IV by a caring EMT who was both efficient and sympathetic. She promised to keep Bree's pregnancy confidential and let only the medical staff know.

Meanwhile, Bree wanted to curl into a ball until it all went away.

The ambulance stopped and before she knew it, she was being wheeled into the emergency room and immediately into a curtained area and transferred to the bed there.

Nick peeked his head into her cubicle a few minutes later. "How are you? Any better?" He'd obviously followed the ambulance in his own car.

She was on her side in a fetal position, the most comfortable she could get. "Not really."

He stepped over to the bed. "Have you seen a doctor yet?"

"No." She sucked in a breath to talk. "They're busy."

"That's true. The waiting room is packed." He pulled up a chair. "Can I do anything for you?"

"You've…you've been so sweet," she said. "Can you call Roxie to come?" She moaned and curled up tighter when the cramping continued in earnest. She inhaled and exhaled a few times before speaking. "You don't have to stay."

"I already called Roxie. She's on her way. And I'm not going to leave you alone." He squeezed her hand.

A few minutes later, a young male doctor appeared and introduced himself.

"I'll give you some privacy," Nick said before leaving.

"Has there been any bleeding with the cramping?" the doctor asked.

"Not that I know of. It came on very suddenly."

He asked her to roll onto her back and he did a thorough exam, followed by an ultrasound. "What were you doing when this began?" he asked.

"Having lunch," she got out, wanting to roll onto her side again. "Am I having a miscarriage?"

"Everything appears fine according to the ultrasound. Cramping isn't uncommon in the first trimester, although not normally severe enough to require a hospital visit. That's why I had to make sure you didn't have an ectopic—a tubal—

pregnancy." He made notes on a clipboard. "I'd like to keep you here until the cramping subsides just to be sure everything's okay."

"But why did this happen?"

"It's one of the mysteries of pregnancy," he said. "Your body is changing as the baby grows, and between that and the different hormones, your body sometimes balks. Don't be surprised if this happens again. But if you have severe bleeding with the cramping, then get yourself to your doctor or the hospital quickly."

"Okay. Thank you." She realized that the cramping had gotten milder, and she began to relax a little. This pregnancy hadn't been planned, but she certainly didn't want to go through the trauma of a miscarriage.

Right after the doctor left, Roxie entered the curtained area. "Are you okay? I was so worried when Nick called."

"He doesn't know about the pregnancy, does he?" Bree asked her friend.

"Not that I know of. He just said you were here and that you were in a lot of pain. He mentioned possible appendicitis, so I figured he didn't have a clue about what was really going on. Did he go home?"

Bree shrugged. "I don't know. I told him to, but that doesn't mean he listened to me." She pointed to the corner. "He put my purse over there. Someone from Billing was here asking for my insurance info, but that was before Nick showed up with my purse. Would you mind getting her back here now that I have my info?"

"I will, as soon as you tell me what happened."

Bree filled her in, and then Roxie went to get Bree's paperwork. Bree was anxious to leave now that she felt so much better. A nurse finally came in and removed her IV, and Roxie returned just as Bree was being helped into a wheelchair to go home.

"I'll go get my car and meet you at the ER entrance," Roxie told the nurse, who nodded her approval.

Bree felt on display as she was being wheeled out. The trip seemed to take forever, but finally the automatic doors at the ER entrance opened, and she saw Roxie get out of her car and come around to help Bree get in.

The nurse set the brake on the wheelchair, and Bree was standing up carefully when she heard the nurse speaking to someone behind Bree.

"You must be the daddy," she said. "I'm sure you're relieved that everything is just fine."

Bree spun her head around, and Nick's gaze flew to Bree's. She couldn't breathe.

Still oblivious to the drama surrounding her, the nurse took Bree's arm to help her into the car. "You go home and rest now. Take care."

The nurse unset the brake on the wheelchair and turned it around, disappearing into the emergency room.

"Bree, wait." Nick finally spoke. He stood next to the open door of Roxie's car where Bree sat in the passenger seat.

"Not here, Nick." Roxie must have realized that Bree couldn't form a sentence. She walked around the back of the car to open the driver-side door.

Nick ignored Roxie, still staring at Bree. "You're pregnant?"

Bree swallowed thickly. She nodded because no words would come. Never before had she felt such a swirl of emotions as she was experiencing now. Guilt, regret, shock. The list went on and on.

"The baby's mine?"

"Yes," Bree whispered. "I'm—"

"You're sure?"

Bree stared at him in amazement. "Yes, it's yours."

"Please, Nick, not now," Roxie pleaded. "It's cold out here and she's been through enough this afternoon."

He didn't ignore Roxie this time. Instead, he looked pointedly at her when he said, "And for some reason you think I haven't?"

Roxie wisely kept her mouth shut.

Nick glared at Bree. "Were you ever going to

tell me?" She'd never seen him angry in the short time she'd known him, but this was definitely rage bubbling below the surface. He was about to explode.

When she didn't answer, he asked again. "I want to know if you were ever going to tell me I'm the father of your baby."

She closed her eyes, breathed in and out, then opened her eyes to look at him. "I don't know. Probably not."

NICK WAS FURIOUS. He couldn't remember a time when he'd ever been this angry at someone or something. So he focused on the most important thing at the moment. "Is the baby okay? You were in a lot of pain."

Bree nodded. "Everything's fine."

Relieved, he pulled his cell phone from his pocket and looked at Bree. "Give me your address."

Bree didn't say anything.

"She'll get in touch with you, Nick," Roxie said from the driver's seat. "I'll make sure of it."

He ignored Roxie and repeated his question to Bree. She slowly recited her address.

He put his phone into his pocket. "I'll meet you at your apartment as soon as I take care of a few things." He needed to make sure everything was set at his restaurant for dinner service.

Bree didn't react and he left before he said anything he'd regret.

His heart was practically beating out of his chest as he drove. He began putting all the pieces together. Her symptoms, the reason she wasn't drinking and telling him she had food allergies. That's why she'd passed out. He had to give his mother credit—she'd been right about the pregnancy.

Mom.

What would she say? She'd be over the moon about having a grandchild. It's what she'd begged for. But this wasn't the way she'd wanted it to happen. He knew that for sure.

It wasn't that she would be upset about them not being married. She'd be more concerned that they barely knew each other.

Or maybe he was projecting his own concern onto his mother.

After checking in at the restaurant, he headed straight to Bree's apartment building. By the time he paid for metered parking and walked a block and a half to her building, the sun had set completely and the streetlights and open businesses provided the only illumination.

He had to sign in with the guard after he called up to Bree's apartment to get her okay. Nick wasn't sure what he'd have done if she'd turned him away. He wasn't a violent person by nature, but this was a situation he'd never had to face before.

"Seventh floor, apartment 708," the guard told him, pointing to the elevator. "Turn right when you get off the elevator."

"Thank you." Nick wasn't in the mood to be polite, but he didn't need to take his frustration out on the innocent man behind the desk, either.

A few minutes later he stood in front of Bree's door and raised his hand to knock. He'd been gritting his teeth, so he relaxed his jaw before rapping on the door.

Bree opened the door almost immediately. She wore pajama pants, thick socks and a tank top with an open sweater over it. More casual than he'd seen her since they'd come back from the island. "Come in." She stood back so he could enter and shut the door behind him. "Would you like something to drink?"

"Water, please." He hadn't realized until she'd made the offer how parched he was.

She pointed to the exquisitely decorated seating area that must have been done by a professional. "Have a seat. I'll be right back."

He took his time, looking at the things she had on display. Nothing personal, except for a photograph of her with her three friends. He picked up the frame to get a better look. They were much younger, maybe in college. They looked different now. Not so much older as more mature. They'd gone from girls to women.

"Here you go." Bree handed him a glass and they sat down.

Bree chose the end of the tan sofa and Nick sat in the paisley armchair across from her. He took a long drink of his water while Bree placed two coasters on the coffee table. He put his glass on one and sat back, resting his foot on the opposite knee.

He realized from her silence that he'd have to be the one to start the conversation.

"How long have you known about the pregnancy?"

She shrugged. "Not that long." She sipped her water. "When the doctor took blood to figure out what was wrong with me, she also ran a pregnancy test. Twice."

His eyes widened. Double the proof. "So what's your plan?" She obviously had one that hadn't included him.

She bit her bottom lip and pulled her sweater closed as she crossed her arms. "I've thought it through," she began, "and I think the best thing would be to put it up for adoption."

He stared at her. "Adoption? Are you kidding me?" He paused. "You said you probably weren't going to tell me about the baby. Then how were you going to let someone adopt it? I'm pretty sure you'd need my signature."

She shrugged. "I figured eventually you'd need to know. But—"

"Eventually? Was dinner on Sunday night not the right time? Lunch today? How about when you had to go by ambulance to the hospital? You couldn't even mention it then?"

She still held her glass and sipped her water. "I didn't want you to find out this way."

"It's not the way I'd have chosen, either." He figured sarcasm was better than anger. "I just can't believe you didn't tell me. Instead, you made up all those excuses about food allergies and antihistamines and cats. No wonder Roxie didn't know what I was talking about." It was all becoming clear the more he pieced it together.

He cocked his head to one side. "So how did this happen? We used protection."

She pursed her lips. "Not in the shower."

The memory came flooding back, but he refused to let the recalled experience influence his current feelings. "You said you were on birth control." They'd shared that they hadn't been with anyone else in quite a while, so he hadn't worried about their lack of caution.

"I honestly didn't think I could get pregnant. Turns out that being on a low-dose pill isn't always foolproof."

Great. "So the baby's okay? The doctor said everything was fine?"

She nodded. "He said cramping like I experienced sometimes happens in the first trimester."

"You were in a lot of pain. You're okay now?"

"I am. Just tired, but that's been pretty standard the past few weeks."

"In the future, will you let me know if you need anything?" After voicing his anger, now he needed to make sure she took care of herself and his baby.

"That's not necessary."

"You're having my baby," he pointed out.

"But we're not raising it. I told you, I'm going to put it up for adoption."

"I haven't agreed to that."

Her eyes widened and she leaned forward. "What do you mean you haven't agreed? There is no other option." She gasped. "You're not asking me to end the pregnancy, are you?"

He was shocked by her question. "No, of course not. I'm just saying that I haven't agreed to let my child go off to be raised by strangers." He uncrossed his legs. "You've had time to process this, but I haven't."

"I'm sure you'll come to the same conclusion when you've thought about it," she said.

"I doubt it."

She was quiet for a few long seconds before

speaking. "Then there's only one other option available." She looked him in the eyes. "If you don't want to give it to a loving family, then you can raise it on your own."

AFTER NICK LEFT Bree's apartment, she wasn't sure if she was angry or sad or any mixture of the two. She curled up on the sofa and cried until she had no more energy left. She must have fallen asleep because the ringing phone woke her.

She got up slowly, dried tears on her cheeks. "Hello."

"Hey, Bree, it's Hannah. I wanted to make sure you're okay. Roxie told me what happened."

Bree assumed that Roxie had told Hannah the entire story. "Nick came over, and we talked everything out."

"How's he doing?"

"Not good. He's furious."

"Doesn't he realize it takes two to make a baby?" Petite Hannah was being her usual protective self.

Bree padded to the kitchen for some water while she talked. "He's more upset that I didn't tell him about the pregnancy than the pregnancy itself. He's not seeing what the future holds."

"Oh, gotcha. What else did he say?"

Bree sipped her water and went back into the

living room to curl up on the sofa. "He's not happy about the adoption plan."

"Really?" Hannah sounded concerned. "Does he have another plan?"

"No, but I do. I told him if he didn't want to let someone adopt it, then he could raise it himself."

Bree heard Hannah's intake of breath. "What did he say to that?"

"He didn't say another word," Bree told her. "He just left. So I don't know what will happen, but there's a lot of time before a decision needs to be made. I'm sure he'll come to his senses and see that he can't be a single parent and run a successful restaurant at the same time."

"But would you agree to let him raise it if he decides to do just that?" Hannah asked.

Bree mulled it over. "I don't see why not. I just know there's no way for me to raise a baby when I have to spend so much time working."

"You could delegate more so you wouldn't have to put in so many hours."

"Why would I do that?"

"So you can be a mother," Hannah said. "Don't you want that someday?"

"Not really," Bree answered automatically. "I know nothing about being a mother, thanks to my dad paying off my own mother after I was born. I have no idea what it's like and, frankly, I'm not interested."

"But you might change your mind when you see this baby and hold it."

"I really doubt that, Hannah. My company's not going to suddenly manage itself."

"But you have Roxie and Amber and me to help you. Not just with the company, but with the baby, too." Hannah's voice was filled with emotion. "Plus, you're financially stable and able to pay for help."

"There's no way I'd do that." Bree was emphatic. "I was raised by nannies, and I won't allow that to happen to this child."

Hannah was quiet for a few seconds. "Please just think about it, Bree."

"I'm sorry, Hannah. My mind is made up."

Hannah must have realized she was getting nowhere with Bree, so she changed the subject. "How are you feeling? Did the cramping go away completely?"

"It seems to have. I get a twinge every now and then, but I'm trying to take it easy."

"That's good. Please let me know if you need anything."

"I will. Thanks, Hannah."

Bree disconnected and set the phone down on the coffee table, thinking about what Hannah had said. Bree disagreed completely. There was no way she was going to change her mind about keeping it. She could never make it work by herself. She wasn't sure Nick could do it alone, either, but that would be up to him to decide. At least he had family around when he needed a hand.

She only had a father who kept his distance, and now a new stepmommy who was also pregnant.

If only she could go back in time. Back to their working vacation on the island when she'd slept with Nick.

If not for her best friends coaxing her to let her hair down, get out of her comfort zone and have a vacation fling, none of this would have happened.

"I'M REALLY WORRIED about Bree," Hannah told Roxie that evening as they were leaving spin class. "She doesn't seem to be showing any emotion at all about this baby. It doesn't even bother her that Nick is upset about it."

"I know," Roxie agreed, blotting her face and neck with her towel before stuffing it into her bag. "She acts like this pregnancy is just one more business deal to handle."

"What are we going to do?" Hannah sounded defeated. "We can't just ignore what's going on with her."

They exited the building and walked to the

parking lot. "I agree," Roxie said, "but beyond talking to her I don't know what else we can do."

"Has she told you what happened between her and Nick? She told him he could raise the baby if he didn't agree to give his permission for adoption. I would have loved to have heard that conversation."

"You're kidding—she actually told him that?" They stopped walking before splitting off to their own cars. "He looked pretty mad at the hospital. I can only imagine how he's feeling now that they've talked."

Hannah tilted her head, freely swinging her blond ponytail, which made her look as young as a teenager. "Can you blame him?"

Roxie shook her head. "I warned her that she should tell him about the pregnancy before he found out on his own. She wasn't going to mention it at all unless she absolutely had to."

"I don't usually disagree with Bree on major things, but this time I think she was completely wrong."

Roxie shrugged. "I do, too, but it was her decision. Now she's going to be the one to suffer because of the way Nick found out."

"How do you think he's going to handle it?" Hannah's eyes widened. "Do you think he'll actually raise the baby on his own?"

"No clue," Roxie said.

Hannah shivered. "It's freezing out here." She rubbed her upper arms. In their exercise clothes, neither was dressed for the thirty-degree weather.

"I'm cold, too," Roxie agreed. "And hungry. Let's go home, shower and I'll pick up some Chinese takeout for the four of us—we'll meet at Bree's. I'll call to let her know we're coming, and you call Amber to meet us there." They agreed on an approximate time and went their separate ways.

Roxie was the last to arrive. Although Bree hadn't been happy with the plan when Roxie had called, she seemed to have reluctantly accepted their appearance.

"I got a mixture of entrées," Roxie said to her friends. "Hopefully, there's nothing in any of them that you can't eat, Bree." She'd purposely chosen Chinese food for that reason.

"Thank you, Rox, I appreciate it," Bree said quietly.

They were seated at Bree's oak dining room table when Bree made an announcement. "I know you came over to find out what happened between Nick and me, so let me end the suspense." She took a sip of her water and set it down slowly before continuing. "It turns out that right now Nick is vehemently against giving up the baby for adoption."

"He is?" Amber asked.

"What does that mean?" Hannah wanted to know.

Only Roxie waited for Bree to continue.

"It means that he's probably not going to give me permission to put it up for adoption. And without his signature, I'm unable to do anything legally."

"Do you have a plan B?" Roxie asked.

"Yes. I told him that if he didn't give permission for adoption, then he would have to raise the baby on his own."

Amber gasped, as she was the only one who hadn't heard this latest piece of news. They all stopped eating. "Did he agree to that?" she asked.

Before Bree could answer, Roxie posed a question of her own. "Do you think you'd be okay living this close to your child and not being involved in its life?"

Roxie could tell from Bree's startled look that she hadn't taken that into consideration.

Bree was saved from answering the question by her ringing phone.

"We'll be waiting for your answer when you get back," Roxie reminded Bree as she left the room.

Amber leaned in and whispered to Hannah and Roxie, "Do you think we're getting through to her?"

"Even if she gets that how she's handling the situation isn't healthy," Roxie replied quietly, "there's really nothing we can do to change the situation."

"There has to be something," Hannah insisted. "We can't just give up."

They ate in silence as they waited for Bree's return to the table.

"Well, this day just keeps getting better and better," Bree said as she slowly took her seat. "I hired a private investigator after I learned I was pregnant. I decided that I needed to find my mother and figure out if this child is inheriting any medical issues. Well, it turns out he keeps hitting dead ends."

"Your mother?" Hannah's eyes grew wide. "You want to find her, after all these years?"

"I do. I'd always assumed she'd died when she didn't show up on my twenty-first birthday, and now it seems I might have been right all along." Sarcasm oozed from Bree's words. "But my PI can't even find proof of her death." She looked down at her food, not touching it and not saying anything more.

"I'm sorry, Bree," Hannah said softly.

"You've had a tough day," Roxie stated, as if they didn't all know it already. "Why don't you eat some dinner and we'll clean up and leave so you can get some rest."

As if Roxie hadn't spoken, Bree said, "I guess if she'd wanted to be found, then she'd have made it easier. It's as if she's disappeared from the face of the earth."

No one said anything, waiting for her to continue.

Bree began to rise from the table without eating another bite. As she pushed in her chair, she said, "Please excuse me. I'm going to take Roxie up on her suggestion and go to bed. Maybe tomorrow will be a better day." Bree headed to her bedroom and shut the door with more force than necessary.

Hannah stood up, gathering her plate and anything else she could carry. "Come on, let's clean up and leave. She needs to rest. She's going to end up back in the hospital with the way this day has gone."

Roxie couldn't agree more.

In all the years they'd known each other, Roxie couldn't remember a time when Bree hadn't been in absolute control of every aspect of her life.

Until now.

CHAPTER ELEVEN

WHEN HE ASKED Pete to meet him at a bar in Old Town, Nick was pretty sure there wasn't enough alcohol in the building to make him forget what a lousy day it had been.

"Hey, buddy, what's up?" Pete clapped Nick on the shoulder as he arrived at the bar and sat down next to Nick.

"This has been one hell of a day," Nick told him, emptying his beer glass and lifting it to get the bartender's attention.

"I'll have what he's having," Pete told the bartender when she came to refill Nick's glass. "Tell me about it," Pete said to Nick. "What happened?"

Nick breathed in and out. "Bree's pregnant."

"Good for her," Pete said, without realizing what Nick was telling him. "So what's that got to do with you?"

Nick lifted his glass as if to make a toast. "Congratulate me. I'm going to be a dad." He took a long swallow, realizing that Pete was staring at him. Nick swallowed his mouthful and sputtered, "Shut your mouth, dude."

Pete did so and then drank half of his beer at once. He set down the glass. "I didn't even realize you'd been with her—or anyone. Not since you and Tracy broke up."

Nick nodded. "On the island."

"Ah! That explains why you've hesitated asking for her financial help." He took another swallow of beer. "You're sure she's pregnant? Sometimes those pee tests give false positives."

"If only that were the case. Nope, she had a blood test. Run twice, apparently. No mistakes there." He raised a finger, realizing he was well on his way to being drunk. "In fact, she had an ultrasound today. No denying it now." He filled Pete in on calling for an ambulance when they were at Gabriella's restaurant and how he actually found out by accident that she was pregnant.

"She wasn't going to tell you?" Pete shook his head. "That's rough, man. So now what? You're not going to get married or anything, are you?"

"It's not that simple. She doesn't want to raise a child, says she'd make a terrible mother. So she plans on putting the baby up for adoption."

"Adoption?" Pete seemed to let that sink in. He shrugged. "You know, maybe that's the best option. You barely know Bree and if she doesn't even want to raise it—"

"I told her I wouldn't agree to adoption." Nick set his glass down too hard on the bar, causing several patrons to look their way.

"Okay. So then what?"

Nick swallowed. "She told me that if I didn't agree to adoption, then I could raise the baby on my own."

Pete's eyes grew wide. "You can't do that!"

"Why not?" Was he actually considering it?

"You don't know anything about babies," Pete reminded him. "And babies grow up to be teenagers. I've heard they can make your life hell."

"I can learn. Other people do it."

Pete's expression screamed doubt.

"I can," Nick repeated. "And I have Mom to guide me."

"But is that what you really want to do? It'll be a complete lifestyle change, man. And what about the restaurant? It's barely surviving as it is."

"I know there's a lot of details to work through, but I can't just let some strangers raise my child." He scratched his cheek through his beard. "Besides, do you really think Mom would allow that to happen?"

Pete laughed humorlessly. "We both know the answer to that."

"Yeah. So that leaves me no choice." He swallowed thickly. "I'm going to be a single dad."

"Listen, before you make any decisions, there's

plenty of time until the kid arrives. A lot can happen between now and then."

Nick nodded. "True. Maybe Bree will change her mind."

"Exactly, so play it cool. No quick decisions."

"Right. No quick decisions."

Pete raised a hand to get the bartender's attention. "This round's on me." When they had their drinks, Pete changed the topic. "So what's the story on getting financial help from Bree's company? I'm guessing you haven't said anything to her about it?"

Nick shook his head. "Nope. I've got a few things going on that I'm hoping will help us out." He reminded Pete about the bartending class, and then told him about Nick's consultant position with Bree's company. "That's what we were doing when Bree suddenly moaned in pain. We'd been having lunch at this Latin-fusion place. Great food, but large portions for the money. I think that's where they're going wrong, but I won't know until I go back to look at their books."

"So she doesn't know how badly The Fresh Pantry is doing financially?"

Nick scowled. "Do you think she'd ask me to be a restaurant consultant if that were the case?"

Pete nodded his agreement. "Actually, I'm surprised she offered you the position, knowing she was pregnant with your kid."

"I hadn't thought about it that way. She didn't seem to mind using the restaurant for bartending class, either, although she wasn't actively involved in that." He pursed his lips and shrugged one shoulder. "This is just a short-term commitment, so maybe she figured she could hide her pregnancy until our business was concluded."

Pete nodded. "You're probably right. Or maybe subconsciously she wanted to be near you... wanted you to find out about the baby."

They had been running into each other a lot since returning from vacation. "Anyway, back to saving the restaurant," Nick said. "I'm also thinking about renting out the restaurant for use as a pop-up. That tapas one gave me the idea. Turns out, there are websites where you can list your space for rent. So once the bartending class ends, The Fresh Pantry will be available to rent out on Mondays."

"Is it really worth the money?"

"For our space, I think we can get fifteen hundred a day."

Pete's eyes widened. "That would be an extra six thou every month."

"*If* we can rent it every Monday. There's no guarantee. But I figure this close to DC we can pick up some takers. Old Town is a great location." Nick drank the last of his beer, deciding he'd had enough.

They talked over details about Nick's idea, but he couldn't stop yawning. "I'm gonna get going, Pete. Thanks for meeting me tonight. It really helped to talk it out."

"Anytime," Pete said before calling the bartender over and paying the entire tab.

"Let me give you some money." Nick reached into his back pocket for his wallet.

Pete shook his head. "Nope. It's the least I can do. Besides, you need to save your money to buy diapers." He laughed at his own joke.

Nick didn't think it was funny. "I grabbed an Uber over here, what about you?" Nick hadn't taken any chances after the day he'd had. He knew overindulging would be hard to avoid.

"Same here," Pete said. "I figured something must be up because you're never game for going out to a bar on a weeknight." He paused. "Hey, let me ask you something."

"What's that?"

"You've met Bree's friends. What's Roxie's story?"

"I don't really know much about her. You interested?"

"Maybe."

"Let me guess, she's not interested." Nick couldn't help giving him a hard time. "Maybe she's seen too much of the real you."

"Hey!" But Pete grinned at the jab. "Seriously,

can you find out what's up with her? She says she's involved with someone."

Nick sighed. "I'll do what I can. You do remember that I'm the one with the major life change, right?"

IF BREE HAD learned anything from her high-stakes businessman father, it was to always have a lawyer on speed dial.

So the first thing she did the next morning when she got to her office was to call Larry Schwartz III, the lawyer she kept on retainer for the company because they weren't in the position yet to have one on staff full-time.

"Hi, Larry, this is Bree Tucker," she said when she was put through.

"Good morning, Bree, what can I do for you?" Larry was in his fifties and had become a lawyer just like his father and his father before him. Larry liked to joke that he was born with scales in one hand and a gavel in the other, since he would probably become a judge at some point, just like his father and grandfather had.

"I have some questions about adoption," she said. "Can you answer them or do I need to talk to an adoption lawyer?"

"I can answer general questions, and we can go from there if you need more information."

Bree inhaled deeply. She trusted Larry implicitly and knew he wouldn't divulge her secret, but she wasn't ready to tell him about her pregnancy. "I have a woman who is pregnant—she's early in her pregnancy—and plans to put the child up for adoption. The father is against it. So where does she stand legally?"

"Hmm. Are they married?"

"No."

"Living together? Common-law marriage?"

Hell no. "No, they're not. My understanding is that this was a short-term thing. Neither of them is invested in a relationship." Amazing how freely she could convey her own situation in the third person.

"Well, every state has its own laws, but in Virginia he would be required to sign an affidavit giving up his rights to the child, just like the mother would."

"And if he refuses?"

"Then there would be a hearing in front of a judge and he could plead his case. He'd probably have his own lawyer."

Sounded messy. "There's no way around getting the father's permission? Even if she doesn't name him on the birth certificate?"

"Not that I know of. But I can put you in touch with an adoption lawyer, and maybe you'll get a different answer." Larry paused. "By the way, I'd suggest that she not lie on the birth certificate about the father's identity because that could be a punishable offense."

"I'll keep your advice in mind as the pregnancy progresses. Thanks, Larry." They disconnected and Bree stared at the notes she'd made, doodling on the corner of the page while she considered what to do next.

"Nothing," she said aloud. She had several months to worry about this. Who knew what would happen between now and then?

Although that wasn't how she liked to run her life. She preferred to do research, make a decision and then take action. Her handling of this situation was completely foreign to her.

Her desk phone rang and she answered it. "Bree Tucker."

"Hello, Bree, how are you feeling?" Gabriella Carrera's slight Columbian accent was immediately recognizable. "I'm so sorry I wasn't at the restaurant yesterday when you fell ill."

"Thanks for your concern, but I'm doing well, Gabriella. Nothing to worry about."

"I hope it wasn't my food that made you sick. I should have been there, but my son had a doctor's appointment and my husband is on a business trip in California."

"No, no, your food was delicious and I completely understand about your son," Bree told her. "Nick Harmon was with me—the consultant I hired—and he agreed that your food was spectacular."

"I'm so glad to hear that."

They spent the next few minutes talking about what else Nick would be looking at in respect to the day-to-day running of her restaurant.

By the time she had hung up with Gabriella, Bree realized that there was no way she would be able to avoid Nick now that she'd hired him as a consultant. At least it would only be for a short period of time. Originally, she'd hired him knowing he'd finish the job and be out of her life by the time her pregnancy began to show. But, *surprise*, now he knew about the pregnancy, and wasn't that going to make things uncomfortable between them.

"No time like the present." She picked up the phone to call Nick, realizing that talking out loud to herself wasn't exactly healthy behavior.

"Hello," Nick said when he picked up after several rings.

"Hi, Nick, it's Bree."

He was silent.

"Are you still there?" she asked, thinking they'd been disconnected.

"I'm here. What do you want?" His tone was brusque.

"I'm calling about business." If that was the

way he wanted to play it, she could go along. "I was wondering when you might have time to go back to Gabriella's to finish assessing her restaurant."

He didn't say anything at first. "Do we need to go together or can I go alone?"

Ouch. She thought for a second. "I think the next time you go, I'll go, too, so I can introduce you to the owner. Gabriella wasn't available to meet with us yesterday because of a family obligation. I'd told her ahead of time that it wouldn't be necessary for her to be there."

"Then I can be available midafternoon any day this week, or next Monday when my restaurant is closed."

They decided on the next afternoon because Bree didn't want to waste time. She wanted this consultant job done quickly so she wouldn't have to deal with him unless it was absolutely necessary.

After they ended their conversation, she called Gabriella to let her know their plans. The next thing on her agenda was to call her father to find out if he could give her any other clues to figuring out how to find her mother. That had been her investigator's suggestion, but Bree had been too tired to make the call last night. Her dad had told her things over the years in answer to Bree's questions, but as she'd become an adult, Bree had questioned whether he'd been completely truthful with her.

It turned out that she couldn't get through to her father. She'd forgotten that he was leaving today on his honeymoon in Aruba, and he wasn't answering his cell phone, so she left him a message to call her.

Why hadn't her mother ever contacted her? For money, even? Had her dad paid her more money to keep staying away? Bree had heard her father say over and over that if you had money, people wanted your money—and he knew how to use it to his advantage.

BREE WAS THE first to arrive at Gabriella's the next afternoon. She'd already eaten two small meals to hold her over until she ate at the restaurant. Her entire life was suddenly revolving around food. What to eat, what not to eat, when to eat, how much to eat. How was she going to endure this for months on end?

"I hope I'm not late." Nick's sudden arrival startled her.

"Not at all," she said. "Gabriella has some other food she'd like us to try…since our tasting was interrupted the other day."

Nick raised an eyebrow, words unnecessary.

"Here we go," Gabriella said as she expertly carried several plates and placed them on a table for them. Then she put a hand out to Nick, "I'm Gabriella Carrera and you must be the fantastic Nick."

He grinned at her compliment, maybe even blushed a little. It was difficult to tell in the dim lighting.

"I don't know about the fantastic part. We'll see if I can make suggestions that will help your business."

"Excellent. I'll leave you while you taste the food and I'll be back after I check on something in the kitchen."

When Gabriella was gone, Nick gestured to Bree to take a seat. They were in the same intimate booth as last time, the curved tufted seat giving them ample opportunity to be either right next to each other or to sit across from one another. Unlike Tuesday, they sat as far from each other as possible.

"Are you feeling okay?" he asked after several minutes of silence while they tasted the food.

She nodded. "I am. A few little twinges since I left the hospital, but the doctor said that's to be expected."

"Good." He took a long drink of water. "You're not working too hard?"

"I'm fine." Was he going to be this solicitous of her every time he saw her? His words of concern didn't exactly match his cold tone of voice. "Work's the least of my problems."

He gave her a questioning look. "Are you referring to me?"

"No, no." She waved a hand at him. "You, I can handle." She debated confiding in him and figured why not? Together they'd made a baby that he was probably going to raise, so why not give him some of her family's background? She lowered her voice so no one would overhear their conversation. "When I found out I was pregnant, I hired a private investigator to find my mother. I feel that knowing her medical history is something I should pursue. The PI called last night to tell me he's come up empty so far."

"So now what? Is he giving up?" Nick asked.

"Not exactly. He wants me to get information from my dad. See if there are missing pieces to give the PI a better lead."

"Do you think he'll be helpful?"

Bree shrugged. "I don't know. His story about her has changed over the years and I don't know what to believe."

"So your dad raised you by himself, or did you have a stepmother?"

Bree chuckled. "I've had several stepmothers over the years. None of them lasted very long and I wouldn't call any of them very motherly. I always had a nanny to take care of me, though."

Nick nodded. "Will you tell your dad about the pregnancy, since that's why you're interested in finding your mom?"

"I guess I'll just see how it goes." She hadn't considered that she might have to tell her father about the pregnancy. With the length of time they usually had between visits, she could easily give birth by the next time her father wanted a face-to-face get-together. "If I can avoid telling him, I will. Besides, he's got his own new arrival coming. That should keep his focus off why I want to find my mother."

"New arrival?" Nick's eyebrows shot up. "Isn't he, what? In his midsixties or something?"

Bree smirked. "Yeah, but if you marry someone in their late thirties, then it's not a problem." She knew she sounded snarky, but she couldn't help it.

"Wow, you've really gotten hit from all sides, haven't you?"

She gave him a slight smile, appreciating that he understood how topsy-turvy her life had become recently. "So what about you? Have you told your mom yet?"

He frowned. "Funny you should ask."

"Why's that?"

"Remember when she helped you at the tapas pop-up? She thought you might be pregnant then."

He paused and narrowed his eyes. "You didn't know that night, did you?"

Bree shook her head quickly. "No, I didn't have a clue. I thought maybe I was sick from something I'd picked up on the island. Pregnancy wasn't even a consideration." She paused. "So… have you or haven't you told your mom yet?"

"Not yet. I decided I needed a little more time to figure things out before I tell her."

"That's probably a good plan." She didn't ask if he had decided definitely that he would raise it. They still had a few months to work things out.

"When was the last time you saw your mother?" His change of focus back to her was pretty obvious.

"I don't remember."

His brows furrowed and he scratched his bearded cheek. "It's been that long?"

Bree nodded. "She was very young when she got pregnant with me, and my father didn't marry her. Instead, he got full custody of me, and shortly after I was born she was forbidden to see me until I turned twenty-one. But she never even came to see me when she was finally able to. For all I know, she might be dead." Bree tamped down the fragile emotions that were bubbling to the surface. Damn these pregnancy hormones. "I've got one old picture of her and that's about it."

"You know, I can't help noticing that the agreement between your parents sounds vaguely similar to our situation," he said wryly.

"Are you saying you'd ban me from this child's life like my father did to my mother?" She didn't like where this conversation was going.

"Of course not. But you're the one who doesn't want to raise him or her. Are you saying you've changed your mind?"

"No, I'm not saying that. I just don't like the idea that you might go to that extent to keep me away."

"No decisions have been made yet," he said. "I don't see any circumstances where I'd forbid you to see the child."

She didn't know what else to say after that.

The next few minutes were painfully silent until Gabriella and her bright personality returned.

"Was everything to your satisfaction?" she asked, folding her hands at her waist.

"Delicious," Nick said succinctly as he wiped his mouth with his napkin.

Her nervous expression turned into a smile. *"Gracias,"* she said. "Opening this restaurant has been a dream of mine since I was a little girl, and to know that you don't think the food is why we're not making a profit makes me very happy." She sat down on the bench, forcing Bree to scoot closer to Nick.

Bree glanced at Nick, but he was concentrating on making points to Gabriella about portion sizes and food costs.

"I'd like to see where you're spending your money," Nick said. "And whether you've hired too many staff members for the amount of business you're doing."

"Absolutely. Let's go back to the office, and I can pull it up on the computer." Gabriella rose.

"I have nothing to add to the discussion, so I'll leave and let you two do what you need to do." Bree was going to take the opportunity to make a quick getaway. She turned to Nick, "You can call me and let me know what you find."

"I will," he said. "And good luck with your dad."

"Thanks, I'm afraid I'm going to need it."

AFTER BREE LEFT Gabriella's restaurant, Nick kept thinking about Bree and her mother. Maybe, if she got her questions answered, she might be able to see things more clearly in regard to her own situation.

He had a difficult time concentrating on Gabriella's finances, but he forced himself to figure out what her problem might be. After he had spent time looking over everything, the two of them carried Gabriella's laptop and files out to a table in the dining room to spread them out.

Nick took a piece of paper and began writing numbers. He pointed to them as he explained to Gabriella. "Right here, using your empanadas as an example, I'm seeing that this is what it costs for the actual food, and this is what you're charging. That leaves you only twenty percent to pay for overhead."

He went on to explain how much she should be making on each meal and how she should either make smaller portions or charge more.

"Which way would you go?" she asked.

He thought about it and what he'd learned in his time as a restaurateur. "I would pay attention to how much food people take home. If most people box up their leftovers, then I'd do smaller portions. Otherwise, you need to charge more for the food." He thought of another idea. "*Or* you can do both."

"This is very helpful information," Gabriella told him. "How did you learn so much?"

"Part of it was from experience," he said. "But before I opened my restaurant, I earned a business degree and then went to culinary school. I worked as an assistant manager and then the manager of a DC restaurant. Both were good experiences and taught me a lot."

"Oh, my!" She shook her head. "I don't have any of that. My restaurant started as a food truck, and we did so well that I thought it would be a natural thing to open a restaurant. But there's so much more to consider now."

She wasn't the first inexperienced person to open a restaurant when the only thing they knew was how to make good food.

He could see she was overwhelmed by everything he'd told her, so they planned another meeting when he could come and watch the staff to see if she had the right number of employees.

She walked him to the exit. "Thank you so much, Nick. I'm learning a great deal from you."

He smiled. "I'm glad I can help."

"Bree's lucky to have found you. Smart, good-looking, and you two make a very cute couple."

"What?" He thought maybe he'd heard her wrong. "Oh, no, we're not a couple." Maybe they were a couple of idiots, but that's not what Gabriella meant.

She winked at him and gave him a broad smile. "I've seen you two together, how you look at each other. Take it from me, I know these things. Maybe you're a couple and you don't even realize it."

CHAPTER TWELVE

ON THE LAST DAY of bartending class, Roxie made sure to show up at The Fresh Pantry before the students were done for the day. She wanted to congratulate them and make sure they updated their résumés. She also had referral letters for them to present when they interviewed with prospective employers.

What she hadn't expected, when she walked into the restaurant, was for Pete to also be there.

"Hey, Roxie, good to see you." Pete flashed his sexy grin. He was dressed casually in jeans and a black henley that accentuated his broad shoulders and muscular physique.

She smiled back, slightly hesitant. "Hi. What are you doing here? Don't you have to work today?"

"I'm on my way to the airport," he explained. "I have a business trip to Chicago. I just needed to drop off something for Nick first."

"Taking any time for fun?" Who was she kidding? Of course he was going to take time for pleasure. That's how he rolled.

"I might have a little time one evening, but most of my schedule is booked with meetings." He leaned closer and lowered his voice, "Hey, can we talk a minute?"

"Um, sure." She agreed only because she was curious.

"Step back here." There was a hallway that led from the dining room to what Roxie assumed were back offices, as well as where the restrooms were located.

He stood close to her, close enough that she felt the heat come off his body. She fisted and unfisted her hands, trying to keep herself from reaching out to touch him while plastering her back to the wall.

"I wanted to talk to you about this situation between Nick and Bree," he said. "I'm concerned. What do you think about what they're planning to do?"

"About what?" She wasn't going to be the one to verify Bree's pregnancy.

"The baby. What else could I be talking about?"

She nodded. "Just checking." This was a subject she didn't mind talking about. "Truthfully, I think Bree's nuts. If she's not going to raise the baby, then she should put it up for adoption. There's no way she can let Nick raise it. They live too close to each other, and she's bound to run into Nick and the baby."

"I agree. Mostly with the part about Nick raising the baby." Pete ran a hand through his thick, dark hair. "He doesn't have a clue how to do it, and he certainly can't raise a baby on his own."

"Baby?" Nick's mom suddenly appeared. She'd stepped into the hallway from one of the doorways close by. "Nick is having a baby?" She stood with her eyes wide, waiting for Pete to reply.

"Damn," Pete said under his breath. "Listen, Auntie Em, I don't know what you heard—"

"I heard you say something about Nick raising a baby." She put her hands on her hips. "I want the truth right now, Peter Mitchell Buchanan."

Peter Mitchell? She must be pretty upset if she was using Pete's full name.

"I think you should talk to Nick about this." He spoke calmly, but he was obviously aware of whom he was dealing with.

"Who's pregnant?"

"I told you—"

"I know, I know. Talk to Nick. Well, I'm talking to you right now." She looked at Roxie then. "Will *you* tell me the truth? It's your friend, Bree, right? I knew it. He was very concerned about her being sick, and then they had dinner together here at the restaurant. How long have you both known?"

Roxie looked to Pete for what she should say, but he was no help when he merely shrugged and raised an eyebrow. She turned to Nick's mom. "Mrs. Harmon, it's not my place—"

"You two are quite a pair. Fine. I guess I'll have to go directly to Nick to get the truth." She didn't seem pleased at all. But who would be in her situation?

"Please don't go to Nick," Pete begged.

"Don't worry, I won't tell him how I found out." She started to leave and then turned back to Pete. "Unless he asks."

"Now what?" Roxie asked when Nick's mom was gone. "Should we warn Nick?" Her heart was beating hard. "I feel so bad that we were the ones who spilled the beans."

"I don't know what to do." Pete checked his watch. "I've got to get going or I'll miss my flight."

She'd never seen Pete this unsure of a situation, not that she'd known him for that long. "Can you call Nick from the airport?"

He nodded. "Right. I'll call him before I get on the plane."

"You should probably call him sooner than that. You don't want his mom to get to him first. I'll call Bree right now, too."

"Good thinking." He reached out and put a hand on her cheek. "Thank you. I'm glad you were here. This entire situation has me really torn up." He moved his hand from her cheek to the back of her neck and he put his lips on hers for mere seconds before pulling back far enough to look into her eyes.

Just long enough for her mouth to begin to tingle.

He continued to stare into her eyes, and then he kissed her again, this time for longer than a few seconds. He deepened the kiss and it became more like a kiss hello than a thank-you kiss or even a goodbye kiss.

He finally moved away and she wanted to pull him back to continue, but she didn't. She couldn't put words together to either tell him he was out of line or that she wanted him right there, right now.

She was definitely confused.

"I have to go," he whispered. "I'll miss my flight."

"Right," she whispered in return.

He straightened as if trying to gather himself together. "Can we get together when I come back? My return flight is Friday night."

She wanted to say yes, absolutely, but her good sense remained intact. "I don't think that's a very good idea." And not just because she was technically still in a relationship with someone else, even if she hadn't heard from Jim in almost two weeks. He claimed his new job was taking over his life and she was almost getting used to his long silences.

His eyes widened. "You were right there with me during that kiss."

Something she didn't need a reminder about. Her lips were still singing, but she refused to give in to her attraction to him. "That may be true, but I don't want to be next in your long line of broken hearts. And you already know that I'm in a long-distance relationship."

"Maybe you think you are," he said. "But deep down you know you've already broken it off with that guy."

NICK HAD JUST showered after a long run when he got a text from his mom. He'd been running more often lately as a stress reliever. Not that it had helped very much.

Where are you? Need to see you.

He replied, At home. Everything OK?

Instead of answering his question, she wrote, I'll be there in ten minutes.

She actually arrived at Nick's Alexandria condo in less than that, appearing extremely agitated.

He was in the kitchen when she walked in the door. "Something to drink?"

She shook her head. "No, we just need to talk."

"Sure. Do you want to sit down?" He headed to

the sofa and turned to her. "Did something happen at the restaurant?" She'd planned to go there today to get some things done while it was closed.

"The restaurant's fine." She followed him to the seating area, but remained standing. Her hands were folded and she kept running one thumb over the top of the other. "Nick, do you have something you want to tell me?"

"About what?"

She didn't say anything more, and he knew immediately that she had found out about the baby.

"I was going to tell you—"

"Say it."

He hadn't been this nervous talking to his mom since he'd broken a neighbor's window with a baseball when he was a kid. "Bree's pregnant, and I'm the father." He paused. "It's not an ideal situation, but it is what it is."

His mom surprised him by coming over and hugging him tightly. She had tears in her eyes as she sat down next to him on the sofa. "Tell me about Bree. My goodness. I don't even know her last name."

"Tucker. Her dad is Cal Tucker."

"The multimillionaire?"

"More like billionaire, I think."

"You've made plans to get married?"

Nick's mouth went dry. "No."

His mother's eyebrows rose. "Why not?"

"Mom, we met on vacation." How did you tell your mother that her grandchild was conceived because of a vacation fling? Probably better than calling it a one-night stand. "She'd never agree to it anyway."

"Have you asked her?"

He sighed. "She wasn't even going to tell me about the baby. I found out by accident."

"Sounds familiar."

"What do you mean?"

"You haven't asked how I knew about the pregnancy. *I* found out by accident."

The only ones who knew about the pregnancy were Bree and her friends and Pete. He'd told no one else.

"I overheard Pete and one of Bree's friends—Roxie, I think—talking. The one in charge of the bartending class." She rubbed her temple. "When I confronted Pete, he wouldn't confirm or deny it. And when he told me to talk to you, that confirmed my suspicions."

"It's not the way I wanted you to find out. I just needed time to figure things out first."

She nodded. "I understand. But you know you can come to me with anything. You're an adult and can make your own decisions. I'm not going to judge you."

He was relieved that she was taking this so well. Although he should have known she would.

"So tell me what the plan is now that you've decided not to get married." She smoothed her hair back from her face. "Shared custody?"

He shook his head. "That's probably not going to happen. Everything is still up in the air. The only definite thing I know is that Bree has no plan to end the pregnancy." He hesitated. "Actually, there are two things decided. Bree doesn't want to raise the baby and wants to put it up for adoption."

"Adoption!" His mom jumped up from her seat. "You can't let her do that."

"Calm down, Mom." He gently pulled on her arm until she sat down again. "She can't just put the baby up for adoption without my approval, and I already told her I wouldn't give it."

His mother brushed a tear from her cheek. "So now what?"

He nodded. "She told me that if I wouldn't agree to adoption, then I can raise the baby on my own."

Her eyes widened. "Really? She'd do that? Just give her baby to you with no looking back?" She got up again, pacing over to the single chair across from the sofa and turning to him. "She's got plenty of family money to hire enough help. What's keeping her from being part of her child's life?"

"I think it has to do with the way she was

raised. Her father never married her mother, and he even paid her mother to stay out of Bree's life until she was twenty-one. With her father off making money, she was essentially raised by nannies."

"So she doesn't think she knows how to be a mother?"

"I'm not sure if it's that or if she's just following in her father's footsteps and putting her child's welfare in someone else's hands." He held up one finger. "But I'm not sure she even realizes that's what she's doing. From the way she talks about her dad, I don't think they're close."

"And she wouldn't like being compared to him?"

He nodded. "Correct."

"So what are you going to do?"

"I'm not sure. I'd love to hear any advice you have for me."

She gave him a hint of a smile. "You know I'm always full of advice." She pursed her lips. "I think that first you need to make sure you go to every doctor appointment she has. If she's going to give you this child to raise, then you need to be there throughout the pregnancy."

"That's a good point." He stood and walked over to her. He took one of his mom's hands in both of his. "I've been going over and over this situation. One minute I know I can deal with anything that comes along, and the next minute I have no confidence when it comes to being a single parent. None."

She smiled and patted his cheek with her free hand. "Don't worry, dear, it'll work out. You have me in your corner and there's no way I'll let anything happen to my grandchild."

"Thanks, Mom." Once again, he was extremely relieved that she was taking the news so well.

She patted his hands. "Now the first thing to do is to invite that girl over to dinner. I'd like a proper introduction to the mother of my grandchild. Meeting while holding her hair while she vomits into the toilet just won't cut it."

"BREE, I'M SO SORRY," Roxie said over the phone after she'd confessed that she and Pete had inadvertently given away Bree's secret. "I had no idea Nick's mother was even in the building."

"That's okay, Rox." She leaned back in her office chair. "I'm sure Nick was going to tell her soon anyway."

"But that's a terrible way to find out about your first grandchild."

"It was an accident. She seemed nice when I met her, and I'm sure she'll realize that there was no malicious intent at play." Bree really wasn't that concerned.

After Bree assured Roxie several times that all

would be okay, they disconnected. Not a minute went by before Bree's phone rang again. "Bree Tucker."

"Hello, Bree, this is Emily Harmon. Nick's mother."

Uh-oh.

"Hello, Mrs. Harmon. How are you?"

"I'm doing well, and please call me Emily or just Em. There's no need for formality, is there?"

Bree swallowed thickly. "I guess not." She paused. "You've spoken to Nick?"

"Yes, I have," she said. "I know all about the baby and that's why I'm calling."

"Nick explained our plans?" Bree could only hope that Mrs. Harmon—Emily—wouldn't try to influence Nick or Bree about their decisions. So far, she seemed warm and friendly, but things could turn on a dime.

"Oh, yes, that's why I'm calling. I'd like to invite you to dinner with Nick and me, maybe Thursday night? I thought you'd probably want to get to know me since I'll be part of your baby's life."

She didn't know what to say. "Um, sure. Dinner? Thursday?" She quickly checked her schedule. "I think that works for me."

"Great! Why don't you come by my house around five." She recited her address. "That'll give us plenty of time to get to know each other better."

"Five is fine, Mrs.—I mean Emily." From the

little Bree knew about Nick's mother, she was petite, looked younger than her age, and now Bree could see that she was a woman who got what she wanted.

Perhaps Emily was a woman much like herself.

"I hope you won't be disappointed," Emily said. "We're a little more casual than what you're probably used to."

This woman said exactly what she meant. Bree liked her already. Besides the fact that Emily had helped her when she was puking her guts out at that pop-up. Not everyone would be that hands-on.

"I'm sure everything will be wonderful," Bree told her. "Can I bring anything?"

"Oh, how sweet! I'm going to say no this time since it's our first dinner together. But maybe next time you can bring your favorite side dish or dessert. How does that sound?"

"That's great. If you're sure." Bree hadn't expected that response. When she and the girls got together and each brought something, hers was always store-bought. Wine, dessert or bread from the bakery. Never anything she'd cooked herself. She didn't even have any favorite recipes. Growing up, their cook had prepared meals, and she had never shared cooking tips or recipes. Unlike Nick, who not only cooked, but prepared food from recipes handed down in his family.

No sooner had their call ended than Bree's phone rang yet again. She wasn't going to get any more work done at this rate. "Bree Tucker."

"Hey there, Bree." Her father seemed chipper and had actually called her the correct name.

"Hi, Dad. Are you in Aruba?"

"We are," he said. "We're having a wonderful time."

Not that she'd asked.

"I got your message," he continued. "You wanted to talk to me about something?"

She drew in a deep breath. "Yes, I've decided that I'd like to find my mother."

There was silence on the other end.

"Dad?"

"I'm here. Why do you want to find her? Can't you leave things the way they are now?"

"I'm not looking to have a relationship with her. I only want to talk to her about her medical history. I know nothing about her or her side of the family." Bree had decided to tell her father that it was for her own benefit that she wanted the information.

"I can't say I'm happy about it. What do you want from me? I haven't seen her since shortly after you were born."

Bree didn't need a reminder of that. "I was hoping you have some idea where she might be." Saying it aloud, she was reminded that it had been thirty-three years since her father had seen her mother.

"Not a clue. What about a PI?"

"I already hired one. He's come up empty."

"Hmm. I think I have an address for her parents. It might be a dead end—"

"That's okay. It's worth a try." She waited anxiously for him to get his laptop and find the address. She copied it down, not surprised that he would keep the information within reach. "Thanks, Dad. I'll give this to my PI, and maybe he can talk to some of their neighbors if they don't live there anymore." She felt her excitement grow. This was the first piece of good news she'd had in quite a while. "If you think of anything else, please let me know."

BREE WASN'T SURE what to expect at the Thursday-evening dinner. Emily lived in a modest home in Fairfax. A three-bedroom split-level that was built in the sixties according to the website Bree had found when she'd mapped the address.

When she arrived at Emily's front door, it swung open before she could knock. "Come in, come in," Emily greeted her, followed by a warm hug after she closed the door. "How are you feeling?" She gestured to the living room. "Come, sit, make yourself comfortable."

The room made it easy for Bree to do just

that. The colors Emily had chosen were warm and inviting. A neutral tan on the walls and dark hardwood floors were a great backdrop to the different shades of green in the area rug, sofa and coordinating pillows.

"These are for you," Bree said, holding out a bunch of flowers to Emily.

"Oh, they're beautiful," Emily exclaimed as she sniffed them. "I'll go put them in water."

Just then, Nick joined them. "Hey, Bree." He'd come from the back of the house, presumably the kitchen since he handed her a glass of ice water. "I can get you something else if you don't want water."

Her mouth went dry when she saw him in his jeans and plaid shirt with the sleeves rolled up to his elbows. "No, this is fine. I'm drinking water almost exclusively these days." She emptied half of her glass before setting it on the coaster in front of her.

"There we go," Emily said when she returned with the flowers. She set them on the coffee table and took a seat across from Bree. "You're feeling good, I hope? No more trips to the hospital?"

Nick must have filled her in on everything. "I've been doing fine. Still a little nauseous at times, but it's getting better."

"Glad to hear it." She turned to Nick, who stood at the other end of the sofa. "Don't you have something for us to nibble on while we wait for dinner?"

He nodded. "Right." He disappeared into the kitchen.

Bree didn't think it was her imagination that Nick seemed a little unlike himself tonight. Nerves, maybe?

"I hope you'll be able to enjoy dinner," Emily said. "We tried to choose things that you can eat."

"It's been difficult between what I can't eat and what makes my stomach turn," Bree told her. "But I'm sure dinner will be fine." She searched for a neutral subject. "You have a wonderful home. Is this where you raised your family?"

Emily nodded. "It is." She rose and went to the fireplace, where she picked up one of several framed pictures in different sizes. She came back to the sofa to show Bree. "This is our last family picture." She pointed to the tall man whom Nick resembled. "This is Nick's dad, and of course you recognize Nick and Pete."

The picture was of them sitting on the front porch of a beach house, all wearing white shirts and blue denim jeans. "Looks like a happy time."

Emily smiled, her eyes glassy. "It was. Every summer we went to the beach. After they grew up, the boys always tried to make sure they came, but some years were impossible. So Joe and I—

Nick's dad—would have the place all to our-selves. At least until extended family descended."

"It wasn't just the four of you?" Bree asked.

"Oh, no! We always rented a large house, and extended family would come for a day or two here and there. We never knew how many would be there at the same time."

"Sounds like chaos." Bree couldn't even imagine trying to plan for something like that.

"It was, but well worth it."

Nick returned with a plate of cheese and crackers, as well as some grapes and melon balls.

"Your mother was just telling me about your beach vacations." Bree turned to Emily. "You must be looking forward already to going this year."

Nick stiffened. "We stopped when my dad passed away." He sat down on the other end of the sofa from her.

Bree felt awful. "Oh, I'm so sorry. I had no idea. I didn't mean to bring up a painful subject."

Emily patted Bree's hand. "Don't worry about it. I'm the one who brought up the vacations at the beach." She rose from her seat. "Excuse me a minute while I check on something."

As soon as Emily was out of the room, Bree said to Nick, "I feel terrible. I hope she's okay."

"I'm sure she's fine. She just used that as an excuse to leave us alone."

"She did?"

He nodded. "We need to talk about what's going to happen."

Bree narrowed her eyes. "Are you saying I was tricked into coming to dinner tonight so you could blindside me?"

"No, no, nothing like that. My mom really did want to have you over for dinner to get to know you. It's just that since you're here, I thought it would be a good time to broach the subject."

"What exactly are you trying to say?" She could feel her heart beating faster and faster.

"I want to be part of this pregnancy."

"What do you mean? I think you were a major part already if I remember correctly." The images that floated through her head weren't helping her keep up her defenses.

He smiled. "True, but I'm talking about from here on out. I'd like to be part of the journey. I want to be involved by going to doctor appointments with you."

She thought about it a moment. "I guess that'll be okay."

"Good. I want to know everything that's going on, so my other suggestion is that we get together for dinner or lunch once a week to catch up."

"Now that's a little too much. Once a week?" She had a company to run.

"How else will I know what's happening?"

"I can send you an email or we can talk on the phone. One meal a week is out of the question."

"I disagree."

"Convince me, then."

"Fine," he said. "If you want me to be able to raise this child, then it needs to hear my voice so it recognizes me when it's born."

She'd done her homework thoroughly and, obviously, he had, too. He also had his mom to advise him.

And as soon as he'd said it, she knew he was right.

"Then I have one caveat," she said. "We get the details in writing so there are no misunderstandings."

CHAPTER THIRTEEN

NICK WAS SURPRISED that Bree had agreed so easily to his requests. Shocked, in fact. "That was much too easy," he joked. "You're not usually that agreeable. At least not with me."

She shrugged. "What can I say? I've done a lot of research on pregnancy, and you brought up good points. It wouldn't be right for me to deny you prenatal access if you're determined to raise this baby on your own."

Raise this baby on your own. Hearing the words aloud was a shocking revelation he hadn't quite gotten used to yet. "I'm glad we can work together, then."

"Besides, I have to eat anyway," Bree said. "So having a meal together won't cut into my work time."

He wasn't sure how to take that.

"But I'm serious about drawing up a legal contract," she said.

He nodded. "That's not a problem."

His mother returned then, almost as if she'd

been listening from around the corner. "I hope you two are having a nice chat."

Nick exchanged glances with his mom, and she nodded in understanding. "Let me go check on dinner," he said as he rose.

"Can I do anything to help?" Bree asked.

He decided that keeping their friendship moving along would be a good plan. "Sure. How good are you at chopping vegetables for the salad?"

She seemed surprised that he'd take her up on her offer. "Um… I'm okay, I guess." She stood up and straightened the dark red knit dress she wore with a silver belt, even though he'd told her to dress casually when she'd asked. "You're not going to be a tough critic, are you?"

He grinned and held out a hand. "Come on, let's check out your skills." He already knew about her excellent skills in bed, but now wasn't the time to dwell on them.

"Do you do much cooking?" he asked after he got her set up with a cutting board, knife and a variety of vegetables.

She grimaced. "The kitchen isn't really my thing, but I'm trying to teach myself so I can eat better over the next several months. It's not going very well, though."

He laughed. "I'm surprised."

"Why's that?"

"Because you seem to be good at whatever you set your mind to."

She considered him for a few moments and then shrugged. "You're right. I'm always determined to do the best I can at things. I'm not sure why I'm so bad at cooking." She held up a finger with a bandage on it. "This is from trying to learn how to cook actual oatmeal, not the instant kind." She showed him her other hand. "This one is almost healed. It was when I burned myself frying an egg." She paused. "In fact, I burned both me and the poor egg."

He laughed harder this time. "Eggs? Oatmeal?" He shook his head. "I think maybe we should spend those weekly meals teaching you how to cook."

She raised her eyebrows. "You'd do that?"

"Of course. Once you get the basics mastered and can read a recipe, it's all downhill from there."

"Yeah, downhill into the trash, you mean." She smiled as she said it, though.

"We'll see. If we write it into that contract you want, then you can't get out of at least trying to learn to cook." He opened the oven to remove the whole chicken he'd baked. He checked the doneness and decided it needed a few more minutes. He closed the oven door, set the timer and straightened. "So why is it that you never learned to make even the simplest things, like oatmeal?"

"Cooks," she said. "I wasn't even allowed in the kitchen at home."

"Then how are you able to live on your own if you can't even feed yourself?"

"The easy answer is that I rely a lot on carry-out food." She brushed her hair back from her face. "The truth is that my dad always assumed I'd accept his money and be able to afford cooks of my own."

"But you didn't take his money?"

She shook her head. "Nope. I wanted to make it on my own. He and I don't usually see eye to eye when it comes to business practices." She paused. "With a little help from an inheritance my great-aunt left me, I was able to have seed money for my business. It wasn't a lot, a few thousand dollars, but enough to get started before I was even out of college."

"It seems like you're doing okay for yourself now. Have you thought about hiring a chef?"

She laughed, a pleasant sound that made him happy. "No, the funny thing is that I've gotten so used to not having any hired help in the house that I really like my privacy. Having dinner at my dad's recently made me realize how intrusive they really are." She raised an eyebrow. "Although I do have a cleaning crew come in once a week.

I'm not *that* eager to do everything on my own." She smiled, and his insides warmed.

They went back to their respective jobs preparing dinner. He looked over to see how she was doing. "Wait." He stepped behind her and reached around to position his hand over hers as she held the knife. "Hold it like this." He removed her extended pointer finger from the dull edge of the knife to grip the handle with her entire hand. "There you go."

Her hair smelled citrusy, reminding him again of the island. And he would have been fine if she hadn't turned her head around enough to glance at him. He took the knife from her hand and laid it down before grasping her shoulders and turning her body to face him.

Her tongue darted out to wet her bottom lip, and he couldn't stand it. He leaned in and gently touched his lips to hers. When she didn't protest, he deepened the kiss and slid his hand through her hair to the back of her neck.

She wrapped her arms around his body, holding him close. She tasted so good and the memories they'd made on vacation came flooding back. He wanted to lay her back on the kitchen table and do his best to replicate those memories.

But two things happened simultaneously that stopped him. The timer for the chicken went off, and his mother returned to the kitchen.

"I'm so sorry," his mom said quickly while he stared into Bree's wide eyes. "You continue with what you're doing, and I'll just leave—"

"No, Mom, come in." He reluctantly let go of Bree and turned off the buzzing timer. After all, they couldn't do more than kiss. "Dinner's almost ready. I just need to mash the potatoes while the chicken rests."

"Then what can I do to help?" his mom said quickly.

For some unknown reason, he couldn't shake the feeling that his mother had her own agenda that she was promoting and she was deliberately keeping him in the dark.

On second thought, he knew exactly what her plan was. She wanted grandchildren and she also wanted him to be married to their mother.

BREE WAS *SO* EMBARRASSED. Having Emily catch them making out was humiliating. What must she think of Bree? Probably that she was some easy woman who couldn't keep her hormones under control.

And she'd be absolutely right.

These crazy pregnancy hormones were making her so horny and she just wanted to quiet them. Preferably by having incredible sex with Nick. No one but him caused these flare-ups. Like it or not, he was the only one she wanted.

Not that she was out looking for a suitable man. She didn't have time for a man.

Unless it was Nick. She fanned herself, flushing from thoughts of them together.

Just once. She was sure that was all it would take for her to get sex off her brain.

She finished chopping the vegetables for the salad, something she'd actually accomplished only because she'd eaten chopped vegetables in her lifetime and knew how they should look.

Not that hers looked exactly as she'd planned. The mushrooms were different widths and so were the carrots, but tossed in a salad, they'd be fine. At least they weren't burned.

While Emily set the table and poured drinks, Nick carved the chicken. Bree was fascinated as she watched his talented hands work quickly and efficiently. She nearly groaned aloud as she recalled how expertly he'd used his hands on her.

"Are you okay?" he asked.

She realized she was staring. "Um, yes. I was just watching and trying to learn how to do that." Their eyes met, and she knew immediately that he could see right through her. He was well aware that she wanted him.

He winked at her. "I'll be sure to add carving a chicken to our lessons."

She turned away, feeling her face heat. What was it about him that affected her like this?

They sat down to eat at the kitchen table, and unexpectedly Bree found she was enjoying herself. The meal was more like when she ate with her girlfriends than when she had dinner with her dad. The conversation went from one subject to another seamlessly, and before she knew it, she'd cleaned her plate.

When they were finished eating, Nick and Emily got up to clear the table. "Here, let me help," she found herself saying as she carried her plate and the leftover salad to the counter. "Dinner was delicious," she told Nick. "That chicken tasted better than any I think I've ever had."

He grinned at her compliment. "Thanks. I'll definitely teach you that one. It's just some herbs and butter and then you bake it. Not difficult at all."

"Easy for you to say. I'm not sure I even know how to turn my oven on. Oh, wait. I've used it to heat up carryout. Once. When my microwave was on the fritz."

Nick smiled at her joke, and she smiled back. He really did have a very nice smile.

Emily edged her way to the sink, where she took over the cleanup. "You two go sit and relax. I'll finish up here."

"Are you sure?" Bree asked. "It doesn't seem fair."

"Go on," she repeated. "Nick cooked, and I'll

clean up. That's completely fair." Before Bree could argue, Emily added, "And you're our guest, so go relax."

Nick ushered Bree back into the living room, where they sat close to each other on the sofa. "I really like your mom," Bree told him.

He smiled. "Thanks. I'm pretty lucky." He took her hand in his. "So should we schedule our next dinner slash cooking lesson?"

"Sure. What works for you? Maybe Mondays when the restaurant's closed? I'll keep my schedule clear."

"That would be perfect. Tonight was okay for me to be gone because it was a weeknight and my sous-chef is very capable. So capable that I'll probably lose him in the next year when he opens his own restaurant."

"That's too bad. It's tough to lose good employees. I've been there." She pursed her lips. "So next Monday. I'd suggest my place for dinner, but I have very few cooking utensils. Every time I try something new, I have to go shopping first."

He laughed and squeezed her hand. "Not a problem. I don't mind cooking at my place. Unless you want to go out? Although that wouldn't allow the opportunity for a cooking lesson." He held up his pointed finger. "Wait! I've got it. Next week is restaurant week in Old Town. If you want, we can go try some new dishes at different restaurants. Appetizers here, entrées somewhere else, dessert at a third place. What do you think?"

"That sounds great."

"You don't mind putting off the cooking lesson a week?"

She laughed. "I don't mind at all. You should be warned that you have no idea what you're getting yourself into with these lessons."

They made definite plans and Bree realized it was getting late. Not actually late, but late for her these days. "I really should go," she said as she rose.

"I'll walk you to your car," he offered.

She knew what that meant. A good-night kiss, maybe more than one. So she gratefully accepted his offer.

"It was a lovely dinner, Emily. Thank you so much." Bree was about to shake Nick's mom's hand when the woman put her arms out and gave her an honest-to-goodness hug. Bree felt her eyes tear up at the emotion she felt from a simple embrace.

Then Emily took Bree by the upper arms and said, "Don't be a stranger, Bree. You're family now, whether you think so or not."

While Bree and Nick walked to her car, Bree wasn't sure how she felt about what Emily had just said to her. Did she think Bree wanted to stay in touch after this was all over? Bree had only agreed to dinner because she'd had an urge to show Nick's mom that she was more than the fainting, vomiting person she'd first met. The same one who'd had a vacation fling with her son and wasn't planning to marry him now that she was pregnant.

"You're being very quiet," Nick said when they reached her car.

She hit the button on her door handle to unlock it and opened the door before turning to him. He was closer than she'd realized, the heat coming from his body giving her added warmth on the chilly night.

"I guess I'm just tired," she said, part truth and part fib. She was always tired these days.

"I'll let you get home to bed, then." He tipped her chin up and touched his warm lips to hers.

She automatically leaned into him as his arms came around her. He was fulfilling the promise he'd made to her when he'd offered to walk her to her car.

OVER THE NEXT few weeks, Bree gradually began to feel a little more energized and she was rarely nauseated anymore as long as she kept something in her stomach.

She and Nick were keeping things friendly, no matter how much his mom so obviously wanted them to be more than friends. Truthfully, Bree wouldn't mind if they were more than friends, either. At least for one night. Too bad she hadn't been brave enough to add that into the contract they'd drawn up.

Damn these pregnancy hormones.

Later today they were meeting at the doctor's office, their first time at an appointment together. Bree had scheduled it for a Monday morning because Nick's restaurant would be closed. But first she'd come into work early so she could take care of some things before their appointment.

Bree was growing more and more comfortable with Nick, although going to the ob-gyn together would be substantially different from their other outings.

They'd enjoyed participating in restaurant week and tasting a variety of foods from different restaurants. Usually there was a set price for three courses at a restaurant, but because Nick's restaurant was participating, he could divide the meal into courses at different restaurants. He'd told her that his restaurant had done a lot of business during that time and even throughout the weeks afterward. Bree wasn't surprised. He was an accomplished chef and once you tasted his food, you definitely wanted to come back.

He'd also been trying to teach her how to cook, *try* being the operative word. She wasn't very good at all. He told her she needed to have more confidence in herself, which was something she'd never been told before.

Her cell phone rang. Caller ID showed her PI. "Hello." She'd given him the information her dad had provided about her maternal grandparents, but so far all the PI's weekly updates had been disappointing.

"Hello, Ms. Tucker. I think I finally have some useful information for you."

Her heart beat faster. "What did you find out? Did you locate my mother?"

"Not exactly. But I did get a lead. It turns out that your mother's parents moved from the address you gave me almost twenty years ago."

"Wow. That's a long time."

"Exactly. Like I told you before, I spoke to the neighbors. Most of them weren't living there when your grandparents resided in the area, and finding their former neighbors has been difficult." He cleared his throat. "It seems your grandparents lived several places after that address until they moved into an assisted-living facility about two years ago."

"Where is it located?"

"It's in Delaware. A small town near the ocean."

"Then I can go see them," she said.

"Slow down. I've already tried to pay them a

visit. It turns out that all guests to see your grand-parents have to be approved by some relative of theirs. I'm not on the list, so I couldn't even talk to them."

"Could my mother be the relative?"

"Possibly, but it could also be another relative. I get the feeling that whoever is behind all this secrecy is very concerned about the family's privacy."

Was it because of her dad? Had he made threats against her mother and her family to keep them from being easy to locate?

"I'm going to visit them," Bree said. "I'll do whatever it takes for me to talk to them."

"I think that's at least worth a shot. Just let me know if you get any more information that I can use to find your mother."

They disconnected after he gave her the exact address, and Bree saw that it was time to leave for her appointment.

Nick was already sitting in the waiting room when she arrived. "Sorry I'm late," she said to him as she walked over to check in at the desk.

"You're right on time," he told her. "I was early." When she sat down next to him, he whispered, "I'm a little anxious."

She smiled and patted his hand. "You'll be fine. They won't ask you to put your feet into stirrups."

He chuckled. "Thank goodness. I wore the wrong shoes to ride a horse today."

She laughed, enjoying their continued camaraderie.

Not long after that she was called back. "How are you feeling?" the nurse asked as she showed her to the exam room.

Bree filled her in on how much better she was doing, while Nick sat quietly in the chair in the corner of the small room.

"You can have a seat on the table," the nurse said before taking her blood pressure. "Looks good. The doctor will be in soon and you'll get to hear your baby's heartbeat."

Bree's eyes widened. She hadn't expected that. She looked at Nick, who appeared just as surprised. "That's great."

The nurse left them alone and they were silent until Nick said, "I didn't think you were far enough along to hear the baby's heartbeat."

"Me, neither." She was still trying to process it. She was going to hear an actual heartbeat.

A few minutes later, the doctor knocked and came into the exam room. "Good morning, Bree, how are you?" Before Bree could answer, the grandmotherly doctor looked at Nick and said, "Welcome. I'm Dr. Bell. Are you the father?" She put a hand out to shake Nick's.

He stood and shook her hand. "Yes, I am. Nick Harmon." He returned to his seat.

Dr. Bell looked at Bree and said, "I take it the two of you have worked things out since you told him about the baby. You're planning to keep it?"

Bree swallowed. "Actually, Nick is going to raise it. He won't agree to adoption, so he'll have sole custody."

The doctor's eyebrows rose, but she wisely kept her thoughts to herself.

Bree continued explaining. "Nick would like to be involved prenatally, so he'll be coming to as many of my appointments as possible."

"I see." Dr. Bell looked from one to the other. "I'm glad you could come to such a civilized agreement."

Bree's thoughts exactly. Which was why she'd suggested a written contract.

"Let's take a listen to this little one's heartbeat, shall we?" The doctor had Bree lie down and she put some cold gel on her lower abdomen. "This is the fetal Doppler. I may have to move it around a bit to find a good heartbeat."

Bree couldn't see Nick right now, but she had the feeling from the look he'd given her a few seconds ago that he was as nervous as she was. She had never imagined this would be such an emotional moment, but then again, everything these days made her emotional.

The three of them were silent as they listened to the swishing noises coming from the device as Dr. Bell moved it around.

"There," she said finally. "Listen closely. Yours is the slower beat and the faster beat is the baby's."

As Bree lay on the table, staring up at the ceiling, she listened to the rhythmic beat of her heart mingled with the baby's. Then she blinked and a river of tears flowed from her eyes, over her temples and into her hair.

A FEW MINUTES LATER, the doctor left after stating that everything appeared as it should. Nick remained silent while Bree straightened her clothes, and then he followed her to the front desk, where she made her next appointment.

He was in awe of hearing their child's heartbeat, and he could only assume Bree felt the same way since she'd spoken only in short phrases afterward. Before exiting the medical office building and going to their separate cars, Nick stopped Bree.

"Is everything okay?" he asked.

"Sure. Why?" Her voice was a little raspy.

"That was pretty awesome back there."

"Uh-huh." She was looking through the glass door to the parking lot, not at him.

"That's it? Uh-huh?" Couldn't they even share

this little step in their weird but obviously amazing situation?

She looked at him then. "What do you want
me to say?" She crossed her hands on her chest
and raised her voice an octave. "Oh, my! Wasn't
that just spectacular?" She dropped her hands
and scowled. "I can understand how you would
feel differently. You want to raise it. I believe the
books call it 'bonding.'"

His eyebrows rose and he stared at her with
wide eyes. "I saw your tears. I don't believe you
have no feelings whatsoever when it comes to
our baby."

"Your baby," she corrected.

"Fine. *My* baby." He ran a frustrated hand
through his hair. "What is it? Are you putting
up a wall between yourself and the baby? Is it to
avoid getting emotionally involved, so that it's
easier to give the baby to me?"

"I don't need to put up a wall. I'm fine with
you raising it, or a good family raising it. Either
way, that's how it's going to be. So why should I
get emotionally attached?" She brushed her hair
back from her face with a gloved hand. "In about
seven months, I'll go into labor and it'll be born.
Soon after, you'll take it home and raise it. Then
I'll go back to the life I had before you and I met
on the island."

He didn't know how to reply. After a few seconds of silence, he said, "You obviously have everything all figured out." He swallowed back the harsh words he'd love to hurl at her. Now wasn't the time or place. "Are we still on for dinner tonight?"

"If you still want to," she said without enthusiasm.

"And a cooking lesson?"

She nodded. "Oh, wait. I can't. I need to go to Delaware this afternoon and I won't be back in time for dinner. The trip came up suddenly this morning."

"Delaware?"

"My PI found my grandparents at an assisted-living facility there."

"And you're going to drive there to see them today?"

"Yes. I want answers about my mother, so I can't afford to wait."

"I agree." He quickly reviewed his day. "I'll go with you."

Her eyes widened. "Why would you want to do that?"

He shrugged. "Because I don't think you should be alone if you don't get the news you're hoping for. And because what you find out today could affect our child."

She seemed to think about it, and then said, "Okay."

"Okay."

They made plans to meet, and they each went their separate ways, giving him more time to consider her attitude toward the baby.

He obviously needed to work on making her realize that this wasn't a business deal they had going on between them, despite the signed contract. This was a human life that they'd created.

He also couldn't let her miss out on this child's life, the way her mother had missed out on Bree's.

Besides, he was beginning to have feelings for the mother of his child, and he was pretty sure he didn't want things to end between them when the baby was born.

CHAPTER FOURTEEN

BREE HAD CALLED AHEAD to the assisted-living facility where her grandparents were supposedly living. She'd been told she would need to be approved to visit them, even though she'd related that she was the couple's granddaughter. She didn't tell the person she spoke to that they'd never met or that it might turn out that they weren't related at all. The woman said she would convey the information and get back to her about whether she would be able to visit the couple.

"You understand that this might be a wasted trip," Bree said to Nick when she picked him up early that afternoon. He'd offered to drive, but she'd insisted on taking the wheel. After all, it was *her* family she was searching for. He didn't even need to make this trip.

She'd never admit it to him, but she was actually glad for his company.

It turned out to be a pleasant drive, just under three hours, with no more talk about how he thought she should feel about the pregnancy or the future.

They were pulling into a parking space at the Waterside assisted-living facility when Nick asked her the same question that had been eating at her since she'd decided to come to Delaware. "What happens if you can't get in to see these people? Or what if they're not actually your grandparents and this is a dead end?"

She turned off the car's engine and stared straight out the windshield. "I don't know. I haven't allowed myself to think much past getting in to see them."

He reached out, took her hand in his and gave it a gentle squeeze. "Thank you for letting me come with you. If this does turn out to be your grandparents, then they'll probably want to stay in contact with their great-grandchild. Something I'm happy to facilitate."

She nodded when words wouldn't surface. If she turned her head to look at him, she knew her emotions would come pouring out in the form of tears. And she tried to avoid that at all cost. One thing was for certain—she wouldn't miss these stupid hormones when this pregnancy was over.

They exited the car and walked together to the front entrance. "At least it's a sunny day and pretty warm," Bree commented as the automatic doors opened for them. "I've always found a car drive to be a stress reliever."

"That's a good way to look at it," he said.

They stepped to the front desk, where they were greeted by a woman in her early sixties with salt-and-pepper hair. She was about as tall as she was wide and had a welcoming smile. "Hello, what can I do for you?" Her tone was soothing, and Bree's hopes of seeing her grandparents rose.

"I called earlier about seeing Frank and Alice Greeley. I'm their granddaughter, Bree Tucker." At least that's what she'd been led to believe.

"Let me check the approved list of visitors for them." The woman clicked some keys on her computer keyboard and then ran a finger down what was presumably a list of names on her screen. She shook her head. "I don't see you listed here. I'm sorry. Only approved visitors are allowed."

Bree's heart sank. She didn't know if this meant the person who needed to approve visitors hadn't been contacted yet or if she'd been turned down as a potential visitor. "But I came all the way from DC—"

"Is there a way to contact the person who approves visitors for them?" Nick asked. "I'm sure that person would be interested in knowing that Bree is here."

The woman seemed to think about it for a minute and finally said, "Let me check with the supervisor on duty." She stepped away from the desk and into an office behind her.

Bree turned to Nick. "Right now I wish I was

the kind of person who would turn that screen around and figure out where my grandparents were located. Then I'd take off to see them while no one was around."

His lips twitched. "I'm glad you're not that kind of person, because that would only get you kicked out of here and banned permanently."

"If I wasn't arrested first."

"True." He nodded. "Here she comes."

"I spoke to our supervisor, and she's going to speak to Mr. and Mrs. Greeley. If they give permission, then you can have the name and contact information for the person who authorizes visitors for them."

"Thank you so much." Bree was relieved that at least they'd made a bit of progress. "Can you tell us what the relationship is between the couple and this person?"

"Sure, I think that would be okay. It's the couple's daughter who determines who can visit them."

Bree suddenly felt light-headed and grabbed onto the counter for support when her knees began to buckle. She may have found more than she'd bargained for by coming here today.

"Thank you for that information," Nick said when Bree couldn't speak. "We'll wait over there." He nodded to the sofa and chairs that were off to the side and took Bree by the elbow to guide her there.

"Are you okay?" he asked quietly when they were seated next to each other on the sofa. He rested her hand in his, passing his strength to her.

She nodded slightly and tried to speak. "She caught me off guard." She turned to look directly at Nick. "It could be my mother who's making the decisions. I might have found her." She sucked in a breath with difficulty as her heart pounded in her chest.

"Do you know if your mother had any sisters or brothers?"

"No, honestly, I know almost nothing about her. My information is from my dad, and even from the little he's told me, I don't know how much to believe."

Nick nodded. "I'm thinking that you need to be prepared. This could be your aunt and not your mother."

"I know. I keep telling myself that, but even if it is my aunt, at least she might be able to give me a clue about my mother's whereabouts."

"Looks like this might be the supervisor," Nick said, nodding in the direction of a tall woman in her thirties with shoulder-length light blond hair and large dark-framed glasses.

Bree and Nick stood up, and the supervisor put a hand out to Bree. "Hello, Ms. Tucker, I'm Sharon Waters. I just spoke to Mr. and Mrs. Greeley and explained the situation. They have allowed me to give you the contact information for their daughter so you can see if you can convince her to allow you to speak with the Greeleys. I will say they were confused about who you are, and they seem to be interested in finding out more."

"Thank you so much," Bree said. "You have no idea what this means to me."

"I'm glad to help. I believe someone on the staff tried to reach the Greeleys' daughter earlier today, but was unable to connect with her. I hope you have better luck."

Nick spoke up then. "Do all the residents here have such tight restrictions on visitors?"

"Oh, no. The Greeleys are the only ones who require authorization. We have no idea why, but the daughter is adamant that she knows who comes and goes. Just very protective, maybe."

"I see." Nick looked at Bree. He was obviously as stumped about the situation as she was.

"Come with me, and I'll get you the information."

Once Bree had the name and phone number, she knew immediately from the first name that this wasn't her mother. She could only hope it was her aunt. Nick excused himself to use the restroom, but she suspected it was to give her privacy.

Her hands shook as she sat on the sofa in the

waiting area and touched the numbers on her phone. After two rings, a woman answered. "Hello."

Bree swallowed the lump in her throat, unprepared for the nerves she was experiencing. "Hello, is this Karen Monroe?"

"Yes, it is." The woman sounded suspicious already.

"My name is Bree Tucker, and I'm calling about Mr. and Mrs. Greeley. I'd like to get your permission to visit them. I have reason to believe they're my grandparents."

There was silence on the other end.

"That's impossible," the woman finally said. "Why would you say such a thing?"

As Bree told her about not knowing her mother—and leaving out who her wealthy father was for obvious reasons—she explained how her PI had found the couple. "So you can see that it's important for me to speak with them." She paused. "Unless you might be able to help me, instead?"

"I'm afraid you've reached a dead end. My brother and I are the only ones who have given my parents grandchildren."

"Do you think we could meet in person?" Bree asked. "My PI seemed pretty sure that your parents are my grandparents. Maybe if we sat down and discussed it. My mother's name is Marianne Greeley. Do you know of someone with that name?"

After another period of silence, Karen said, "I can be at the Sands Diner in fifteen minutes. It's three blocks south from Waterside on First Street."

"I'll see you there." Bree hung up and went to find Nick. He was over at the front desk chatting with the first woman they'd spoken to.

"Thank you for your help," Bree told her. "I really appreciate it."

"I hope you find what you're looking for," the woman said.

As they exited the building, Nick asked, "So what happened? Did you reach the daughter? Where are we going?"

She stopped and looked at him, butterflies dancing in her midsection. "We're going to a diner down the street. I'm pretty sure we're going to meet my aunt there." She quickly filled him in on her phone conversation.

She drove them to the diner and parked in the small lot beside the building. When they entered, Bree checked out all of the patrons though she realized they were early.

"Two?" the hostess asked them.

"Three," Nick said. "A table where we can keep an eye out for the third person in our party if that's possible."

The young woman nodded and showed them to a table with an excellent view of the entrance.

"Would you like me to give you and this woman privacy?" he asked. "I can go for a walk while you two talk."

Bree wasn't sure why, but she wanted him there. Maybe in case she was disappointed by the outcome. "No, I'd like you to stay." He could also verify that the meeting had actually happened and she hadn't dreamed it.

They put their coats on the backs of their chairs, which were positioned at a ninety-degree angle from each other, and sat down. "Are you hungry?" Nick asked.

"Not at all, which is probably the first time I've said that in about two weeks. Once my stomach settled down, I got my appetite back and it's never satisfied now." Their knees were touching and Bree didn't move, not wanting to lose physical contact with him. There was something about his presence that gave her strength. Something she'd never thought she lacked until now.

They chatted a few minutes and ordered drinks, and Bree tried not to mentally jump ahead. Every time the door opened and a customer came in or went out, Bree looked them over.

When the woman she'd spoken to on the phone finally arrived, Bree was sure that she was her aunt, even from a distance. She waved and the woman came over to their table. Bree and Nick stood up while introductions were made.

"Have a seat," Bree suggested as she and Nick both sat back down, too.

"I have to say, you do have a family resemblance," Karen said. "Why don't you start from the beginning and tell me why you think you're related to us."

Bree laid out the story as she knew it, starting from where her dad told her he'd met her mother and ending with the fact that she hadn't shown up after Bree turned twenty-one. She did, however, leave out her own pregnancy. She wasn't sure why, but she felt she needed to hold back a few things back. Including her rich and famous father's identity.

When she finished, she opened her purse and dug through her things to come up with her mother's picture. "This is the only photo I have of her." She held it out to Karen, who looked much like her mother probably would at the same age.

Putting a hand over her mouth as she took the picture, Karen gasped, looking from the picture to Bree to the picture again. She set it down and said, "This is my sister, Marianne. I had no idea that she ever had a child."

Bree's heart pounded. "Where is she? Can I see her, get in touch with her?"

Before she spoke, Bree knew the answer from

the tears in Karen's eyes. "I'm so sorry, Bree. She died shortly before her twenty-fifth birthday."

A weight on her chest made speaking difficult. "What happened?" Bree felt the devastating loss even before she heard the story of her mother's demise. She'd never even met the woman, at least not that Bree could remember.

But it was as if a part of Bree had died in that moment, along with her mother.

NICK WATCHED BREE'S reactions as Karen told her what she knew about Marianne's life and early death.

"Marianne and I weren't really that close," Karen told her. "She was the oldest, then came my brother and then me. I had just left for college when we found out she'd died. No one had seen or heard from her in over two years." Karen folded her hands on the table and breathed in deeply. "She'd dropped out of college with only one semester to go before graduating. She told our parents that she had a great opportunity, but never explained more than that. Whatever it was, it paid well."

"How do you know that?" Bree asked.

"Because she would send money orders home to my parents, anywhere from five hundred to a thousand or more a week."

Nick wasn't sure he'd heard correctly. "A week? That's a lot of money."

"Didn't anyone question how a girl in her early twenties came to have that much disposable income?" Bree asked.

"She refused to say much about it on the few occasions that my parents spoke with her," Karen said. "And after she died, a few people came around inquiring about her, which we found odd."

Nick's first thought was that Bree's mother had been prostituting herself, but then reality set in. She'd met Cal Tucker, not yet a billionaire, but well on his way. "What year was this?"

Karen pursed her lips as she calculated the answer. "It must have been eighty-three or eighty-four." She looked at Bree. "When were you born?"

"Eighty-four."

Karen nodded. "So she was pregnant with you, and that's why she wouldn't come home or answer my parents' questions about where she was."

"That sounds like a logical assumption," Nick said.

Karen narrowed her eyes. "So who raised you? My sister must have been twenty-two or twenty-three when you were born, and she died by the time you were only a few years old."

Bree didn't answer at first. Nick reached under the table to take her hand, and she turned to look at him. He had the feeling she was about to reveal who her father was.

"I was raised by my father." She paused, blinking slowly. "He told me he paid off my mother to not contact me until I was twenty-one." She sipped from her glass of water. "When she never showed up, I figured she was unable to visit for some reason." Bree left unsaid that she had considered her mother might not want to see her.

Nick squeezed her hand again and she squeezed back.

Bree continued. "You should probably know that my father is Cal Tucker."

Karen's eyes widened. "*The* Cal Tucker?"

Bree nodded. "I think that explains where she got the money to send home to your parents. I know he gave her a lot of money when she gave up custody of me."

Relief showed on Karen's face. "This is such good news. You can't imagine the thoughts that have been tossed around about how she came to have that money. As well as the amount she had in the bank when she died."

"She had a lot?" Bree asked.

"Over half a million dollars."

"Whoa!" Nick said automatically.

"What happened to it?" Bree asked.

"She left it to my parents in her will."

"That seems pretty young to have a will," Nick

said, "but I guess with all that money she felt it was necessary."

"She also probably knew she was dying and had to get her affairs in order," Karen said sadly. "She died of ovarian cancer." She cleared her throat. "We didn't know until near the end. She called my parents, telling them that she'd tried the best treatments available but she wasn't going to survive. She also said that she wanted to tell them something in person before she died. They immediately traveled to where she was living in upstate New York, but she was already gone."

"She never told them or you about me?" Bree asked.

Karen shook her head. "If we'd had any idea, we would have come for you. I'm sure now that that's what she'd wanted to tell my parents."

Bree shook her head. "I'm afraid that wouldn't have worked with my dad. After kicking my mother out of my life, he certainly wouldn't have let you near me."

"You're probably right," Karen said. "But still we would have tried."

Bree smiled a little. "Thank you. I believe you would have." She turned to Nick. "I wonder if my father knew that she'd died." She looked at Karen then. "You said people inquired about her?"

Karen nodded. "Yes. I'd have to check with my

parents, but I'm pretty sure they told me the men said they were private investigators. They were supposedly looking into a check-fraud case, but the whole thing seemed odd. Once they found out that Marianne was dead, they seemed satisfied and left. But that wasn't the last time anyone came around asking about her. That's why I'm so careful about who can visit my parents. My dad has a heart condition, and he wouldn't be able to take the stress if anyone came asking about Marianne now. My parents took her death very hard, blaming themselves."

"The men definitely could have worked for my father," Bree confirmed. "He was probably keeping an eye on my mother to make sure she never made contact with me. He tends to be paranoid about such things."

"Now that I know about you and who your father is, I completely agree."

"Do you think I could see them while I'm here? My grandparents, I mean."

Karen reached out to take Bree's hand. "Of course you can. Come on, I can't wait to introduce you."

They both rose from their seats and hugged for a long time. Nick couldn't see Karen's face, but Bree's eyes were definitely bloodshot, with tears running down her cheeks.

NICK INSISTED ON not going to Bree's grandparent's apartment with her, saying he'd be fine in the lobby. Bree ultimately let him win the argument and was amazed when she finally met her grandparents. They were in better physical shape than she'd expected given that they resided in an assisted-living facility. She imagined her grandfather's heart condition was the reason they had decided to move here.

Her grandmother took her hands in hers, looking closely at Bree's face. "You are definitely my granddaughter. You have your mother's beautiful eyes and hair color."

Bree smiled. "Thank you."

Her grandmother smiled in return. "And that dimple in your cheek."

Bree laughed, putting a hand to her cheek. "I never realized that was hereditary."

"Oh, yes!" She pointed to Bree's grandfather. "See, your grandpa has it, too."

"So you like to be called Grandpa?" Bree hadn't thought about what to call her grandparents. Her father's parents had died when she was too young to remember them.

"If you're comfortable with that," he said with a warm smile, "then Grandpa it is."

"My other grandkids call me Grammy, but I'll

answer to anything," her grandmother said as she laughed nervously.

Bree felt completely comfortable with them. She'd never imagined that she'd find more family than her mother on her quest to discover her medical background.

"Do you have any family pictures you can show me?" Bree pulled her worn picture of her mother from her purse. "This is the only picture I have of my mother."

Grammy—she forced herself to think of her by that name—took the photo, and she put a hand to her mouth, shaking her head back and forth. "Some days I still can't believe she's gone. I keep expecting her to call." She looked at Bree. "Do you remember her at all?"

Bree shook her head. "No. My father got sole custody of me shortly after I was born. Their agreement was that she wasn't allowed to see me until I turned twenty-one."

Grandpa shook his head. "I can't believe he'd take you away from your mother. What kind of person does that?"

Her aunt Karen—another title Bree was getting used to—spoke up then. "Bree's father is Cal Tucker."

That caught her grandparents' attention. "Cal Tucker?" Grammy repeated. "The billionaire?"

Bree nodded. "The one and only." She swallowed before continuing. "I feel like I should apologize for him and his behavior."

"Oh, no, no, dear," Grammy said. "You mustn't feel that way. We don't know exactly what happened between him and our Marianne, but look at you. He took real good care of you."

Bree cringed internally. Her father had had very little to do with her upbringing. Basically, all he did was hire the nannies who'd raised her.

"Let me get you some pictures," Grammy said as she went back down the hallway in their small apartment.

Bree remained seated with her grandpa and Karen, who asked, "How long have you been looking for your mother?"

"It's been a few weeks," she replied.

Karen's eyebrows rose. "That's all? You never came looking for her before?"

Bree shook her head slightly and decided to be candid. "No, I always assumed that she didn't want anything to do with me when she didn't show up when I turned twenty-one. I'm easy to find through my father."

Karen nodded. "So why did you change your mind and begin the search now?"

Before Bree could answer, Grammy returned with several photo albums that she placed on the dining room table. "Come over here, Bree. The light is better."

Bree did as Grammy suggested, and she was amazed to see the pictures of her mother. "That looks just like me," she said of one of her mother sitting at a picnic table. She'd probably been six or seven at the time.

"That was at a family reunion in Maryland," Grammy told her, and then went through the pictures one by one, relating the stories behind them.

"I'd love to meet your children," Bree said to Karen when they had finished looking at pictures.

"I'm sure they'd love that, too." She proceeded to tell Bree about her two sons and daughter, all in their twenties.

Bree looked up at the time on the clock over the dining room table and suddenly realized how long she'd been there. "I should go." It wasn't fair of her to leave Nick on his own for so long.

They said their goodbyes, and Grammy gave her a long hug, then pulled back to look into Bree's eyes. "Please come back to see us soon. We'd really like to get to know you."

"I feel the same way," Bree said. "Don't worry, we'll keep in touch." They'd already exchanged phone numbers and email addresses.

"I'll walk you out," Karen said. They headed down the hallway to the lobby and Karen stopped suddenly. "You never answered my question about why now?"

"Why now?"

"Why did you suddenly come looking for your mother now?"

Bree swallowed the thick lump in her throat. She hadn't shared her pregnancy with anyone except her girlfriends and Nick and his mom. "It's because I found out I'm pregnant."

Karen's eyes lit up and she quietly clapped her hands. "How wonderful! I'm so happy for you. I know my parents will be thrilled to have a great-grandchild."

"It's not that simple."

Karen tilted her head. "What do you mean?"

"I've decided not to raise it."

"Not raise it? Are you putting the baby up for adoption?"

"That was my original plan, but the father won't agree."

"So what are you going to do?"

"The father's going to raise it."

"Is it Nick? The man with you?" Karen asked.

Bree nodded. "Yes."

"Is this definite? No chance you'll change your mind?"

"There's no way I can raise a child," Bree explained with care. "I have a company to run, and I don't have enough time to give to a baby. Besides, I know nothing about being a mother."

"But you could learn."

"I don't think so. I just don't have the maternal

instinct. Probably because I never had a mother
to emulate."

Karen gave her a quick hug, and Bree gave a
little wave as she walked the rest of the way to
the lobby.

As soon as she was close to where Nick was
sitting, she turned to see if Karen was gone. Seeing that she was, Bree faced Nick as he stood up,
and she fell into his arms with a sob.

CHAPTER FIFTEEN

"ARE YOU OKAY?" Nick whispered into her hair. He had never seen her like this in the short time they'd known each other and was worried that something terrible had happened during the meeting with her grandparents.

"Uh-huh," she moaned into his chest, and then sobbed again. She reached up to wipe at her face.

"Here," he said as he guided her to the sofa. "Let me find some tissues." He saw them on the end table and brought the box closer. He pulled one out and handed it to her.

"Th-thank you," she said, wiping her cheeks and nose. "I guess this was more emotional than I'd expected."

"Do you want to talk about it?" He put an arm around her shoulders and pulled her to him.

She shook her head. "Not here. Wait till we're in the car."

"Sure."

"Let me visit the ladies' room first and get myself put back together."

She began to move and he held on to her.

"Don't go yet," he said. "Just sit here a minute with me."

She took his advice and leaned her head on his shoulder. "You do realize that you being nice to me is going to make me cry again," she warned. "Stupid pregnancy hormones."

He chuckled. "If you run out of tissues, I'll find more." He squeezed her shoulders and felt her relax against him.

They were silent for a while before she finally got up and faced him. She patted under her eyes with a tissue and said, "I'll be right back."

He put out his hand. "Give me the keys and I'll bring the car to the front door."

She hesitated a second, then dug into her purse.

He took the keys and squeezed her hand in the process. "Don't worry," he said with a wink. "I won't leave without you."

Her lips twitched, but it was far from a smile.

They each went their own way, and he didn't have long to wait for her after pulling the car to the entrance. He'd decided the moment she'd fallen into his arms on a sob that he'd drive them home because she wasn't in any mental condition to do so.

She came around to the driver-side door appearing extremely weary.

"I'm driving," he said. "Get into the passenger seat."

She glared at him for a few seconds and then did as he'd requested. They both seemed surprised at her lack of confrontation.

The first few minutes of the drive passed in silence, and then Bree began to fill him in on her visit with her grandparents. "They're both very nice and want to see me again."

"I'm glad you made the connection," he said. "Did you make any definite plans?"

"Not yet. It was a little overwhelming for all of us, I think." She had a balled-up tissue in her hand, and she dabbed at her nose. "I don't think Karen—Aunt Karen—was too happy to find out that I'm not going to raise this baby."

"You told her I'm raising it?" He was surprised the subject had come up at all on their first meeting.

"I did. Her reaction was the same as everyone else who knows about our situation. She doesn't get that I have no maternal instincts."

"I think you have them and don't realize it, but I don't want to fight about that right now."

She turned her head in his direction. "Thank you. I appreciate that. I'm not sure I have any fight in me at the moment."

"So how did the pregnancy come up in the first place? I can't imagine you just blurting out, 'Hey, I'm pregnant with Nick's kid, and he's going to raise it.'"

She made a sound that was half cough and half chuckle. "Yeah, that doesn't sound like me at all. Actually, Aunt Karen asked me why I began my search now and not years ago. I felt backed into a corner and had no other explanation."

Nick nodded. "I'm not sure what other reason you could have come up with either except maybe that you were dying and needed an organ or bone marrow."

"And she would have seen through those reasons pretty quickly when I kept living and my pregnancy began to show." She chuckled lowly at her dark joke.

They chatted amiably on the rest of the drive and before Nick knew it, they were at his building.

"Would you like to come in?" he asked as he pulled around to a parking spot before she even answered. "I could make us some dinner. You're probably getting hungry."

"You don't have to do that."

He looked into her eyes. "Maybe I want to."

"Why?"

He narrowed his eyes. "You're asking me why I want to make you dinner?"

She nodded. "Yes. Why do you want to have anything to do with me? All I've done is turn your world upside down. You should be enjoying this time before you have all the responsibilities of fatherhood."

He hadn't thought about it that way, and he didn't want to. "I'm just as responsible for this situation as you are." He turned off the engine and opened the car door. "Now, come on. Let's go see what's in my fridge to eat."

He came around to her side of the car and opened her door. He reached in to give her a hand as she got out and then, as if completely natural, she leaned into him and their lips met in a hot and passionate kiss.

A kiss filled with the promise of things to come.

NICK'S ARMS AROUND Bree felt like a cocoon of warmth and comfort. She was so intent on his mouth and body that she didn't realize at first that a light rain was landing on them.

Not until Nick pulled back to tell her exactly that. "Come on," he urged, closing the car door and locking it. He passed her the keys and put a hand to the small of her back to guide her into his building.

The first time she'd come here weeks ago, she hadn't known what to expect when she'd stepped through two sets of doors and into the lobby. From the outside, it was a brick high-rise from an earlier decade, but the inside public areas had been redone with neutral colors and contemporary furniture.

Nick took her hand in his and led her to the elevators. He pushed the button for the sixth floor when they entered. All she wanted him to do was kiss her again, but she wouldn't beg. The thrill of knowing that they were going to be alone together in his condo was almost more than she could stand.

Right now she didn't care if this was her pregnancy hormones making her feel this sexually excited or not. She knew how she felt and she wasn't leaving here until Nick did something about it.

They walked down the hallway to his door. He unlocked it and opened it, allowing Bree to walk in first.

Even though she'd been there before, she was still impressed by how gorgeous and comfortable his place was. She loved the neutral colors on the walls and the warm hardwood floors, with furniture covered in browns and tans. She turned to Nick as he closed the door. "Did you decorate this place yourself?" The question had suddenly popped into her head.

He scowled. "Long story. Let's get dinner started and I'll tell you all about it." He took her coat and hung both his and hers in the closet next to the door.

"This is a great view," she said as she looked out the windows in the living room.

"Yes, it is." His tone was deep, sexy, smooth.

She turned to look at him and found him watching her, not the view. His expression revealed hunger—for her. She actually felt her face heat, and she was definitely not prone to blushing.

He made her nervous all of a sudden, so she asked, "What's for dinner?" *Besides me.* Her insides quaked at the thought.

"Any preferences?"

She followed him as he walked to the large, modern kitchen that was probably the main reason he'd bought this place.

He opened the freezer drawer in the stainless steel, French-door refrigerator. "I have chicken, ground beef, pork chops." He spoke over his shoulder. "Anything sound appealing?"

Just watching you lean over the drawer like that. Seeing his butt from this angle made her remember how firm it had been when she'd gripped it as she—

"Bree?"

She blinked. "Oh, whatever you want is fine. I'll eat whatever you make."

He closed the freezer and turned around to face her. Their gazes met and he stepped toward her. "I can't stop thinking about you. About us. Together." He slowly unknotted the long scarf she wore, the backs of his hands brushing her sensitive breasts. He pulled the scarf from her neck in a leisurely manner and tossed it onto the counter. Then he placed a hand on each side of her waist and pulled her pelvis to his. He was already hard and she wanted him more than she'd ever wanted anything in her life.

She moved against him and loved when he groaned into her neck. "You're killing me," he whispered, before kissing her neck with his open mouth.

She sucked in a breath, snaking her arms around him to grasp his behind. She ran her hands up and down his butt and upper thighs, loving the solidness of him.

He turned them around so her back was against the fridge. They kissed then, hot, passionate kisses that made her legs weak. He cupped her breast, teasing her nipple through her sweater with his thumb and forefinger. She wanted to rip her sweater off and bare herself to him. She wanted his touch everywhere all at once. She couldn't get enough.

When he slipped his hands under her sweater to her bare back, she could hardly breathe. His mouth moved again to her neck, and she desperately wanted it on her breasts.

The next thing she knew, he'd placed a large palm on each side of her behind and lifted her.

She automatically wrapped her legs around his waist and shifted her hands to cup his bearded face while they continued to kiss.

He carried her that way down the hall to what she assumed was his bedroom. She didn't care. She just craved release.

As they tumbled onto his bed, he flipped her on top of him. He pulled his mouth from hers and looked into her eyes.

"Two questions," he said as he gasped for air.

"Better be quick ones," she managed to answer.

"Is this what you want? I don't want you to regret it."

She couldn't help laughing. "If you only knew how much I want this—"

"Second question," he said, cutting her off. "Is it safe?"

That one stopped her. "Safe?" Then she realized what he meant. "Yes, it's safe." From all the reading she'd done—unless specifically told not to—sex was safe all through the pregnancy. "But I like that you're concerned." She kissed him quickly. "Now can we get on with it?"

He laughed then. "Some romantic you are."

"Hey, you're the one who stopped to ask questions," she reminded him. He lifted her long sweater above her waist and started undoing the zipper fly on her skinny jeans.

She nearly stopped breathing when he planted

a kiss on her bare skin just above her panties. After he helped her wiggle out of her jeans, she crossed her arms in front of her body and stripped off her sweater over her head. She tossed it onto the floor, not caring that the move was completely out of character for her.

She lay back in only her bra and panties, watching Nick take in her entire body with his eyes as he removed his own clothes. By the time he was down to his skivvies, which showed every inch of his erection, she could hardly stand it anymore. "If you don't get over here soon, I'm going to melt into a puddle right here on your bed."

He grinned, a sexy grin that spoke volumes. He slid on top of her then, playing with her nipples and kissing her skin from the back of her ear to the inside of her thighs.

But she was still wearing clothes and so was he.

So she maneuvered under him to scoot down low enough to reach into his boxer briefs to wrap her hand around his erection. He buried his head in her neck and moaned before taking the hint and removing his underwear.

Before he could get back onto the bed and onto her, she wrapped her hand around him again. She bent her head and put her lips around the tip, teasing him with her tongue.

"Bree," he gasped as he held both sides of her

head. "If you don't stop now, I can't promise—"
He didn't need to finish his sentence. She got
the picture.

She gave his penis a loud smacking kiss and
reached around to unclasp her bra. She tossed it
with the rest of her clothes and fell back onto the
pillows, her legs spread in invitation.

Nick didn't need more incentive than that and
he went straight for her panties, first rubbing her
crotch erotically with his fingers over the cloth
and then moving it aside to play with her flesh.

When she could stand it no more, she pulled
at her underwear and Nick dragged it down her
legs. He rubbed his erection against her wetness
and she wrapped her legs around him, urging
him inside her.

When he finally slid all the way into her and
quickly brought her to orgasm, she realized that
this was the absolute best way to end her already
wonderful day.

ROXIE WAS WORKING late at the office that evening
when she had a visitor. "Pete? What are you doing
here?" She hadn't heard from him since he'd left
on his business trip several weeks ago. He must
not have liked that she'd turned down his dinner
invitation. But she wasn't the kind of woman who
cheated on her boyfriend.

Now he stood in her office doorway in navy

dress pants and a navy-and-white-checked shirt with the sleeves rolled up to reveal his strong forearms, his navy tie hanging loose. How easily she could forget that she was in a relationship.

"I thought you might still be here. I had to talk the guard into letting me in. I was hoping you might have heard from Nick or Bree today," Pete said as he stepped through the doorway and put his hands on the back of the chair facing the other side of her desk. "Nick's not answering his phone, and his mom can't reach him, either. There was a problem at the restaurant."

Roxie's eyes widened. "What happened?"

"Nothing serious." He didn't elaborate.

"I haven't heard from either one of them. Bree took the afternoon off to go to Delaware on personal business. Maybe Nick went with her."

Pete nodded. "With the way this day is going, I hope the fact that Nick's not answering his phone isn't a harbinger of bad news on their end, too."

"I thought the restaurant was closed on Mondays," Roxie said.

"It is. We rented it out for use as a pop-up restaurant." He came around the chair and sat down across her desk from her.

She really wished she wasn't as attracted to him as she was.

Pete leaned forward, his folded hands on the

desk, and lowered his voice. "A fight broke out and some furniture was broken."

"Oh, no! That's terrible."

He nodded. "I know. The police were there and broke things up, but I really need to let Nick know as soon as possible."

"Let me try Bree," Roxie said as she picked up her office phone and began dialing. "Hey, Bree," she said when voice mail picked up. "Please call me when you get this. And if Nick is with you, have him call Pete. It's important." She hung up the phone and looked at Pete, who nodded approvingly. "I don't know what else to do," she said. "I hope nothing's wrong."

"The only other thing I can think to do is to go to his condo to see if he's there. I can't believe he's not answering his phone."

"I could go check at Bree's condo, too," she suggested.

They both stood at once to do just that, when their phones rang almost simultaneously. "It's Bree," Roxie told Pete with a sigh of relief.

He nodded and gestured with his cell phone. "It's Nick."

They answered their phones. "Where have you been?" Roxie asked Bree. "Is Nick with you?"

"Calm down, Rox. Yes, Nick's here. He's talking to Pete right now."

"Are you all right?" Roxie demanded. "You weren't in an accident or anything, were you?"

"Of course not." Bree sounded upbeat and happy.

"Well, you had us worried."

"Us?"

"Pete and me. He just showed up at my office to find out if I'd heard from the two of you. Seems there was a problem at Nick's restaurant."

"Oh, no. Hey, I'm going to hang up and see what's going on. I'll fill you in later on what happened in Delaware."

"But—"

Bree disconnected before Roxie could ask where she and Nick were. Obviously, they were together from what she'd just said. But, for all Roxie knew, they were still in Delaware.

"Nick's filled in," Pete told Roxie after he'd disconnected. "He's going to contact insurance. Man, I told him there were easier ways to make money, but he wouldn't listen to me."

"Make money? Is The Fresh Pantry in trouble?"

"I shouldn't have said anything. Keep it to yourself, okay? Everything's fine. I'm just a worrier." He made it sound like he was backpedaling for some reason.

"So the restaurant is financially healthy?" She wondered if Bree knew there might be a problem. Roxie couldn't imagine Bree hiring Nick as a restaurant consultant if she thought his restaurant was in financial trouble.

"Oh, sure, it's all fine." Pete seemed to be trying hard to sell her on that fact. "He's just a little overprotective after what happened about a year ago."

"A year ago?"

Pete nodded. "Yeah, he pretty much got left at the altar. Not figuratively—she actually called it off a week before the wedding. He was pretty torn up about it. They'd been together over three years. It took not only a toll on his heart, but on his finances, too. He insisted on buying back her part ownership of their condo."

"That's awful."

"I know. I just hate seeing him busting his butt to make some extra money and then have things like this fight mess things up even more."

AFTER BREE AND NICK had returned their calls, they set down their phones. When their phones had gone off simultaneously, Nick realized he'd missed several calls and texts from Pete while his phone had been on vibrate. Instead of answering, he'd only wanted to throw the devices out the window and continue snuggling with Bree in his bed. After they'd exhausted themselves and grown chilled, they'd burrowed under the covers and must have drifted to sleep.

Waking up with Bree in his arms was something he could get used to. She fit perfectly against him and her skin was so soft. He couldn't stop touching her.

Now they looked at each other from opposite sides of the bed. "I need to go to the restaurant," Nick said softly. "I don't want to, but there was a fight and the police were called." He came around the bed to her side and reached for her hand. He told her what he knew about the situation. "I want to stay with you. I want you to spend the night."

Bree smiled sadly. "I'd like that, too." She leaned closer to kiss him. "But I understand. Go. You need to get to the restaurant."

He kissed her quickly, then deepened the kiss to taste her once more. He ran one hand down her neck, over one breast and lower until he touched her most intimate place. He chuckled when she wiggled against his hand at the contact.

Finally, she pushed him away. It was a good thing, because he wasn't sure he would have stopped himself otherwise.

"Come on," she said. "Let's get dressed, and I'll go with you to the restaurant."

"You don't have to do that."

"I know. But you went with me to Delaware. It's the least I can do."

He kind of liked that she'd do that, so he didn't try to talk her out of it.

"Mind if I jump in the shower first?" She'd gathered her clothes and held them in front of her.

He grinned. "I'd suggest I join you, but we'd never get out of here. Go ahead. Give a yell when I can get in." From the look he gave her, he was recalling their shower on the island, too.

They were pretty quick getting to the restaurant and under normal circumstances, Nick would have been more upset about what happened. But he'd just had incredible sex with the mother of his child, and he was feeling pretty damn good. He wasn't about to let this incident get him down.

He and Bree drove his car to the restaurant. And he thought it was a good sign that she was willing to come back to stay at his condo once things were straightened out here. They entered by the alley door and walked through the kitchen to the dining room, where several people were cleaning up.

He'd left his assistant manager in charge while the pop-up was renting the space, and he came right over to Nick. "What happened here?" Nick asked while Bree stepped away to walk around the dining room to assess the damage.

"Some patrons got into a fight. I don't know what it was about, but it seemed like a domestic dispute. A few tables were overturned and there was glass all over the place. The police were called, and I have a report number for the insurance company."

Nick nodded. "Was anyone hurt?"

"An ambulance came at the same time the police arrived, but they just treated a few people for cuts and then left."

"Where's the chef who was hosting the pop-up? John something?"

"He just left a little while ago. He feels awful about it."

"I'm sure he does. He'll feel worse if our insurance decides not to cover it and finds him liable." Nick had made sure to double-check his insurance coverage before agreeing to allow anyone to use his restaurant for pop-ups or bartending classes or anything else.

They spoke for a few more minutes, and then he caught Bree's eye across the dining room. She'd taken a seat at a table and had been looking at her phone.

He smiled, and she smiled back. He wanted to take her home again and spend the night with her. She appeared so young and vulnerable with her long, wet hair pulled into a ponytail and sans makeup except for some lip balm she'd had in her purse.

Suddenly, Pete showed up with Roxie in tow. They'd come in the back way, also.

"Hey, guys," Nick said. "You didn't need to come down."

Roxie gave him a little wave and continued walking over to where Bree was seated.

Pete said, "I wanted to make sure you didn't need my help here." He looked around. "Seems pretty well cleaned up. So where were you? Several of us tried to get ahold of you, but you weren't answering your phone."

Nick shrugged. A gentleman never told. "Sorry. I guess I had it on vibrate." It wasn't even a white lie, just not the complete truth. Certainly a better way to go than to discuss what had gone on between Bree and him.

"You slept with him again?" Roxie's voice carried to where Nick and Pete stood.

Bree shushed her, but it was too late.

Nick couldn't even look at Pete because he knew he was about to take a boatload of crap about his sex life.

CHAPTER SIXTEEN

"MAN, YOU HAVE a big mouth," Bree informed Roxie after she'd practically shouted to the entire room that Bree had slept with Nick. Again. Not that there were that many people in the restaurant's dining room, but enough to embarrass Bree.

And for Nick and Pete to overhear…

"Sorry," Roxie said, appearing adequately apologetic. "I was just surprised. You've been saying that you don't want a relationship, don't want to raise your baby. But here you are sleeping with the baby's father."

"That doesn't contradict anything," Bree insisted. "Sleeping together doesn't make a relationship, and it hardly makes me change my mind about raising children."

"Does Nick know that? Or does he think you're coming around?"

Bree hadn't thought about it. "I'm sure he knows that this is just sex." Really, really great sex. She put her cool hands to her warm cheeks.

"I have no interest in a relationship with anyone, and I've made that quite clear to him."

"I hope you're right." Roxie looked over at Pete and Nick, who were deep in conversation. Then she turned back to Bree. "So what happened today? Did you find your grandparents?"

"I found a lot today." Bree gestured to Nick. "Looks like he's going to be a while. Can you give me a ride to his condo to pick up my car? I'll fill you in on the drive."

"Sure."

"Let me tell him, and I'll meet you out behind the restaurant. I'm assuming that's where you parked?"

Roxie nodded. "Pete said it was okay."

Roxie left the building and Bree went to speak to Nick. "Sorry to interrupt," she said to the two men. "I just wanted to let you know that Roxie's going to give me a ride to pick up my car."

"That's not necessary," Nick said. "I'm just about done here." He appeared confused, probably because she'd changed her mind about spending the night with him.

She felt more than a twinge of guilt. "I know. But Roxie doesn't mind."

Nick said to Pete, "I'll be right back." He turned to Bree again and took her elbow. "I'll walk you out."

From his brusqueness, she knew he was pissed

off and she knew why, but she asked the question anyway. "Why are you so upset?"

He stopped suddenly, in the middle of the restaurant's empty kitchen. "Why am I upset?" His eyebrows rose. "Oh, I don't know. Maybe because one minute we're having incredible sex, and now you're brushing me off like I'm a piece of lint."

"That's not true." Well, maybe it was a little true. Incredible sex, indeed.

"It certainly *is* true. You use this excuse about not being interested in a relationship, but you have no problem jumping into bed with me. Is that what you do? Sleep with guys and then disappear before any feelings are involved?"

Now he'd succeeded in making her angry. She put her hands on her hips and spoke very distinctly. "I do *not* sleep with strange men, and I'm appalled to hear you say something like that about me. How dare you!" She took a step toward the exit. There was no way she was going to admit to him that it had been a really long time since she'd had sex before he'd shown up in her life. A hell of a long time. Because that's the way she rolled.

"Don't just walk away," Nick said. "Stop acting like nothing happened between us." He ran a hand through his hair. "We have a connection that's not going away. We made a baby. There's no denying that."

Her anger was about to push her to tears, which

made her even more angry. "Don't you think I know that? Don't you think I blame myself for my own screwup?" She sucked in a breath. "You know, I could have just ended this pregnancy, walked away as you describe my behavior. But I'm not. I'm going through with it."

"And walking away after that to let me raise it."

She had nothing to counter. He was right, but she wasn't about to admit it. "My life, my business."

"Well, now your life is *my* business. You've made it that way, whether you want to admit it or not."

"Look, we both know where the other stands," she said with as much patience as she could muster. "Roxie is waiting for me. I need to go."

He stood silently, not saying another word. She had turned to leave when she felt an odd sensation in her abdomen. She stopped and put a hand on the spot where she'd felt it.

"Are you okay?" Nick had walked up behind her, concern replacing the anger in his tone.

"Yes," she whispered, and then felt it again. "I think I just felt it move."

"Really?"

She nodded. Then she took his flat palm and placed it where she'd felt the flutter. They waited, his breath warm on her neck, until it finally happened again.

Their gazes met, and even though her own eyes began to fill with tears, she could see Nick's eyes were glassy, too.

ROXIE WAS ABOUT to go back into the restaurant for Bree when she finally exited through the alley door.

"Hey, what happened to you?" she asked Bree when she opened the passenger-side door and got into Roxie's car.

"Nick." As if that answered the question sufficiently.

"I take it you don't want to talk about it?"

Bree didn't say anything right away. "He's not happy that I'm not going back to his place for the night."

"Are you sure you two aren't in a relationship?" Roxie said as she pulled out onto the main thoroughfare from the alley.

Bree put her hands to her face. "I don't know. I'm so confused." She paused. "We were fighting, and then I felt movement."

Roxie's head spun to look at Bree. "You felt the baby move? Already?"

"I'm into my second trimester," Bree said in a clinical tone. "Everything I read says this is about the time when you can begin to feel it move."

"Did you tell Nick?" Surely that was a moment that would bring them closer.

"Sure. He was right there when it happened. He felt it, too." Bree shifted in her seat. "But I could tell when I left that he was still mad that I wasn't going home with him."

"Why don't you start at the beginning and tell me what happened in Delaware? Then maybe I can get a feel for where you are now with Nick."

As Bree began to tell Roxie the tale of meeting her grandparents and aunt, interspersed with directions to Nick's condo, Roxie was struck by how dispassionately Bree spoke about her deceased mother.

"So most of that money your dad paid your mom actually ended up with your grandparents?"

"That's right. She must not have had very long after I was born to even enjoy her financial freedom."

"Do you think she regretted not fighting to keep you?"

Bree didn't answer right away. "I never thought so before, but maybe if she had told her family, then they would have convinced her to fight for me. They seemed very welcoming today, but I don't know how they would have reacted back then."

"You told them about your baby?" Roxie asked.

"Just my aunt. She wondered why I began searching for my mother now and not years ago. I felt I had to tell her the truth about being pregnant and that I felt like it had been up to my mother to find me earlier, if she'd wanted to. As Cal Tucker's daughter, I'm pretty easy to locate."

"That's true. You know, I never even considered what will happen when the tabloids get ahold of this news about your baby."

"With any luck they'll be more interested in my father's newest addition instead of focusing on me."

"Let's hope." Roxie had never gotten used to the occasional picture of Bree in the grocery-store tabloids.

They were nearing Nick's building and Roxie turned where Bree told her to. "I'm parked over there." Bree pointed to the right side of the parking lot.

The sun had already set on the early May evening, but the parking lot was well lit, enabling Roxie to pick out Bree's car without help.

"You're sure you're doing the right thing by going home?" Roxie asked.

Bree had opened the car door and was partially out. "Spending the night with Nick isn't going to change anything. We have no future together. I don't want him to get the wrong idea."

"But you'll always have a child together," Roxie pointed out.

"A child doesn't make a relationship. And I don't want a relationship. You know that. I have enough people and responsibilities in my life without working so hard to have one more."

Roxie didn't know how to counter that, and Bree was already out the door.

"Thanks for the ride. See you at work tomorrow," Bree said before closing the car door and heading to her own vehicle.

Roxie just sat there a minute, wondering how she could help her friend realize what she was doing with her life.

Or what she *wasn't* doing.

SEVERAL WEEKS WENT BY before Bree heard from Nick. She'd been bogged down with work and had tried hard not to think about how they'd left things. He hadn't even pushed for their usual Monday dinners, and she told herself that she was fine the way things were.

Then one evening she was unlocking her condo after work when she got a text. She reached into her purse and checked her phone. Nick. Funny, since she'd just been thinking about him.

My mom wants us to attend a family reunion in Pennsylvania this Saturday. She'd like you to meet her family.

Bree didn't know how to respond. After their argument in the restaurant, he'd been acting like he didn't want to have anything more to do with her.

She let herself into her condo and locked the door behind her. He texted again as she put her purse on the hook in the coat closet.

I'll understand if you don't want to go. Just say the word.

That would be the easiest thing to do, but she wasn't a coward and didn't like to go back on her word. She'd promised to spend time with him to enable bonding, and she saw no reason not to go with him to this reunion.

What time Saturday? she texted.

Will pick you up by 8. Takes about 2 hours. It's west of Harrisburg, he responded.

OK, she ended.

She had set down her phone down and begun to change into more comfortable clothes when her phone sounded again. This time Nick was calling instead of texting.

"Hello," she answered.

"Hey," he said. "I wanted to thank you for going to this reunion. I know it's a last-minute invitation. I wasn't going to ask you, but my mom can be pretty pushy about this stuff."

"That's okay. I like your mom, so I don't mind doing this for her."

"What about me?" he asked.

"What about you?"

"Do you mind doing it for me?"

She didn't even have to think about it. "No, of course not."

"Good." He was silent a few seconds. "I like you, Bree. A lot. I want us to get along."

Her heart began to race. She hadn't expected this conversation, especially after not hearing from him for weeks.

She cleared her throat. "I know you were upset about me going home instead of your—"

"I'm sorry about that. I've thought about it a lot and I think I understand completely," he said before she could finish. "It was a work night, and I know you like to be at the office early in the morning. Your work is your life. It only makes sense that you'd want to sleep at your own place."

"Thanks for understanding." She didn't correct him. That was only part of the reason she'd chosen not to go home with him, but she wouldn't get into that now. She was anxious for them to get along together, as well.

"I can't believe we felt the baby move," he said, catching her off guard.

She put a hand to her abdomen, remembering the moment they'd shared. "I know. I wasn't expecting it."

"I was thinking that the baby probably heard

us arguing and was trying to get us to stop. What do you think?"

"I think that's pretty crazy thinking." She actually smiled at his nonsense. "Fetuses can't hear this early." She had obviously done more research than he had about this pregnancy stuff.

"Oh." He chuckled. "Well, I'm still going to believe what I want."

She laughed at him. With him, actually, because he was laughing now, too.

"Do you feel it move often?" he asked.

"Sometimes. I notice it more when I'm being still."

They talked details about the family reunion and then he said, "Sleep well. I'll talk to you soon."

As she finished getting ready for bed, she couldn't help wondering if she'd made a mistake by coming home that evening a few weeks ago instead of spending the night with Nick.

ROXIE WAS THROWING TOGETHER a salad for dinner Tuesday evening when her phone rang. "You want me to what?" she said to Pete, who'd called out of the blue.

He spoke slowly and distinctly as he repeated his request. "I'd like you to go to a family reunion with me this weekend."

"Why?"

"Why not?" he countered.

"Because we barely know each other. Why would you take me to a family reunion of all things? That's just plain odd."

"Okay, so truthfully it's Auntie Em's idea. She talked Nick into bringing Bree to this thing, and she thought it might go better if I brought someone, too."

"But why me?" Hadn't she turned down his date requests enough times already?

"Because anyone else I take will assume that I'm getting serious about them. But you've made it clear that you're in a relationship, and you also understand why I'm taking you. That it's just to make my aunt happy. I think she doesn't want people to take too seriously the fact that Bree will be with Nick since they're not planning a future with the baby."

"Oh. Sure. I actually see your reasoning." She wasn't sure how to answer. "So Bree and Nick will be there, too?"

"According to Nick, Bree has agreed to come."

"I thought they weren't speaking to each other," she said.

"I don't know what's going on with those two. They've got a strange situation."

"That's for sure. So give me the details about this weekend."

He did that and they disconnected shortly afterward. Roxie stared at her phone, wondering how he'd persuaded her to go with him. It hadn't even taken much convincing to get her to say yes.

She popped a cherry tomato into her mouth and tried to figure out what kind of influence he had over her when he was so obviously a guy who would never settle down. She shook her head—why did she even care?

She was contemplating texting her boyfriend Jim when her phone rang again. "Now what?" She picked up her cell phone to see it was Bree. She finished swallowing the tomato and answered. "Hey, Bree."

"Help," Bree said dramatically.

Roxie's pulse soared. "What's wrong?"

"I can't zip my jeans anymore!" Bree sounded more upset over her clothes than she had when she'd found out she was pregnant.

"That's all?" Roxie sighed in relief.

"That's all! What am I going to wear? It's like it happened overnight. It's not even that I've got a visible bump. I'm just thicker around the waist. In fact, it's as if I don't have a waist anymore. I just go straight from chest to hips."

"Okay, calm down. We can get you new clothes."

"But I'm not ready to wear maternity clothes. Once I do that, everyone will know I'm pregnant."

"It's going to happen sooner or later," Roxie reminded her.

"Later is what I'm counting on."

Roxie could see no way to delay the inevitable, so she made a suggestion. "Why don't we all go shopping one night this week. Hannah's really good at picking out flattering clothes. Maybe you just need something a size larger for now, until you actually look pregnant."

"Okay, that might work. I don't mind if people think I'm putting on a few pounds. It's really none of their business anyway."

Roxie agreed. "I'll call the girls and we'll plan on tomorrow night if that works for you."

"Perfect. Thanks, Roxie. I knew I could count on you. I figure I can make it through work with long tops and the button of my pants undone, but I've got a thing to go to this Saturday and I'd rather not be wearing clothes that don't fit."

"I understand. And you should know that I'm going to the family reunion, too."

"You are?"

Obviously, Bree hadn't heard the news, so Roxie filled her in.

"I'm so glad you're coming, too," Bree said, not even questioning the part about how Pete had asked Roxie. She knew Bree and the other girls weren't huge fans of Jim. "Things have been pretty cool between Nick and me, so having you there should help."

"Glad I can be of service," Roxie quipped before they discussed details of their shopping trip and she hung up to call Hannah and Amber.

"This is so much fun," Hannah said as the four women entered the maternity section in the high-end department store the next evening.

"Easy for you to say," Bree countered. "You're not the one with the expanding waist."

"How do you decide on size?" Amber asked. "Don't you keep getting bigger and bigger?"

"Thanks for the encouragement," Bree said gloomily. "According to what I read, you buy your prepregnancy size. I guess as long as I don't put on eighty or a hundred pounds I'll be okay."

The girls pulled clothes off the racks and finally decided on a few for Bree to try on.

"Hurry up so we can see," Roxie said.

"I will say that these jeans are pretty comfortable," Bree said when she stepped out of the dressing room. "I don't think I'm ready for big shirts yet, but pants and skirts that expand will get me through for now."

They all agreed, but talked her into buying two maternity dresses that were actually cute. She could wear them to work when she couldn't fit into her regular clothes anymore.

Bree paid for her purchases and didn't mind when the others wanted to wander through the store for clothes for themselves.

"Oh, look!" Hannah said as they were walking toward the exit. "We've got to check this out." Hannah sidetracked into the infant-clothing section, and the others followed her, oohing and aahing as each new find was cuter than the last. Bree stood there, wondering why miniature clothes were suddenly making her friends hear their maternal clocks ticking.

"Come on, guys, let's get something to eat," Bree begged. "I'm starving."

"Doesn't this make you even a little sorry that you're not going to raise this baby?" Roxie held up a pink frilly dress that was less than a foot in length. "Look how cute this is."

Bree shook her head. "You're nuts. Do you know how much work is involved in raising a kid?"

"But it's time well spent," Hannah told her. "I think if the right guy came along, I'd be ready to settle down and have kids."

The others agreed with her, while Bree stood there in shock.

"But what about the company? If you're all getting married and having babies, then who's going to help me run the company?"

"Don't worry, Bree, we're not going anywhere," Amber said. "And if that's what it comes to, then maybe our next step is to provide day care for our employees."

That began a conversation about starting a program now since they already had employees with children who would benefit from on-site day care.

Bree didn't mind talking about the work-related subject, as long as it got the group out of the infant-clothing department and off to dinner.

She was hungry enough to eat anything.

While the other three ordered cocktails, Bree chose a decaffeinated soda. She'd been feeling a little odd all afternoon, figuring it was just one more phase in this pregnancy odyssey. She was sure that eating a healthy dinner would make her feel a little more normal.

"You're pretty quiet tonight," Roxie commented to Bree. "Are you okay?" All three women looked at her as they waited for her answer.

"I'm fine," Bree said. "Stop worrying about me. I'm just a little tired."

Their server came to their table then and took their orders.

"I'm going to the ladies' room," Bree said as she rose from her seat. "I'll be right back."

While walking through the casual restaurant, she got a sudden cramp and stopped for a few seconds until it subsided. Then she continued on to the restroom without another incident.

"I think I need to call my doctor," Bree said when she returned to the table. Again, they all turned in her direction. She lowered her voice so no one else would hear. "I'm spotting and I just had a fairly severe cramping episode."

It took only a few seconds after what Bree had said for them to respond. "Do you want me to call her for you?" Roxie asked.

Bree was still standing at the edge of their table. "No, I'll step outside to call. At this time of night, I'll probably get her answering service."

"I'll go with you." Hannah was already on her feet and ready to go.

Just as she'd suspected, Bree got the answering service. "I can wait out here alone for a callback," Bree told Hannah.

"I'm not going anywhere, Bree. Who knows what's going on, and I don't want to leave in case you get worse."

"Thank you." Her emotions came bubbling to the surface. "I'm really lucky to have the three of you."

Hannah gave her a hug. "I know. We're all lucky to have each other."

Bree's phone rang and she spoke to the doctor on call—not her usual one—who asked several questions before giving her advice. "Thank you," Bree said before disconnecting.

"Well?" Hannah appeared anxious, folding and unfolding her hands.

"The doctor suggested I go home and rest. As

long as the spotting is minor and the cramping has stopped, he thought I'd be fine. He said it's not unusual, as long as it's minimal. He would like me to come in tomorrow for an exam to make sure everything's okay. But if it gets worse at all, then I should head directly to the ER."

"I can drive you home," Hannah suggested as they walked back into the restaurant.

"I'd appreciate that." She'd had enough scares with cramping to realize that she probably shouldn't drive.

"Would you like me to call Nick and let him know?"

Bree was surprised at the question. "Absolutely not. There's nothing he can do to help."

"Don't you think he should know what's going on?"

"If there was something to tell, then yes. But right now, no."

Bree related what the doctor had said to Roxie and Amber, and they had their food packed up to go. Hannah drove Bree home, but she insisted that Hannah not walk her to her door.

Bree was letting herself into her condo when her cell phone rang. Nick's name was on the caller ID.

"Hello," she answered.

"Are you okay?" Strange question for him to ask, unless—

"I'm fine. Who called you?"

"That's not important. Are you and the baby okay?"

Knowing the girls, it likely wasn't Hannah who'd called, because Bree had specifically requested that she not. Of course, she hadn't told Roxie or Amber not to call him.

"Everything's fine. I just need to rest." She related the conversation she'd had with the doctor on call.

"I'll go with you tomorrow to the doctor."

"That's not necessary," she said. "I'm sure everything's fine. I'll call you afterward."

"Let me know what time your appointment is and I'll be there." He obviously wasn't taking no for an answer.

CHAPTER SEVENTEEN

BREE HADN'T DOUBTED that Nick would show up for her ob-gyn appointment the next day. She had had to put her foot down, insisting he meet her there rather than drive her to the doctor's office. She wanted to be able to go directly to work afterward. This was an unscheduled appointment, so she couldn't afford to be gone from the office longer than absolutely necessary.

"Hi," she said, when she walked into the waiting room and he was already seated there.

He smiled and came over to her. "How are you?" He stroked her upper arm.

"Much better," she said. "Back to normal, as far as I can tell."

He nodded. "Thanks for letting me come today."

"Did I have a choice?" But she smiled as she said it.

He shrugged. "I'm just concerned."

Before she could say more, the nurse opened the door and called her name.

Nick followed Bree and the nurse to the exam

room. He took a seat in the far corner of the room while Bree stepped into the curtained changing area to put on a paper gown.

Her doctor came in soon after, did an exam and pronounced everything was just as it should be.

Bree turned her head in Nick's direction and smiled. "See, I told you." Privately, she'd had a few doubts, but nothing she wanted to verbalize.

He shrugged, wisely not saying a word.

"When are you scheduled for an ultrasound?" her doctor asked after explaining that a little spotting and cramping were normal in some women. She did warn Bree that she should call the office if her symptoms became worse, though.

"Next Monday," Bree replied. Another workday that would be interrupted.

"Since you're both here today, would you like to do it now? A few days won't make a difference in determining growth or the sex of the baby. This way we'll get a good look at the baby to make sure everything's okay."

Bree was taken aback. "Sure. I guess." She looked to Nick, who nodded his agreement.

"Why don't you get dressed, and then we'll set you up in the room down the hall where the equipment is located. A nurse will be in shortly to escort you," the doctor told her before leaving the exam room.

"I wasn't prepared for this," Nick said. "Are you nervous?"

She nodded. "A little." Then she asked, "Do you want to know the sex?" She'd figured that would be a question for next week.

"I hadn't thought about it," he said. "I'm just hoping everything is okay and that the baby is healthy. Do you want to know?"

She shrugged. "I'll do whatever you want." He would be raising it, so he should decide.

"Well, let's find out. I think my mom would like to know. She's anxious to start buying stuff. She's already researching car seats and strollers."

"Okay, then."

He took her hand and squeezed it.

Soon they were shown to another small room, where Bree was instructed to lie back on the table.

After the tech put some cold jelly on her abdomen, she moved the device over Bree while watching the screen until she got the view she wanted. "You can see the heart beating here," the tech said as she pointed to the monitor. She pointed out several other things before asking, "Would you like to know the sex of your baby?"

Bree looked to Nick for confirmation, who nodded. "Yes, we would," Bree said, her heart fluttering in her chest. She'd thought that seeing the actual human being inside her wouldn't affect her, but she'd been wrong. Dead wrong.

"Well, it's pretty clear that it's a girl," the tech said with a smile.

"A girl!" Nick said, grinning widely with glassy eyes.

Bree couldn't say anything. She merely smiled back, realizing then that Nick had been holding her hand the entire time. He squeezed her hand, and she squeezed back.

By the time they left the office, they'd been given pictures of the ultrasound and their next appointment was scheduled.

"Are you okay?" Nick asked Bree when they got to the lobby of the medical building. "You're pretty quiet."

"Sure, I'm fine. Why wouldn't I be?" But that was a complete lie. She steeled herself against the emotions churning inside her.

He turned to her. "Look at me."

She slowly did as he asked. Then she did something she regretted. She looked into his eyes.

And she fell apart.

He pulled her to him and held her tight, whispering soothing words and stroking her hair.

She broke into sobs, unable to remember the last time she'd cried this hard. She wasn't a bawl-her-eyes-out kind of person. She might get a little weepy, more so since she'd gotten pregnant, but nothing like this uncontrollable blubbering.

Especially not in a public place.

Luckily, they were alone, but she needed to get herself together before someone came by. She finally pulled back a little from Nick, then took several deep breaths and swiped at her tears and runny nose.

"Let's go to my car," he suggested.

She nodded. Normally, she'd be able to walk away and take care of herself. But right now, she needed to lean on someone. To lean on Nick.

During the first few months of being told she was pregnant, of being sick, of hearing a heartbeat mixed with hers, nothing had seemed real. She'd just gone through the motions.

But now to actually see through the magic of an ultrasound that she was carrying an actual life—a baby girl—everything had become real all at once.

She was carrying her daughter inside her. She didn't know what that meant right now, but she knew that she'd somehow changed in an instant, and nothing would ever be the same from this moment on.

NICK HADN'T BEEN prepared for Bree's breakdown. She was always so strong, so in control. He didn't know what to do for her except to just be there, and that didn't feel like enough.

They were almost at his car when she stopped walking and turned to him.

"I'm fine now," she said softly. "I really need to get to the office."

She was turning in the direction of her own car when he said, "Wait."

She spun back to face him. "What?"

"That's it? You fall apart back there and now everything's suddenly okay?" His blood pressure was rising as he tried to figure out what was going on with her. "You don't even want to talk about why you're upset?"

"I'm fine. I have things I need to do at work," she said. "I'm sorry for my outburst. I think my hormones are on overload." She laughed, but it was a humorless sound. "I can barely make it through a movie anymore without a box of tissues next to me."

He didn't believe it was just hormones affecting her, but standing in the parking lot of the medical building wasn't the place to have this conversation.

"We're still good for the reunion Saturday?" he asked, instead.

She nodded. "Absolutely." She looked down at her barely protruding belly and then up at Nick. "Will anyone know about the baby? I'm barely showing, so keeping it a secret might be wise. Otherwise, I'm sure you and your mom will have to answer some tough questions."

He'd thought about that, too. "I think keeping it quiet is wise. I'll double-check with my mom to make sure we're all on the same page. Her main reason for having us all there is so that her relatives don't just find out that I'm raising our child alone and think we never had a relationship."

"Which would be the truth," she said.

"I would hope that you'd at least consider us friends after all this," he said, trying to ignore the sting of her comment.

She nodded. "Yes, I do consider us friends."

"Good." He took hold of her upper arms and leaned in to give her a quick kiss on the lips. "That's a start."

She stared at him a moment before turning to head to her car.

"See you bright and early on Saturday," he called after her.

She didn't turn around, merely lifted her arm and waved in acknowledgment.

He watched until she backed her car out of the parking space, drove to the exit and turned onto the main road. Then he got into his own car and headed straight to the restaurant.

He found himself whistling as he drove. He

stopped and smiled. He was going to have a daughter. He couldn't wait to share the news with his mom and Pete.

When he arrived at The Fresh Pantry, his mom was speaking to one of the servers. The restaurant didn't open for lunch for another fifteen minutes, so that gave him time to talk to her before she began seating people.

"Hey, Mom," he said when he came up to her in the dining room.

"Hi, Nick," she said, then turned to the server she'd been speaking to. "Good to catch up with you, Shirley. I want to hear more about that trip you're planning later." The server continued wrapping silverware into napkins, and his mom took Nick's arm to guide him to where they could speak privately. "How did it go at the doctor's? Is everything okay with Bree and the baby?"

He smiled broadly and immediately saw relief on his mom's face. "Everything is fine. Perfect, in fact."

"That's so good to hear. With the problems she's had since the beginning, I was a little worried."

He'd felt the same way. "I have some other news to share, too."

"You're getting married?" She wasn't about to give up hope.

"No, Mom. We're not getting married. You really know how to suck the air out of my balloon."

She feigned sadness. "I'm sorry. What's your news?"

"Well. Since we were both in the office, the doctor thought we could just have the ultrasound today instead of next week."

The moment his mom realized what that meant, her eyes widened to large circles. "And?"

He could feel her excitement building, ready to explode. "And you're going to have a…"

"Just tell me!"

He grinned, loving the power he had over her. "A granddaughter!"

His mom squealed, totally out of character, and grabbed him to hug him tightly. "That's wonderful," she whispered, her voice shaky with emotion. She pulled back to look at him. "After raising you two boys, I'm so happy to finally get a little girl."

"I knew you'd be happy."

She cocked her head. "You're happy, too, aren't you?"

"Of course I am. I really didn't care one way or the other."

"How did Bree take it?" His mother swiped at the wetness on her face. "Was she happy it's a girl?"

He pursed his lips. "You know, she actually had a strange reaction to the whole thing."

"What do you mean?"

"She was very quiet until we got to the lobby, and then she just broke down into tears. Not really happy tears, but sobbing so hard that she had trouble getting herself together."

"Really?" Mom seemed to be considering the reason for Bree's breakdown. "I wonder if she's rethinking her decision to not raise the baby."

"I doubt it," he said, even though the thought had crossed his mind, too. "She said she's been pretty weepy because of the pregnancy hormones."

"I can understand that, but usually there needs to be something that initiates the tears. It can be a lot of things, even internal thoughts. I'd just like to know what was going through her mind after finding out she was carrying your daughter."

"I didn't push her on it today," he said. "I figured I have two hours in the car with her on the way to the reunion on Saturday."

She'd have no escape once they were on the road, and hopefully he'd get some answers.

By Saturday morning, Bree had reconciled the fact that she was actually carrying a tiny human being inside her. The first look at the ultrasound had been her wake-up call, but now everything had become clear.

She was going to be the mother of a daughter. That alone changed her world and what she wanted for the future.

Which, of course, set in motion a whole new set of problems. She'd already agreed to give Nick custody of the baby. To raise her without Bree.

Even just the thought of no contact with her child made tears come to her eyes. She had to come up with a way to maintain custody without a huge legal battle. She wasn't up for a fight like that. She needed to save her energy for her daughter. She'd begun reading about infants, and, judging from what she'd read, they took up a lot of energy. Sleepless nights seemed to be the norm. So how could she run her company without sleep?

She wasn't sure how she'd do it, but she'd figure it out somehow. Which was exactly what she did every time she was challenged.

She was in the lobby of her building when Nick came to pick her up. She stepped outside into the sunny June day. "Good morning," she greeted him as she got into the passenger side of his car and buckled up.

"Good morning," he said. "You look nice today."

"Thank you." She'd worn her expandable waist jeans with a long, casual top that she already owned. Unless the top was pulled tight over her midsection, no one would suspect that she was pregnant.

"Not that you don't always look nice," he added.

She smiled, liking that he wasn't as sure of himself as some other men she'd known. "You look pretty good yourself." He was wearing jeans and a medium-blue T-shirt with an unbuttoned blue plaid shirt over it, the sleeves rolled up to just below his elbows.

"I thought we were all driving in one car," Bree said.

"Mom changed her mind. She's going with Pete and Roxie. I think she was worried about the possibility that you and I might have to leave early after your scare this week."

That made sense.

During the first part of the trip, they discussed neutral subjects as they headed through DC and were greeted by numerous familiar sights, including the Washington Monument and the Air Force Memorial with its unmistakable tall spires.

They were on I-95 in Maryland when Nick asked her about her emotional breakdown at the doctor's office.

She knew the topic would surface sooner or later, but it still caught her off guard. "What about it?"

He glanced at her and then back to the road ahead. "I wondered what it was specifically that upset you."

"I wasn't upset."

"Were those happy tears?" he asked.

"Look, I've told you before. Ever since I got pregnant, my hormones have made me overly emotional. I'm sorry that I burst into tears in front of you. I'll try to do better." She took a deep breath to calm herself.

"I'm not trying to start a fight, Bree. And I'm also not trying to upset you. You know you can be yourself around me. I just want to talk about why the ultrasound made you so emotional."

"Didn't you feel the same way when you saw our baby?" she asked. "You had tears in your eyes, don't deny it."

He didn't say anything at first. "You just said 'our baby.'"

She didn't see what the big deal was. "So?"

He glanced at her again for a second. "So you've never called the baby *ours*. Or even referred to her *as* a baby."

She didn't like where this was going. "What have I called her, then?"

"*It.*"

"*It?*" she repeated.

"Yes." He paused. "Is that that the reason, Bree? Is the baby real to you now, after the ultrasound?"

Damn the tears that she had to keep at bay. "Why would you think this baby wasn't real to me all along? I'm the one who threw up, fainted, couldn't make it through a day without a nap, as well as the one who has to keep a damned restricted diet. Do you think any of those things weren't real to me?"

"I'm not talking about the pregnancy," he said. "I'm talking about the actual baby. Our daughter."

"So what does that mean? You think I had a sudden epiphany?" Which was the absolute truth, but she wasn't ready to admit it.

"I don't know—did you?"

She remained silent, not knowing how to answer. If she shared her feelings, would that make her seem weak? She didn't like to be considered weak. She was strong. Even if she didn't always feel that way, she didn't like anyone to know it.

Plus, she hadn't yet thought through the idea of co-parenting with Nick. And she didn't want her change of heart to cause him to panic.

The next thing she knew, Nick had taken the exit for the rest stop.

"What are you doing?" she asked as she looked at him and then back at the rest area.

He pulled into a parking place and turned to her. "I want you to look me in the eye and tell me you still want nothing to do with our daughter after she's born."

His request came as a surprise. She couldn't form the words to either deny or acknowledge the truth. Instead, she looked down at her hands on her lap.

He waited patiently for an answer that wasn't forthcoming. "If you've changed your mind about giving her to me to raise," he said, "then we can talk it through. We can come up with the right solution that will work for all of us."

She lifted her head. "We can? You'd do that?" She hadn't expected him to be so understanding.

"Of course," he said gently. "Just tell me what you want."

She shrugged. "I don't know what I want." That was a lie. She wanted her daughter and Nick and her company and her girlfriends. But she knew she couldn't have them all at once.

He placed his hand over the two of hers on her lap. "Can I make a suggestion?"

She turned her head and looked into his eyes. "Yes," she whispered.

His hesitation was evident as she saw his throat work. "Marry me."

Her eyes widened as she stared at him, completely confounded by his suggestion. "Are you crazy?" Not once in all of this had she ever considered marriage a viable option.

He put a hand to his chest and groaned to feign injury. "That was a serious blow to my ego." Then he chuckled, a nervous sound that made her realize he wasn't kidding. "I might be crazy, but I really do think it's the right thing to do. For all three of us."

"The right thing to do," she repeated. "Is that a good enough reason to get married?"

He shrugged. "It's a start." He took her hand in his and looked directly into her eyes. "Somewhere along the way during this wild ride we've been on, I've fallen in love with you."

Love? She hadn't expected that. Panic grew inside her, threatening to spill out and take over. She opened her mouth to speak, but he put a finger to her lips to quiet her.

"Let me finish," he said. "I know you're not there yet, but I think you'll admit that we've formed a special bond. More than just making a baby."

She didn't say anything.

"I think we owe it to ourselves to see where this could go." He paused. "Now you may speak." His lips twitched slightly.

She swallowed the lump in her throat and pushed down the panic. "I agree about the special bond. You've been there for the baby and me the entire time." She took a breath. "I'm just not sure that marriage is the way to go. I don't know if it's my father's life and marriage mistakes that I've been watching from the front row, or whether

I just don't have what it takes to be in a marriage. It's not something I've ever strived for. Besides, I know you feel obligated—"

"No, absolutely not." His denial was firm. "I never would have asked if I didn't truly mean it." He scratched his cheek through his beard. "I've been left at the altar before, so there's no way I'd go through with this unless I was sure we were both on the same page."

"You were left at the altar? Literally?" Who would have done such a terrible thing to him?

"She actually called it off a week before the wedding, but there were still a lot of people to tell and professionals to negotiate with, as well as lost deposits. Then there was also the condo we'd bought together."

"She just changed her mind?"

He shrugged. "I'm still not sure why she waited so long to break it off. Cold feet, maybe? We'd been together for three years, engaged almost a year. She said she simply felt we'd grown apart and that she no longer wanted to get married."

"Is the condo you live in now the one you bought together?"

"Oh, no." He shook his head. "I couldn't live there with all the memories, good and bad. I moved in with my mom for several weeks while I sold the condo. Then I took my half of the profits and bought the one I'm living in now."

She nodded. "I can see why you'd be hesitant to ask me to marry you. Which makes me even more curious to know why you did. Despite your protests, it still seems you're doing it because you feel obligated...because I'm carrying your child."

"Don't you think that if I felt any kind of obligation I would have asked you to marry me as soon as I found out you were pregnant?"

She shrugged. "I guess so." She certainly hadn't expected a proposal then or now.

"The truth is, I didn't realize until the words came out of my mouth that I truly do want you to marry me."

"And it's not just because of the baby?"

"Honestly?"

She nodded.

"I can't say that under normal circumstances—"

"If there were no pregnancy." She filled in the blank.

"Right. Without a baby involved, I probably wouldn't have asked you this early in our relationship. But things are different, and there *is* a baby to consider. So I'll ask you again. Will you marry me?"

She'd never planned to get married *or* have children. How could she run her company *and* have a family, too? "I have to say no."

His eyebrows rose. "No?"

"I'm sorry. I just don't see marriage in my future." She decided to be completely honest with him. "I've never wanted a family of my own. I saw how hard my father worked even though he had plenty of money. I also saw how he hired nannies to raise me instead of spending time with me. They were the ones who came to school plays, soccer games, dance recitals. In many ways, I'm just like him. I love my company and don't want to give it up for a family. And I also don't want a family who's always on the back burner because I'm so involved with work."

"I understand that you're confused. There's no reason to rush into any decisions."

"Thank you," she said, and meant it.

"So now what? We just stay with the original plan?"

She nodded.

"How about this? What if we try living together?" He pursed his lips. "To see how things work out for now."

"To make sure that we're all happy in our roles?" she added. "I don't know."

She considered his idea, deciding that she could always end their living situation if it didn't work out. There was no way she'd give up her condo for just that reason. "I suppose it would make life easier if I had someone to cook for me. At least for the next few months." She smiled coyly.

He grinned back at her. "You've been a good

student so far. Maybe we can spend more time on cooking lessons." He held up a finger. "I do have one thing to add to this agreement. That we reexamine marriage in the near future."

"How near?" She didn't want to have this discussion every week.

"Hmm, let's say after our daughter is born?"

She smiled. That she could live with. "Deal." She put her hand out to him to shake on it.

Instead, he grabbed her hand and pulled her toward him. She was pressed into his body while he kissed her passionately.

A much better way to seal a deal.

CHAPTER EIGHTEEN

AFTER NEARLY THREE months of living together, Bree decided that having a professional chef at her disposal was almost worth the price of her independence.

Not to mention the great sex.

The further along in her pregnancy she got, the more her cravings grew, for both Nick and food. French toast at midnight, a broccoli-and-onion omelet for breakfast. No matter what she wanted to eat, Nick was there to make it. Even after numerous cooking lessons, she still could only prepare a few simple things. Nothing as complicated as Nick's repertoire.

He had other good qualities, too. He was fairly neat, picking up after himself and keeping the kitchen spotless in between times when the cleaning crew came. He even made the bed and did the occasional load of laundry.

She'd also found that she was comfortable at his condo. She'd been skeptical at first and had almost called off the whole arrangement because they'd been unable to agree on whose place to move into—with neither wanting to give up their space, just in case the arrangement didn't work out. As a compromise, they'd begun spending weekends at his place and weekdays at hers so she could still walk to work. Not an ideal solution, but this was a trial period, after all. It also made "moving" a nonevent. They merely both freed up space in their bathrooms and closets for the other's things after doing some shopping for duplicate personal items like toothbrushes and shampoos.

Ever since that day at his family's reunion and their warm welcome, she'd begun to feel that she was part of a real family. She'd seen her grandparents every few weeks, as well as her aunt Karen. And meeting her cousins had been a real treat, too.

Bree usually made the trips to Delaware to see them, but this coming weekend her grandparents were coming to visit her. Karen would drive them. Bree had said she was happy to go to them, but they'd insisted that she was too far along in her pregnancy to drive that far from home. She disagreed, but hadn't argued. She'd just been happy that they had accepted her and her baby so quickly.

As she sat in her office that mid-September day, while her daughter did somersaults or dance moves or something wild, Bree reflected on how great her life had become. Not that it hadn't been good before, but she could definitely feel the difference.

She put a hand on her abdomen, loving the feel of the movement beneath it. She was anxious to meet this little one, but she still had several weeks to go.

Her office phone rang. "Bree Tucker."

"Good morning, Bree. This is your father."

She hadn't spoken to him since she'd called him for information about her mother. "Hi, Dad. What's up?"

"I'm calling to tell you that you have a new brother." He actually sounded excited by the news, and she was happy for him.

"That's great." She should probably tell him about her pregnancy. "Is everyone okay? What did you name him?"

"He and his mother are doing well," her dad said. "And we've decided to name him Calvin Tucker Junior."

Surprise, surprise. She should have seen that one coming. "I have news of my own that you should probably be aware of." She breathed in and out to calm herself.

"News? What's your news?" he asked.

She chickened out. "I went in search of my mother." She paused to see if he would respond. When he didn't, she continued. "I found my aunt and my grandparents. Did you know that my mother died a long time ago?"

"How would I know that, Bree?" His tone sounded deceitful, and he'd also answered a question with a question.

This was perhaps not the best time to have this conversation—essentially in the middle of a birth announcement—but she'd already begun. No turning back now. She had to push on.

"Maybe because you were keeping an eye on her after you sent her away." Ever since they'd first spoken, Bree had thought a lot about what her aunt had told her about people coming around asking questions about her mother. The only answer she could come up with was that her father was behind it.

"Why would I do that?" Again, a question. "She had enough money to live on. As long as she didn't bother us, I had no reason to keep track of her."

"But you had investigators checking on her anyway."

After several seconds of silence, he finally admitted it. "So what if I did? I couldn't afford to have her change her mind and come back for you. That would have disrupted our lives."

Bree's pulse pounded in her temples. "And you knew she'd died, but you didn't tell me."

"What good would have come of it? You were

too young at the time to understand, and then i
never seemed important as you got older."

"It didn't seem important? That my mother wa:
dead?" She couldn't believe he had actually saic
those words. He'd always been outspoken, bu
this was downright hurtful.

"I guess I should have told you," he said.

That was about as much of an apology as she
was going to get. "I have other news, too." She
might as well spill it since they didn't talk on i
regular basis.

"Good news, I hope."

"You can decide for yourself." She couldn't
help feeling that him finding out about her pregnancy this close to delivery would hurt him a
little, which would make up for how much he'd
hurt her by not telling her about her mother.
"You're going to be a grandfather." She automatically made the news about him, knowing his ego
needed that.

"What!" His outraged reaction wasn't quite
what she'd hoped. "You're pregnant?" His shock
would have been expected if she'd been a teenager, but she was thirty-three years old.

She needed to calm him down. "I'm having
a girl," she said evenly. "You're going to have a
granddaughter in mid-October."

"Who's the father?"

She swallowed. "His name is Nick Harmon. He's a chef and owns a restaurant in Old Town."

"A chef? How long have you been together? You never mentioned him when we had dinner. Did you know you were pregnant then?" His questions came one on top of the other.

"Slow down, Dad. I met him on vacation." She wasn't about to confess to her dad that Nick had been a vacation fling that had turned her life upside down. "He's a good guy. I'm sure you'll like him."

"Did you run a background check on him?"

"Of course not."

"You've got to do that, Aubrey." There he was, reverting to her former name again.

Visions of her dead cat, Audrey, crossed her mind.

"How do you know he's not out for your money?" her dad asked.

"He's not, Dad. I know him better than that."

"You can't trust blind faith," he said vehemently. "You need to have him investigated." He paused. "You're certainly not planning to marry this guy, are you?"

"Well—" Was she actually considering it?

"Aubrey!" He practically yelled into the phone. "Didn't you learn anything from me? You don't need to marry him just because he got you pregnant."

"I know that, Dad. Listen, nothing's settled. We're just taking our time."

"Well, take that time and check into him. There's no time to waste."

She and her dad disconnected, leaving Bree exhausted. She hadn't expected such a strong re-action from him, and now she couldn't stop think-ing about what he'd said.

"ARE YOU ALMOST ready to go?" Bree asked Nick on Saturday morning. "Class starts at nine." They were taking an all-day Lamaze class at the hos-pital where Bree would be delivering, followed by a hospital tour. He was looking forward to it, but wasn't sure Bree felt the same way.

She stood in the doorway of the smallest of his three bedrooms. The one he'd used to store various items like his bike, his computer, a file cabinet with his important papers and the set of weights he couldn't remember the last time he'd used.

Maybe he should sell the weights since he pre-ferred using the building's gym. "I'm ready to go," he told her. "I was just trying to figure out if some of this stuff will fit in my storage area in the basement of the building."

She looked around at his assortment of things and didn't say a word.

"So I need an opinion. Would it be better for

me to do an identical nursery to what you've done so the baby isn't confused, or should I do something completely different?"

She stared at him. She had to know he'd start on the nursery sooner or later. She'd made no mention of them getting married. And she hadn't come right out and said she wanted to share custody, either. So he naturally assumed that they would continue their current living situation until they decided they needed to change it.

Which meant he needed a nursery.

"It's your place, so whatever you decide will be fine," she finally said. She turned and walked away, saying, "Let's get going."

Nick followed behind her, and they spent the day learning everything there was to know about childbirth, breathing and options for drugs if they became necessary.

"I'll take the epidural right now," Bree said under her breath to Nick after they watched an actual birth video. "In fact, just keep me hooked up until this is all over."

He chuckled softly and took her hand. "You're stronger than you think."

She scowled, and they watched the rest of the video with the class.

After class, they'd been invited to Roxie's for dinner. He was anxious to see Bree's reaction when she found out it wasn't just dinner, but a baby shower. He had no idea how it would go over, which he'd told the girls. But they'd insisted that they had to do this for Bree. They seemed to think that she would change her mind about not wanting to raise the baby, and perhaps already had, even if she hadn't admitted it yet.

He did agree that Bree had more motherly instincts than she realized. She just couldn't see clearly right now.

"I'm pretty tired," Bree said when they were leaving the hospital. "Do you think Roxie would be upset if we didn't go to dinner?"

Uh-oh. Nick didn't know what to say.

"I don't know. Why was she having this dinner tonight in the first place?" He couldn't remember the excuse Roxie had given Bree.

She shrugged. "Something about wanting to show off her new furniture. I'm sure she'd understand."

"Maybe if we walk around a little you'll be more energized. We did a lot of sitting in that class when we weren't on the floor practicing breathing techniques."

"I guess so." But she didn't seem enthusiastic.

Now he was feeling guilty because if not for the surprise shower, he'd have taken her right home and tucked her into bed.

"There's a park down the street. We can get some fresh air." The September day was sunny and comfortably warm, a hopeful sign that the summer humidity and high temps were in the rearview mirror.

"That's probably a good idea," she said. "I could use the exercise. I've been going to that pregnant yoga class, but I miss my old workouts."

So they walked, talking amicably about neutral subjects. When they returned to his car, he opened her door for her and put a hand on her arm to stop her before she got in.

"What?" She looked at him.

"Are you feeling better?" he asked. "Roxie will be disappointed if we can't make it."

"I know." She sighed. "Okay, let's go. But let's not stay too late."

"Deal."

After she was settled in the passenger seat, he closed the door and went around to get in on his side. Whew! He'd dodged a bullet. He hadn't been sure what his next move would have been if she'd decided not to go ahead to Roxie's. He probably would have taken the coward's way out and had Bree call Roxie to cancel. Then it would have been up to Roxie to talk her into coming.

Roxie lived in a small brick row house built in the seventies. According to Bree, she'd slowly been redoing the place since she'd bought it two years ago.

"Parking here is terrible," Bree told him.

"There aren't many visitor spots. Why don't you just park on the street?"

"Good idea." He found a parking place right away, about a two-block walk to Roxie's. Once they had walked past a few houses, he checked the time on his phone and saw that they were within five minutes of when they were supposed to arrive. "Oh, wait here. I need to make sure I locked the car."

Hoping she would wait right there and not go on without him, he walked back close enough to his car to hit the lock button. At the same time he sent a text to Roxie to let her know they had arrived.

"Sorry about that," he said to Bree. "I didn't want to leave it unlocked while it was parked on the street."

She nodded. "You're sure you're good with an early evening?"

He took her hand in his as they walked. "Whatever you want is fine with me."

"Surprise!" The shout came as soon as they entered Roxie's front door.

"What's going on?" Bree looked around the living room to see her friends and relatives—both male and female—as well as Nick's relatives, smiling at her expectantly. Then she saw the banner that read Congratulations, with a background covered in rattles and storks and baby bottles. "A baby shower?" Were her friends really throwing her a baby shower?

Roxie made her way through the crowd to Bree and hugged her. "We thought since Nick would be here that we'd invite some other men, too. Are you surprised?"

"Completely."

"Good." Roxie then said to Nick, "Good job getting her here without giving it away."

He grinned and put a hand on Bree's shoulder. "It wasn't as easy as I'd expected. She wanted to back out."

Bree looked up at him. "You knew about it?"

He winked at her. "They had to tell me so I could get you here at the right time."

Roxie pulled on her arm. "Come on, grab some food and then mingle. I promise we're not going to play any of those silly games you hate, but there are presents to open a little later."

Bree wasn't sure what to think. She should have known that her friends would throw her a baby shower, but they should have also known that it wasn't really her thing.

She inhaled deeply and went to get a plate of food. The girls had gone all out. Looking at the spread, she could tell that they'd had it catered by one of the women who they'd helped get her catering business going. Bree knew the food would be delicious, and she wasn't disappointed when she ate a crab-stuffed mushroom.

After that she worked the room, talking to everyone and thanking them for coming. Nick's mom and Pete were there, as well as several other relatives that Bree had met at the family reunion.

"I can't believe you came all this way for the party," Bree told her grandparents when she got to them.

"We wouldn't have missed it," Grammy said. "You have some very nice friends."

"Yes, I do." Bree continued to greet people, including her aunt Karen and several of Bree's cousins, as well as some of her coworkers at BeeTee, Inc.

She was throwing her plate away when Amber made an announcement. "It's time for presents!" She pointed to a chair for Bree to sit in, right next to a huge pile of gifts.

As the present-opening went on, Bree became more and more convinced that she didn't know enough about being a mother. There were sentimental gifts that made perfect sense, like the crib-sized quilt handcrafted by her grandmother.

But when she opened the diaper disposal thing, she couldn't help wondering what was wrong with a regular trash can. Then there was a video monitor. Was she supposed to watch this baby twenty-four hours a day, even when she was asleep? And the breast pump. Really? Was she expected to pump so Nick could feed their daughter with a bottle when she wasn't around?

Completely overwhelmed, she couldn't wait to reach the end of the torture.

When the last of the presents had been opened and the guests clapped in glee, everyone was invited to have cake. Bree wasn't interested in cake at the moment, but she did need a bathroom.

And a place to hide for a few minutes.

Once she was safely locked inside the bathroom, she looked at herself in the mirror. She'd never backed down from a challenge. But she truly had no idea how she would ever learn everything she needed to if she wanted to be a part of her daughter's life.

On the other hand, Nick hadn't seemed too worried about it. He was calm and usually able to quiet her fears. Maybe she should consider his marriage proposal. They'd proved they were compatible, and she couldn't deny that she loved him.

Not that she'd told him that.

But was marriage the best solution? She was more confused than ever.

Willing herself to not cry, she sucked in a few deep breaths and opened the bathroom door. She was heading back to the party when she heard her name. Nick must be right around the corner in the kitchen. Thinking he was talking about their

Lamaze class, she was about to join him until she heard Pete's reply.

"Bree can help you, man. She's got plenty of money. I know I sound like a broken record, but you don't need to put the restaurant in jeopardy because of your pride."

Bree leaned back against the hallway wall, breathing quickly. Her ears began ringing and she couldn't hear the rest of their conversation because other people were speaking over Nick and Pete.

What was she going to do? Had her father been right? Was Nick after her money? How could she ever marry him if that was the case?

When she couldn't control the tears that flooded her eyes, she walked back into the bathroom, shut the door and leaned over the sink.

How would she make it through the rest of this party without letting Nick know what she'd overheard?

It wasn't easy, but Bree managed to act like everything was fine. It helped that she pretty much avoided Nick the entire time.

As soon as she could reasonably leave, she thanked Roxie and Amber and Hannah profusely, saying she'd had a long day and needed to get to bed. Thankfully, they were very understanding and didn't put up a fuss.

She was silent all the way to Nick's. When

they reached his condo, she began packing up her things.

"What are you doing?" he asked.

"I'm going home."

"Why?"

She was exhausted and hadn't wanted to have this discussion now. But he deserved an explanation.

"I overheard your conversation with Pete tonight."

He narrowed his eyes at her. "What conversation?" He seemed truly dumbfounded about what she was talking about.

"The one where you ask me for money."

He cocked his head. "Take money from you? No way! That's Pete's idea, not mine."

"So you're telling me that your restaurant isn't in financial trouble?"

He hesitated, a definite sign of deception in Bree's eyes. "In the past, yes. But I worked through that. We're doing a lot better now."

"What exactly does that mean?"

"It means that I went through a tough time financially because of several issues all at once, and I came up with various solutions that took care of it."

"Then why was Pete telling you to get money from me now?"

"Because something else has come up, but I

can handle it." He ran a hand through his hair. "Listen, can we sit down and talk about this?"

"I don't think there's anything to talk about. My father warned me that you might be after my money, but I stuck up for you." She could feel her emotions bubbling up again. Damn these pregnancy hormones. "Now I find out that he was right all along."

"Please sit down." His tone was authoritative. He sat down on the sofa, and she reluctantly followed. Only because she wanted to finish this once and for all. "Let me go back to the beginning and explain."

Bree listened with her arms crossed over her chest as he told her about his barback stealing liquor and his food distributor overcharging him. "I admit I wasn't paying enough attention to what was going on at the restaurant with the wedding plans taking up a lot of my time. Then Tracy called off the wedding, and I lost a lot of money in nonrefundable deposits and selling our condo. On top of that, I now had a restaurant that was barely holding on."

"So why didn't you tell me? You had to have known when we met that I had money. Was that your plan from the beginning? Seduce me and get me to save your restaurant?"

"Not at all. I had no idea who you were until later. Pete realized it and wanted me to come to vou for a loan, but I didn't feel right about taking money from you."

"You expect me to believe that?" She started to get up, not an easy task at eight-months pregnant.

"Yes, I do."

"You said you worked through your financial problems, but you still haven't explained why Pete was just saying tonight that you should get money from me."

He rubbed his forehead and explained all the things he'd done to make extra money to keep his restaurant going. The bartending classes, the pop-up restaurants, taking the consulting job with Bree's company. "I even stopped taking a salary until the restaurant was in the black again."

"And tonight was about what?" she asked again.

"We got a tax bill I wasn't expecting. Our accountant made a mistake on our taxes, and now we have a bill and penalties to pay."

"I still haven't heard why you didn't tell me about all this. I know we started out with a business arrangement, but I thought—" She couldn't verbalize what she thought they were to each other because she wasn't sure.

"I know." He shrugged. "I guess it was my pride. I needed to fix it on my own."

She rose, her resolve to end things even stronger. "Fixing it on your own is commendable. But not letting me know is unforgivable. I can't believe you didn't trust me enough to tell me what was going on. Especially after I allowed you to be involved in my personal business." She turned away from him and went back to gathering her things. When she'd found her family she'd opened herself up to him and let him be there for her, but he couldn't do the same with his own struggles.

"So that's it?" he asked, following her around. "I make one mistake and you're done?"

She looked at him. "Pretty much."

"I think you're using this as an excuse."

She narrowed her eyes at him. "An excuse? For what?"

"An excuse to break up with me." She heard his anger as he spoke. "You're afraid to take a chance. Afraid you're going to screw up, and you hate to fail. So, instead, you're not even going to give us a try. You've been waiting for a way out, and now you've found it. You're taking it whether it makes sense or not."

She had her things by the front door when she finally turned to face him. "Actually, earlier this evening I was thinking that I would marry you." She paused, watching the surprise on his face. "But knowing that you can't be completely honest with me is a deal breaker."

"And what about our daughter?" he asked, emotion evident in his voice. "Are we going back to that business arrangement we drew up where I raise her alone?"

Bree put a hand on her protruding abdomen. "I don't know. I haven't decided yet." That was the truth. The baby shower had made her seriously doubt her ability to be a good mother all over again.

"You know I'll fight you for custody if you think you can keep her to yourself." His anger was evident, something he normally kept under control.

Bree should have expected he wouldn't agree easily, but it felt like a punch to the gut. She gathered her things in her arms and opened the door. "I'll let you know what I decide."

CHAPTER NINETEEN

A WEEK WENT BY, and Nick still hadn't talked to Bree since she left with all her things. And he'd been miserable. Everywhere he looked, he was reminded of her. Working on the nursery was almost impossible, but he knew he only had a few more weeks until he would hopefully need it.

He still didn't know if she'd fight him for sole custody. All he wanted was for the three of them to be together. He'd do anything to make that possible. He'd tried calling every number he had for her, texting, emailing. He left messages at work, at home, on her cell. She hadn't bothered to answer him in any form.

He'd contacted her friends, too. They were torn. As much as the women wanted Bree and Nick to be together, they had to take her side. He understood, but that didn't help his situation.

Pete had been no help, either. His attitude was that if she couldn't get past the fact that he hadn't told her about a little thing like the restaurant needing money, then he was better off.

The one person he hadn't yet told was his mom.

She was so excited about being a grandmother and possibly a mother-in-law that he couldn't bear to break her heart. And that's what would happen when she found out.

Surprisingly, his mom was stronger than he'd expected. "We'll do whatever it takes to fight her," she told him firmly when he finally went to her with the news. "She's not going to do to you what her father did to her mother."

"You know she's got money, as well as her dad's money, to back her up." He didn't see how he'd ever win a custody fight. "Besides, that's not what I want."

"What is it you want?"

"I love her, Mom. I want the three of us to be a family. I just can't get that through to her. She won't even take my calls."

"She's afraid," his mom said. "I saw her reaction to the baby shower. Being a mother has never been a goal for her. And she probably feels like she was never given a choice. Which is scary, I'm guessing."

"I suggested that to her, but she denied it. We both know she doesn't like to fail, so she doesn't even want to try. Anyway, at this point, I'm not even sure if she wants custody. On one hand, she doesn't think she has any motherly instincts. On the other, I've watched her become so attached to our daughter." His emotions surfaced. "I don't think she realizes that her attachment is the first sign of maternal instincts."

His mom hugged him then. "You keep fighting, Nick. Keep reminding her that you're here and want her in your life. Don't let her forget that for even a moment."

NICK HAD BEEN RIGHT.

That had been Bree's recurring thought since she'd walked out of his house last week. But the fact that he was right didn't mean it fixed the problem.

She *was* afraid. Afraid to fail, afraid to be hurt, afraid to take a chance. And she hated being afraid.

She also hated not knowing what to do about it.

"There's some water in the cooler in the armrest," her limo driver told her. Her father had sent a car to pick her up. He wanted her to meet her baby brother. This was not going to be a fun afternoon.

"Thank you." She helped herself and took a long swallow.

She'd spent the past week crying her eyes out and when her father called this morning with the invitation, she decided that she needed to pull herself together and move forward. Seeing her father—and probably hearing his advice regarding Nick again—

was a good first step. He'd probably be thrilled to hear that she and Nick had split up.

Just the thought brought her emotions bubbling to the surface again. She took another long drink of water, trying to tamp down her feelings. Some-day she'd get over him completely—stop loving him. She just needed to move ahead to that point quickly.

Her daughter elbowed her in the ribs, remind-ing Bree that she would never get over Nick completely as long as their daughter was in the picture. With Bree's recent luck, this girl would probably be the spitting image of Nick. Which meant she'd be gorgeous.

Damn those pregnancy hormones that were kicking into overdrive and making her work hard to keep her tears at bay.

Traffic wasn't too bad and, before she knew it, the driver pulled up in front of her dad's house. She was invited in by James, the butler, who from his undisguised look of surprise, hadn't been told that Bree was pregnant.

"Congratulations, Ms. Tucker," he said.

"Thank you, James." She handed him her pash-mina.

"Your father is in the den."

She walked down the hall, hearing conversa-tion before she reached the den.

"Bree!" Her stepmother greeted her first. She

had an infant tied onto her in some kind of hammock. Was that something else Bree needed to own? "It's so good to see you." Linda softly smoothed her son's nearly bald head. "This is Calvin Lee Tucker Junior. We're calling him CL."

Bree smiled appropriately or, at least, she hoped so. "He's so little," Bree said.

"Not when you're trying to give birth to him," Linda said under her breath. "And he's gained a pound and a half since he was born."

"Wow." The birth video she and Nick had watched in Lamaze class played through her head. She wondered if she was strong enough to survive giving birth, let alone raising her daughter. As she'd been doing, she shoved away the question of who would raise her little girl. She had no right answer.

"Isn't he a wonder?" her dad said proudly as he kissed his son's head. He'd been talking on his cell phone when she'd arrived, which was the conversation she'd heard. "A hearty, healthy son."

She watched her dad and wondered if he'd ever been like that with her.

"Look at you." Her dad finally greeted her with a pat on the upper arm. "You look ready to pop."

Again she tried to smile, but wasn't sure she was succeeding.

"Come, sit down," Linda told her. "You can put

your feet up if you need to. I know my ankles disappeared those last few weeks before I delivered."

"I'm fine," Bree told her. She was being so nice. "So have you hired a nanny to help out?" She posed the question to her father.

"Oh, no. No need for that. Linda has time off from work and I actually enjoy getting up for those middle-of-the-night feedings."

Bree's eyes widened. "You get up with CL during the night?" She knew for a fact that after she'd been born he'd had three shifts of nannies so she was taken care of twenty-four hours a day.

"Of course he does," Linda verified. "He and CL do their bonding when he's changing his diaper."

"You change diapers?"

Her father laughed. "Yep. Never thought you'd see the day, did you?" He shrugged. "I guess I didn't know what I was doing back when you were born. The nannies kept telling me I needed to spend more time with you, but you know me and work."

Yes, she did know him and work.

Linda excused herself when CL began to fuss. "Speaking of diapers, this little guy needs a clean one."

When Bree was alone with her father she asked a question she'd never considered before now. "So you're not different with CL because he's a boy and I was a girl?"

"Oh, no. Of course not, Bree. I was just too hardheaded to see what I was missing out on back then. I'm truly sorry that you would even think that." He took a seat opposite her and leaned forward. "Now, tell me what's going on with *you*."

She couldn't remember the last time her father had made that request. "Well, Nick and I are no longer together."

His eyebrows rose. "What about custody?"

She shrugged. "We haven't come to a decision yet." Her pride wouldn't allow her to tell him he'd been partially right about Nick needing her money. Not that she even cared about that anymore. She knew him well enough to know that he had a lot of pride and would never be with her for her money. But he should have trusted her enough to tell her about his financial woes.

"First thing you should do is get yourself a good lawyer. You don't want to end up paying child support to that guy." Now he was sounding exactly like the father she knew. And for some reason that gave Bree the comfort she needed today.

Two DAYS AFTER her due date, Bree's water broke. She'd been getting ready for work when it happened.

She placed a hand on her abdomen and spoke

to her daughter. "I guess this means you're ready for us to meet."

She tried to be happy, but ever since breaking up with Nick, she'd been sad. She wanted him there, wanted him by her side as their daughter was born.

But her pride kept her from returning his calls.

Her aunt Karen had told her to give him a chance to make things right. But she'd resisted her advice, as well as that of her well-meaning girlfriends, who had told her the same thing.

Right now she had other things to worry about. She picked up the phone and called Roxie. She barely got out a sentence when her friend said, "I'll be right there." And then she hung up.

"So much for letting me speak," she told her watermelon of a belly. Then she checked her condo for anything that needed doing, and she made sure her packed bag was sitting by the front door. When she was ready, she rolled her suitcase to the elevator and went down to the lobby to wait for Roxie.

It wasn't Roxie who showed up.

"Nick?" Her breath caught in her throat. "What are you doing here?"

"I'm taking you to the hospital." He took her suitcase from her and began rolling it to his car.

"But where's Roxie?"

"She'll come to the hospital when I text her

after our baby's born." He wasn't asking her if this was okay—he was telling her.

"What if I don't want you there?"

He looked directly at her. "You don't have a choice. Now, do you want a ride to the hospital or would you prefer to take public transportation?"

She was silent as she got into his car and buckled up. "I hate being manipulated. You know that."

"Yes, I do know that. And so does Roxie. Right now, we outnumber you." He started the car and they took off to the hospital.

They said very little on the drive and then as they got settled into a labor room.

"Looks like you'll be a while," the nurse told her. "You're only dilated two centimeters. Why don't you do some walking."

"Two centimeters!" she said when they were alone. "It's going to take forever to get to ten."

"Come on," Nick said, holding out his hand. "Let's take a walk. We need to talk."

"Really? You want to talk now? Haven't we said everything there is to say?" Truthfully, she wanted him to say something that would change her mind about him. Make her believe they could make a go of it. Say something to make her believe in herself, in her ability to be a mother. She just didn't know what those words were.

"Now's as good a time as any," he said, and followed her out into the hallway.

"So what do you want to talk about?" she asked softly as they walked past other patients and hospital employees.

"First, I want to tell you that I love you, and I never stopped loving you."

She stopped suddenly and looked at him. He'd taken two more steps before stopping and turning to her.

"Just saying that doesn't make everything right again," she said.

"I know." They began walking. "There's more to it than that."

"Go on."

"I want us to be together. All three of us. I don't care about that damn legal agreement we signed." He looked her straight in the eyes as they walked slowly down the hallway. "I understand that you don't trust me. I should have been honest with you and told you about my financial problems." He ran a hand through his hair. "I was embarrassed. I didn't want you to know. At least not until I fixed them on my own."

She knew him well enough to know that he was speaking from his heart.

He stopped walking and faced her. "I never had any intention of asking you for a loan through your company. Pete urged me to, but I didn't want money to come between us. Especially after we slept together. Even more so after finding out this little one was on her way." He touched Bree's abdomen, the warmth of his hand thawing her heart.

They continued to walk and got to the end of a hall, where they turned around to go back the other way.

"I wish you had been honest with me instead of having me find out by accident. You made it difficult to trust you."

He nodded. "I understand that. So this is what I propose. I'll sign a prenup or anything else you want me to sign. Just as long as you don't rule out the three of us as a family."

She had to stop moving when she had a labor pain. She'd had some easy ones before this, but now she had to do her Lamaze breathing.

"Just keep focused on your breathing," Nick told her as he softly stroked her back. "You can do it."

When the pain subsided, she straightened, and they began to walk again.

"Last week when my grandparents were here," Bree said, "they asked about you. I told them that we'd broken up. I could tell that they didn't approve. And some of the things they said began to make sense to me."

"Like what?"

"At one point, they told me how much I was like my father."

"That must have gone over well," he quipped.

She ignored him and continued. "They compared what I was doing to what my father did to my mother by keeping her away from me. They even asked me if I would hire a nanny to take care of our daughter since I would be raising her alone."

"They knew that I would be involved, too, right?"

"Yes, but they also knew that I'd need someone to live in because of having to get up for work every day."

"Everything they said seems to be right on the money."

"I know. That's why it's been bugging me so much."

He stopped walking and turned to her. "What does that mean?"

She swallowed. "It means that I need to stop acting like my father. I need to believe you when you say you don't want my money. Most important, I need to listen to my heart."

"And what does your heart say?"

She looked into his eyes. "My heart says that I love you and this baby girl, and I don't want to lose either one of you."

"I feel the same way."

"That's not all," she said. "You were right about me. I have so many doubts about becoming a mother. I have no idea what I'm doing, Nick."

He shook his head. "That's not true. You have wonderful maternal instincts. You're just not paying attention. I've seen you bonding with our daughter already. That's the first step. You already know each other."

"But there's so much to learn."

"And that's what you're so good at. You became an expert at pregnancy. So now you'll learn about being a mother the same way, as well as from experience."

"But what if I make mistakes?"

He smiled. "Every parent makes mistakes. It's part of the process. You know they say first children are 'practice children.'"

She gulped. "*First* children? Does that mean what I think it means?"

"Bree, I want more than just one child with you, if you're okay with that, of course." He pulled her close then, as close as they could get with her belly in the way. "I love you," he said into her ear. "I love you more than you'll ever know. And, no matter what the future holds, we're in this together. Mistakes and missteps, as well as wonderful times."

"I love you, too," she whispered. "Promise you'll always be there for us?"

"I promise."

After standing there in an embrace for a few minutes, their daughter once again interrupted when Bree had another labor pain.

When it was over, Bree took his hand and said, "Come on, I think it's almost time for us to meet our daughter."

EPILOGUE

Three months later

"I'M NOT SURE why I let you guys talk me into having the wedding here," Bree told Roxie, Hannah and Amber as they were having their hair done at the salon on Isla de la Blanca. "It would have been much easier to do it at home."

Nick's mom spoke to Bree's reflection in the mirror. "But this is so much more meaningful. Years from now, you'll be happy you chose to do it here."

"You tell her, Emily," Amber said with enthusiasm.

"Yeah, she doesn't have a sentimental bone in her body." This from Roxie.

Hannah spoke up. "Well, she did finally agree to even having a wedding. We need to give her credit for that."

Bree couldn't help smiling. "That's true. But when it came to the actual ceremony, you guys made every arrangement. All I had to do was show up."

"You wanted simple, so that's what we did," Emily said. "Besides, your only job is to take care of my granddaughter."

"I hope she's not fussing for Nick," Bree said. "She refuses to take a bottle even after I've spent the time to pump."

The girls laughed.

"What's so funny?" Bree wanted to know.

Roxie answered, "Who could have guessed that a sentence like that would ever have come out of your mouth?"

"Okay, fine, I get it," Bree said. "You'll see. Someday all of you will be in my position and you'll realize how much a baby changes you." She could hardly believe it herself.

AN HOUR OR SO later, Roxie stood with Hannah and Amber in the resort lobby as they waited to go out to the beach for Bree and Nick's wedding. Bree had asked for a moment alone before coming to meet them.

"So you actually broke it off with Jim?" Amber asked Roxie.

"I did."

"How'd he take it?"

Roxie pursed her lips and then said, "He took it better than I expected. He never even asked why I wanted to do that. Just said that it was probably for the best. Which leads me to wonder why it took me so long to break up with him in the first place!"

Amber raised her eyebrows. "And why *did* you break it off with him?"

"Because it just wasn't working out with him being so far away, and it wasn't like he was going out of his way to work on keeping our relationship alive. I wouldn't hear from him for weeks at a time." She refused to say aloud that her physical attraction to Pete had anything to do with her decision. Not that he'd pushed her to be with him. In fact, he still had a different woman on his arm every time they ran into each other.

Amber turned to Hannah, tilting her head as she asked, "Hannah, are you okay? You've been acting like something's bothering you ever since we left DC."

Hannah shrugged. "It's probably nothing."

"Spill it and we'll decide," Roxie told her.

"I had this strange experience at the airport. When I ran to the ladies' room before we boarded, a guy I thought I knew was walking toward me." She paused. "So I waved and said, 'Hi, Ryan!' He looked right at me but said, 'I'm sorry. You must have me confused with someone else.'"

Amber pursed her lips. "So you thought it was somebody you knew, but it wasn't. *That's* what's been eating at you?"

"No, it's not that simple," Hannah told them.

"I'm *sure* it's Ryan. I just don't know why he wouldn't admit it."

"How do you know for sure?" Roxie asked. "We all have doppelgangers out there. This was probably his."

"How do you know this guy Ryan anyway?" Amber asked.

"We went to high school together. We dated for about six months our senior year." She took a breath and then visibly swallowed. "And then one day, he was supposed to pick me up for a movie, but he never showed up."

"Some guys are really bad at breaking up," Amber quipped. "He probably just didn't want to face you."

"Yeah, I know, but that wasn't like Ryan at all," Hannah said. "He'd never just disappear like he did."

"What do you mean, disappear? You never saw him again?"

She shook her head. "Never. He stopped going to school, his phone was disconnected. I couldn't even contact his parents, because they disappeared, too."

"Maybe they're all secret agents," Roxie suggested in an eerie voice as she hummed a familiar movie tune.

"Or aliens called back to their home planet," Amber added.

"I can see you're not taking this very seriously at all. Remind me not to bring up my deepest thoughts with you guys ever again," Hannah said on a sigh. She pointed across the lobby. "Here comes the bride. Let's get this wedding started."

NICK COULDN'T BELIEVE how lucky he was as he stood on the beach with Pete, watching his bride come toward him. She wore a simple white dress and bare feet. Instead of carrying flowers, she carried their daughter in her arms.

Little Emma Marie wore a dress that complemented her mother's, and his heart was bursting with love for them.

A three-piece string ensemble was playing off to the side. Roxie, Hannah and Amber had already come up the aisle and stood off to the other side in pale green, pale blue and pale yellow dresses, respectively.

Bree's dad had insisted on flying guests to the island, so there were more people in attendance than they'd originally expected. Nick's mother sat alone in the front row on the left, while his relatives took up several rows behind her.

Bree's stepmother was in the front row on the right holding Bree's half brother, CL. To the left of her was an empty chair for Bree's dad. In the second row were Bree's maternal grandparents and her aunt, as well as several newly found cousins and aunts and uncles in the successive rows.

"You ready for this?" Pete whispered to him.

"Absolutely."

Bree and her dad began walking down the aisle then. She stopped at her grandparents to grasp each of their hands, as well as her aunt's. Then she turned to Nick's mom, who held out her arms to take the baby. Nick's vision blurred when Bree and his mom hugged. Then Bree's dad kissed his daughter's cheek and reached out to shake Nick's hand before taking his seat.

Bree turned to face Nick then, and their eyes met. She took the few more steps to reach him, but the next thing he knew, she stumbled and was about to go down face-first when he caught her in his arms. The spectators gasped in unison.

After he helped her stand solidly on her feet again, she grinned with sparkling eyes and said, "I believe we've now come full circle."

He grinned back. "And what a wonderful circle it is."

"I love you," she whispered.

"Not as much as I love you," he responded.

* * * * *

Be sure to look for Lisa Dyson's next
BUSINESS, BABIES & SECRETS *story.*

And don't forget her upcoming book in the
TALES FROM WHITTLER'S CREEK *series.*